DIVIDED HEARTS

THE DIVIDED HEARTS SERIES
BOOK ONE

MICHELLE BOLANGER

Divided Hearts

Published by Risen Fiction Publishing

7522 Timber Valley Dr

Franklin, OH 45005

www.risenfiction.com

ISBN 978-1-969047-00-8 (Hard Case)

ISBN 978-1-969047–01-5 (Paperback)

eISBN 978-1-969047-02-2 (eBook)

Cover Art and Interior by Shonda Ramsey

Printed in the United States of America First Edition 2025

Divided Hearts by Michelle Bolanger was originally published in 2015 with the title *The Kiss* by Michelle Bolanger. Though the story line remains the same, it has been re-edited for clarity and readability.

10 9 8 7 6 5 4 3 2 1

20251111

AUTHOR'S NOTE

It's hard to believe my author journey started 10 years ago. When this story, originally titled *The Kiss,* hit the shelves in July of 2015, publishing a book was an experiment for me. In the years that have passed since, I've learned more than I could have imagined about writing, self-publishing, running a business, and most of all, about myself.

Being a writer is a gift I haven't always nurtured or taken seriously, but I've come to realize that creating worlds and bringing characters to life is my heart's call. I've been privileged with the time to spend learning how to craft better stories; learning how to draw a reader from the first line of a tale to the last page is an art I want to keep perfecting. So, while these early stories aren't perfect, they are mine. They are the beginnings of my journey to being the author I am today, and the one I will grow into in the future.

If you've been with me from the first tentative chapters shared with a few friends, or if you purchased the originals at a book event somewhere in the Midwest all those years ago...

THANK YOU!

If you are new to my writing, I hope you will enjoy these first novels and hop on this crazy journey with me.

I have to directly thank Anita, Katy, and Stephanie. The three of you have been with me from the very beginning, and I never would have published these stories or any that come after without your support.

There are so many new faces who have encouraged me and reminded me that these stories have value, even when I know I can do better now.

To say I am grateful for my newest friend, coach, mentor, and designer, Shonda Ramsey, would be a massive understatement. Your encouragement and wise counsel brought these stories back out of hiding and into new life. Your wisdom and creativity inspires me to keep going. And above all, as the Brand Whisperer, you make me make sense!

There is no amount of thanks or gratitude I can express to my amazing husband, Robert, that would adequately honor him for all his support and encouragement. He is the undisputed spiritual leader of our home, and he is the most selfless man I've ever known. No matter what crazy business idea I come up with, he is always on board as my biggest cheerleader and logistics manager. You truly are Mr. Awesome!

I owe everything I've stated above and everything else in my life to the Creator of all things. To the One who pulled me out of a life of sin and fear to hand me everything I never knew I wanted or needed. Every ounce of creativity I have and every story I write, comes from His gift of inspiration. I am nothing without my Savior and King, Jesus Christ.

Always Hope,
Michelle Bolanger

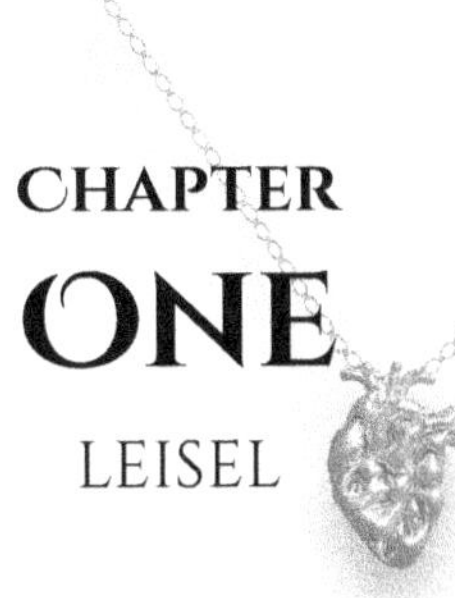

Reigning in her excitement, Leis paused outside her best friend's bedroom holding the two brown envelopes behind her back. She raised her hand to knock but paused at the barely cracked door. She inched it open enough to see Baden sitting at his laptop, the screen black with green letters in neat lines scrolling up as he added text. She could just make out a female avatar in the upper right corner. She pressed the door a bit wider, trying to get a better look when the hinge gave a creak.

She froze as the text and the avatar vanished. Baden snapped the laptop shut and twisted toward her, the surprise on his face easing to annoyance as his brown eyes locked with hers.

"I was going to knock, but it was open," Leis leaned on the door frame. "Can I come in?"

"Sure." He exhaled through his nose and rolled his chair back from the desk. "I was finishing up homework." He cocked his head at the hand she still held behind her back. "What is that?"

"The mail ran." She held them out, one in each hand. "One for Baden Allen Dietrich, and one for Leisel Rene Gottschalk. Do you think they accepted us?"

"Of course they accepted us." Baden snatched the envelopes and playfully pushed her toward the bed, away from the computer. As if she knew anything about them.

She pretended to slip and fell to her back on the mattress. "It seems like the answer came too fast to be an acceptance."

He tore his open and pointed to a red stamp at the top of the page as he dropped onto the bed beside her. "See? Accepted." His weight dipped the bed, making her shoulders tip toward him. "I knew we would both get in."

"Of course you wouldn't worry." Leis poked him in the ribs. "Your four point oh gets you in anywhere." She snagged hers back and tore it open.

He laid back and scanned the letter. "Not always. Besides, your ACT was higher than mine."

"Whatever." She sat up to lean across him, and his amused brown eyes fixed on hers. "You know what this means, right?"

He tucked a strand of long red hair behind her ear. "What?"

His hand lingered against her cheek, and she wished it would spark something inside her. No matter how many times she stared at his boyishly handsome face in admiration, her body stubbornly refused to respond. The gold flecks in his brown eyes seemed to glitter as his fingers traced her cheek. The question in his eyes as he watched her was obvious, but nothing had changed. She wasn't affected by him at all. Her heart tightened, and she leaned closer to him.

"It *means* they have to let us go. Mom and Dad said if we both got accepted, they would let us go to any college we wanted for a year." She froze when Baden slipped his hand behind her neck.

"They did." He rose up to kiss her forehead. "It's my grandmother we have to worry about."

She inhaled deeply and felt his smile against her skin. "Maybe getting away will fix me."

"Leis." He cupped her face. "We've talked about this." When he pulled back to look at her, his eyes were soft. "I'm in no hurry."

"I know," she said. She tucked herself into the crook of his arm, his heart beating steadily against her side. "But I still hope getting away from here will trigger something."

He wrapped an arm around her waist and she sighed. Pressing her face into his soft cotton t-shirt, she drew another breath through her nose. Being born without the ability to smell complicated everything.

"With Andrew and Carol's ceremony tomorrow, I guess ours is on my mind." Her voice came out muffled against his shirt.

"Stop worrying about it. We have plenty of time." Baden rolled them and braced his hands on either side of her ribs. Their legs tangled together but he arched back to keep space between their bodies. His hair fell in a soft curl across his eyes and Leis brushed it away. She bit her lip.

"I know. But what if—"

"Leisel Rene! Get off that bed this minute!" Leis's mother snapped from the doorway.

Baden's face flamed red as he shoved himself backwards to stand at the foot of the bed.

"Leisel, you know better!" Her mother's face was lined with disappointment.

"I'm sorry, Mom."

"I'm sorry, Stephanie."

He reached down to pull her up, and she tugged her shirt straight, mortified it looked far more intimate than it actually was.

"We were just excited to get our acceptance letters," Leis said.

Her mom glowered from the doorway. "I'm sure you are, but you have rules for a reason. Nothing good comes from breaking the rules." She sighed. "The tailor is here for your final fittings before the ceremony tomorrow. He is finishing up with your father. Come to the study in five minutes. Leisel, you and I will talk about this later." She turned away muttering. "I swear I'm tired of you getting Baden in trouble."

Leis waited until they couldn't hear her footsteps anymore. "I'm sorry, B. I'm always causing problems."

He sat at the desk and tossed the paper on top of the laptop. "None of this is your fault," he said and glanced at her.

Leis dropped her gaze to the carpet and said nothing. But it was always her fault.

He rose and crossed the room. "It *isn't*. I love you." He ticked his head toward the door. "What they say doesn't matter."

She studied his face, as familiar to her as her own reflection. His gaze was distant, and her chest ached. She reached up to smooth the tension away from his taunt jaw, and he leaned into her palm, the light scruff of hair pricked her fingers.

No matter what Baden thought, he was pledged to bond with a female who couldn't bond. Without her sense of smell she would never be able to respond to him the way he needed her to.

The Clan had pledged them at birth, before anyone knew about her disability. And now, there was no one else. She was the youngest of three females, and the Clan had been trying for a bonded pair between the Dietrichs and the Gottschalks for almost a hundred years. She and Baden were their last chance because her parents were both over two hundred years old, and no longer able to conceive. His parents could have had more children, but they died in an accident when he was three. No one talked about what happened after he came to live with her and her three brothers.

But he was her best friend. Over the last eighteen years he became her whole world. He defended her, protected her, and he always believed one day, they would be one.

If he could break the pledge, would he? The thought chilled her. A throat cleared, jerking her back before she could follow that thought any further.

"I thought I would warn you both that Mom's in a mood, but I think you just figured that out." Her brother, Andrew, stood in the doorway, glancing between them.

Tomorrow they would be celebrating his bonding. Leis stepped away from Baden then headed for the door.

He caught her arm. "I'll go down with you."

"Dad wants to talk to you, B. He's in his office," Andrew said.

"Great." Leis pulled away, but Baden didn't let go.

"Don't let her get to you, okay?" He kissed her cheek after she nodded. "Go get fitted." He squeezed her arm gently then followed Andrew toward her father's office.

The study was her favorite room in the house. The dark wood floors and floor to ceiling bookcases welcomed her, but her mother's scowling face stole all the warmth from the room.

"Don't keep Johnathan waiting." She waved toward a screen set up in the corner opposite the huge bay window overlooking their back yard. "Get changed, and we'll talk while he's working."

"Yes, ma'am." Leis nodded to the graying man seated in her favorite wingback chair. His face was unreadable, and she hurried to change into the pure white tunic and pants waiting for her.

She undressed quickly, then carefully put on the crisply starched outfit. Though the outer material was made of stiff, rough spun silk, the satin lining slid against her skin. The tunic fell a few inches past her hips and tucked in slightly at the waist. She grimaced at her reflection. The stark white contrasted sharply with her vibrant red hair and gave her pale skin a slight peach glow. The pants were long, and she gathered them up so she wouldn't trip.

Her mother tsked as Leis obediently stepped onto a stool in front of a trifold mirror.

"You creased the pants," she sighed.

Leis looked down. They had wrinkled where she gripped the pants to lift them.

Her mother huffed. "Your brother's ceremony is important. At least *try* to be respectful."

Tears burned the back of her eyes, but she knew better than to let her mother see them. *I won't cry in front of her. It's just a pair of pants.*

"I'm sorry, Mom. I'll be careful," she said.

The tailor and her mother poked and pulled at the garment until they were satisfied with the fit of the tunic, then the man knelt to pin up the hem of the pants. The moment his gaze was fixed on the task, her mother crossed her arms.

"What were you thinking, Leisel?" Disappointment dripped from her tone. "Why on earth were you laying on Baden's bed and tempting him like that? You should be ashamed."

The tears she had tried to blink back earlier welled, and Leis turned to the bright sunlight glaring through the windows in an attempt to keep them from falling.

Her voice was a whisper. "I'm sorry, Mom. We were just excited about the news, and I forgot."

"I know your *disability* makes it almost impossible for anything to happen, but I expect more discretion from you. You are not a human who ruts like an animal!" The tailor stilled then continued pinning. Her mother stepped closer as if he wouldn't hear the rest. "We made a vow before the Elder that you would be an honorable mate to her grandson. Have you forgotten the privilege it is that she hasn't broken the Pledge because of you?"

Leis drew in a shaky breath at her mother's sneering tone. "No, Mom. I haven't forgotten." *You won't let me.*

"Your father agreed to let you go to Ohio with him if you both got accepted. He assured me you wouldn't compromise Baden's status." She straightened to her full height, though Leis still looked down at her from the stool. "I disagree because you're careless." Her eyes narrowed. "Or maybe you're desperate."

Leis flinched. "Am I not supposed to want to bond with him?"

"Not without the supervision of the Elder!" Her mother hissed and gripped her hand hard enough to hurt, but her eyes were hopeful. She lowered her voice. "Did your fangs drop?"

Leis shook her head in shame, running her tongue along the roof of her mouth where two narrow grooves sheathed a pair of viperlike fangs. Without her sense of smell, Baden's scent would never trigger them.

Her mother sighed through her nose and released her hand. "That's good they didn't." She was quiet for a moment as she took a step back to survey the tunic and pants. Finally, she said, "Your father is putting a lot of faith in your disability."

Her mother moved to stand beside her. Seeing both their reflections in the mirror was always startling. They looked so much alike, they could almost be mistaken for twins. Tall and willowy with hair a bright mahogany red and green eyes. Hers were darker than her mother's, but it was hard to tell now when anger darkened her mom's expression.

"If it were up to me, I would keep you both here. The Elder agreed." Her mother shook her head when Leis's tears escaped and fell down her cheeks. She glanced away. "But your father is very persuasive. He is talking to Baden right now to let him know it's all been approved."

"Thank you, Mother." Leis's heart thudded at the news. "I promise we won't disappoint you."

With a snort, her mom turned away. "Don't thank me. It was Baden and your father that convinced his grandmother to let you go." She glanced back. "Don't mess this up for Baden. He's going to inherit a fortune and his family business. *He* needs this education. Don't distract him from his studies, and I expect you to do what he tells you."

Anger twisted her stomach, but Leis didn't respond. There was no point. Baden would never order her around, and she took comfort in the knowledge that in three short months they would be out from under her mother's thumb.

As the last pin went into the hem of her pants, she heard Baden and her father's voices.

"The time away will be good for her." Baden was saying. "I think it will be just what we need."

"I don't doubt it." Her father's German accent was stronger in that way it got when he worked too much. "I know you'll take good care of her."

"Haydn." Her mother's voice and posture softened when he entered the room. "Baden needs to be fitted. Did you get everything worked out?"

"We did." Her Dad's shoes clacked as he crossed the floor and kissed her mother's forehead.

Baden's eyes found hers in the mirror, his expression tight. He gave her a small smile and nodded to let her know everything was all right, then turned to her father.

"When I'm done here, I'll call my grandmother to thank her," Baden said.

Her Dad clapped him on the shoulder as his gaze swung to Leis. He smiled widely. "You look beautiful, Leis."

She might look exactly like her mother, but it was her father she was closest to. She would miss him. His hair was dark blond, not quite brown. He kept it trimmed short, almost military looking. He was a few inches taller than Baden, but standing side by side, she noticed how much they looked alike. They had the same dark eyes and high cheekbones.

Before she could respond to her father, her mother snapped. "You heard them, Leisel. Baden needs to get his fitting done. Go change so he doesn't have to wait."

Lowering her head, she stepped off the stool. "Sorry, Mom."

Baden made a disapproving sound. "Stephanie. I have plenty of time. Don't yell at her."

Leis hurried behind the screen and carefully removed the outfit, making sure she didn't add any new wrinkles. Baden always tried to act as a buffer between her and her mother, but this time her mother lashed back.

"She needs a firm hand, Baden. You'll need it to keep her in line while you're away," she said.

"Stop talking about her like she's a spoiled child! She's your daughter, and a grown woman. This is why I want to get her out of here."

Leis stifled a sob with the back of her hand as her father intervened. "I don't think she meant it that way." Baden snorted, and her father's voice was stern. "Baden. That's enough. Stephanie, why don't you go down and see if dinner is ready? I'll make sure the tailor has everything he needs."

"Fine." Her mother's heels clicked against the hardwood as she left.

Leis closed her eyes and composed herself before she stepped out from behind the screen. Her father was shaking his head, and Baden sat stiffly in the chair staring out the window. The tailor had busied himself on the opposite side of the room.

"I swear mothers and daughters should come with warning labels." Her father chuckled. "Come here, Leis."

"Thank you, Daddy. I'm sorry I made her so upset." She fell against her father's chest, sighing when his arms came around her.

Baden growled. "Stop apologizing for what isn't your fault." Leis pulled away from her dad's warmth to see Baden staring at her. "Three months and we are out of here."

"Baden." Her father's tone was sharp. "Let it go."

The two of them shared a look, and Baden sighed. "I know."

He pushed out of the chair and rested a hand on her shoulder. She stepped out of her dad's embrace and expected Baden to give her a hug, but he backed away stiffly and dropped his hands.

"Go see if your mom needs anything. I'll be down in a little bit." His voice was rough but kind.

Confused, Leis looked up to see her father watching her sadly as Baden turned away and disappeared behind the screen. "Go on. We won't be long,"

With another glance toward Baden, she obeyed.

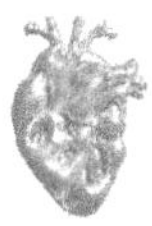

THE NEXT AFTERNOON Leis brushed a non-existent wrinkle from the sleeve of her tunic as she followed her mother down the staircase.

The carpeted steps muffled their feet, and the hum of conversation floated up from the main hallway as her mother turned a critical eye on her.

"Stop picking at your clothes and stand up straight. A lot of very important people will be here today, and I expect you to be respectful," she said.

Leis's chest tightened, but she nodded obediently. All she wanted was to get to Baden. After dinner yesterday he had gone to bed earlier than normal. At breakfast, he sat next to her, draping his arm across the back of her chair and stealing food from her plate like he always did. When they parted ways to get ready for the ceremony, he pecked her on the cheek and told her he loved her.

From the landing, she could see the main hallway full of people, all dressed in the same white silk tunic and pants she and her mother wore. The parquet flooring gleamed under their feet, and they milled around admiring the expensive artwork hanging on the smooth plaster walls. When she and her mother reached the bottom of the stairs, the crowd parted to let them through. Her mother's mood turned syrupy sweet as she greeted her guests and shook hands.

Completely ignored, Leis followed her mother down the long hallway toward the ballroom. The glass double doors opened into a brightly lit space with wide floor to ceiling windows on one side, and on the other, three sets of glass doors were thrown open to the outdoors where the Saddleback Mountains rose in the distance.

A sea of people in white flowed across the intricately laid hardwood floor as the huge grandfather clock beside the fireplace struck the hour. Leis was swept along with the crowd, rising on her toes to search for Baden. As she was about to pass through the doors, a hand clamped onto hers and pulled her to the side.

"Were you looking for me?" Baden's smile didn't reach his eyes.

She turned her hand to lace their fingers together. "Who else would I be looking for?"

His already somber eyes clouded. "Not anyone here."

"What?" She breathed with a laugh.

He shook his head and tugged her toward the doors. "Never mind. Let's find your dad. We'll be standing next to your parents."

"That close?" Leis gripped his hand. "I was hoping we could stay toward the back and sneak out as soon as it was over."

He pursed his lips. "Me too, but the Elder wants all the family in front."

They threaded their way across the flagstones until they found her father. He was talking to a tall red headed man who looked familiar. She thought she'd seen his picture in one of the home builder magazines her father kept in piles in his office, but she wasn't sure.

"Who is that?" Leis tipped her head toward them.

"No idea." Baden's voice lowered. "Just stay close to me, okay?"

Leis held his hand tighter. His words felt like a warning, and her heart rate increased. Until now, she hadn't been nervous, but Baden's demeanor changed when they reached her father's side. The other man was gone, but the tension on her father's face was unsettling. His brown eyes skated across her face and landed on Baden. They exchanged a look she couldn't decipher.

"Daddy?" She reached for his arm. "Are you all right? Where's Mom?"

"I'm fine." He looked back at her and his expression eased. "Mom will be here in a minute. She wanted to see Andrew before the ceremony." He stepped forward. "Come on. It's almost time."

The three of them emerged from the throng, and Leis looked around. Everyone had formed a large circle around a raised platform in the middle of their back patio. She figured there were at least a hundred people milling around. Baden stiffened when, to their left, a gap opened and her mother appeared, flanked by an older couple.

Leis had met Baden's grandparents for the first time at their high school graduation and felt the same unsettling nervousness that something wasn't quite right. His grandmother didn't immediately look threatening. The Elder was a tall thin woman with long grey hair, and though she was dressed in the same garments as the rest of them, she carried herself with such elegance Leis checked to see if she was wearing a crown. Everyone deferred to her, and rightly so. As the eldest of them, her word was obeyed as law. Baden's grandfather trailed behind, almost as a necessary accessory to her wardrobe.

This woman was part of the reason her mother was so hard on her. Leis knew that being chosen as the one who would bond to the Elder's grandson was a great honor. When it was discovered she had a birth defect that could potentially prevent them from bonding and producing heirs, the shame of it devastated her mother, and Leis bore the brunt of her anger.

Baden stood rigid as the trio approached, though his grandmother favored them with a genuine smile.

"Hello, Baden." Her voice was cultured and carried a hint of a German accent. "Leisel."

Leis bowed her head. "Elder."

The woman laughed lightly. "Please, call me Res. You're going to be my granddaughter soon."

Baden flinched and tightened his grip. "Not for another year, Ma'am."

Res patted his cheek. "I know, dear." Something dangerous passed between them before she stepped back to address her father. "Are you ready, Haydn?"

He lifted his chin proudly. "We are." He led her mother onto the platform and the crowd fell silent. "Today we are here to celebrate our most sacred rite. The bonding of two lives and the Exchange of Blood between them that will ensure the continuation of our people."

With a nod, he indicated a family to their right. Carol and her parents stepped onto the platform to stand next to them. Carol's excited eyes darted between her parents and the opening in the crowd as her father rested his hands on her shoulders.

"We pledged our daughter, Carol Beatrice Fertig, to your son, Andrew Simon Gottschalk. Is your son willing and able to take his place as her blood sworn mate and provide the Blood she needs?" he asked.

"I am."

Leis's eyes landed on her brother as he strode from the opening in the crowd. Andrew was tall and impossibly handsome. His brilliant red tunic stark against the white that surrounded him.

His eyes locked on Carol's as he strode forward, followed by two men carrying a large cloth draped rectangle. Under the edges of the pink and blue cloth peeked the legs of the crib Leis and Andrew's parents purchased as was custom.

Leis looked at Carol and her eyes welled with tears. *Will Baden and I ever make it this far?*

She leaned against Baden as Andrew advanced on the platform. The parents backed off the raised surface as Andrew ascended and reached for Carol's hands. Both their hands were shaking.

"Until today, our families have spoken on our behalf. Today, I ask you to leave their care and make the pledge they have made for us not just a promise, but a bond." Andrew's voice was husky.

The two men set the crib on the platform beside them and melted into the crowd. No one breathed as Andrew cupped Carol's face and pulled her toward him.

"As custom requires, I've brought the crib where our children will rest," he intoned.

Carol turned her face into his palm, and jealousy creased Leis's forehead as she watched the other woman's chest expand, her jaw clenching as she inhaled Andrew's scent. Carol's eyes never left his, and Leis blushed at the way she stared at her brother in hunger. His next words were almost growled.

"Carol Beatrice Fertig, I willingly offer you my blood. Are you willing to take your place as my blood sworn mate?" He leaned toward her, and she gasped in pain. "Will you accept me?"

When Carol opened her mouth to speak, blood coated her lower lip, and two glittering fangs peeked from beneath her upper. Instead of speaking, she nodded. At her acceptance of him, the entire patio turned their backs and bowed their heads.

Leis squeezed her eyes closed against the sound of Andrew's short cry and didn't allow herself to acknowledge it wasn't entirely from pain when a similar sound came from Carol.

Hot tears rolled down her cheeks, and she flinched when Baden's fingers wiped them away. She met his warm eyes and more tears coursed down her face. His smile was gentle, and he leaned close to kiss her temple. She inhaled deeply through her nose, desperate for a breath of him that would stir the desire she'd just witnessed between her brother and Carol. But there was nothing. Without a miracle, Baden would never see her fangs. Without a miracle, the crib his family purchased would remain empty.

Baden's thumb caressed her cheek, and he whispered, "Stop worrying. Everything will work out."

Heads turned in disapproval and Leis ducked her head as Baden's hand dropped from her cheek. She did her best to do what he asked, but the chances of things working out for them didn't seem possible.

Head down and feet dragging, Koen made his way up the sidewalk to the performing arts building. It was his third year on campus and not much had changed. Was he a junior? Or sophomore and a half? He missed enough classes last year because of his breathing issues to make even his counselor wonder if he would graduate on time. Trying to ignore the heat and the growing pressure in his chest, he pushed his earbud in a little tighter and let Demon Hunter's new album rattle his ear drums.

A sudden coughing spell made him grimace, and he shook his inhaler. Every puff reminded him he wasn't going to get better. But he was pursuing what he loved, taking the doctor's advice and making the most of his talent while he was young.

When he reached the building's entrance, a flash of red drew his attention to a petite girl who stooped down to retrieve an abandoned soda can. She was having an animated conversation with someone on her phone, but the pounding of the drum solo in his ears drowned out any chance of hearing what was said. She disconnected the call and pushed the bag at her hip around to her back while she opened the door.

Through the glass, he watched her pause to compare her schedule with the board that listed the classrooms. He wondered if he should offer to help her, but she turned and disappeared down the hall before he could.

Huffing in the puff of Albuterol, he held his breath before stepping toward the door with a slow exhale. Though the humidity was doing a number on him and beads of sweat were forming on his forehead, he paused another minute. He was not ready to face his co-star for the next few months. Andrea Summers had been cast with him as the romantic leads for the fall production of an original play written by her brother called *The Kiss.*

He could still hear the piercing squeal she let out when she saw they would be working so closely together. For days afterwards, he tried to replicate the sound on his electric guitar, annoying the heck out of his dorm mates. Grinning ruefully, he admitted he couldn't get his guitar to sound that bad.

Andrea was pretty, and sweet most of the time, but he had no interest in a relationship, and he wasn't into casual hookups. He couldn't play with a woman's heart like that. Leaving the ladies alone just made more sense.

He checked his watch and stepped inside, sighing in relief as the cool building air skittered across his damp skin.

The redhead from outside exited the auditorium, about to turn the corner toward backstage, and he let his gaze sweep over her figure. A light grey tank top and white shorts hugged every curve, and gladiator sandals wrapped around her trim calves. He smiled a little.

Never hurts to enjoy the scenery once in a while, right?

Their eyes connected for a second, and the flash of amused green in her glance arrested his attention so much that he barely noticed the brush of another student passing him in the wide hallway. Then the redhead and her bemused smile disappeared around a corner.

He shook himself out of it and returned to tapping out the complicated drum solo against his leg.

The school's amphitheater was old, but clean and well cared for. The moment he stepped inside he was assaulted by the smell of hot stage lights and dust. Dull blue carpet ran down the center aisle, faded from years of foot traffic. Plain grey paint and sound reducing panels twisted at different angles covered the walls, and the ceiling soared overhead, crisscrossed with lighting trusses and huge speakers.

The overhead lights were on full, and the few cast members milled around just in front of the stage. He skirted the orchestra pit, avoiding the edge and several foot drop off into the recessed floor below. He studied the new director as he greeted each of the actors.

Eric Tate. The man was about Koen's height and dressed in the red Center College theater polo tucked neatly into black slacks. His dark grey hair was slightly curly and trimmed short.

As Koen crossed the space to introduce himself, an arm snaked around his waist. He looked down, unsurprised to see Andrea Summers beaming up at him. With a shudder, he shifted away when her blonde hair whispered across his arm.

Music still hammered through his earbuds, and though he saw her lips move, he couldn't hear what she said. He tilted his head and raised an eyebrow. Annoyed, he looked past her to where the director and rest of the cast stood waiting.

Andrea pulled his earbuds out, shaking her head. "Still trying to ignore me?" she asked.

Even if he *did* want to date, clingy was not his type and Andrea was the definition of it. Her blue eyes offered him an open invitation, and when she let her hands fall onto his shoulders he removed them and gave her wrists a quick squeeze.

"No. Do you ever stop chasing what you'll never have?" he taunted. He quirked a smile in an effort to soften the sting, but he didn't need to worry. She didn't notice his sarcasm or at least didn't respond to it if she did.

Her infatuation with him began when he met her brother, Taylor, last year. Koen hung out with him when their weekends allowed, and the few times Koen visited the Summers' house, Andrea thought he was showing interest in her. Which put Koen permanently in her sights. The more he discouraged her the harder she tried.

Unfazed by his attempt to brush her off, Andrea caught his hand as he headed back toward the stage. His skin itched where she touched him, but he was unwilling to create a scene and allowed her to hold on. Director Tate watched them approach.

"Koen. Andrea. Hope you're ready to hit the ground running. We've got a lot to cover today." Tate's curious eyes dropped to their clasped hands then back up to assess Koen.

Though the man was smiling, his tone let him know he was at least annoyed by their late arrival. He hadn't directly auditioned for the man, but Koen knew the director saw his performances last year and was impressed. He hated making such a poor impression today and hoped the director was the forgiving type.

"Sorry I'm running behind, Mr. Tate." He disengaged himself from Andrea and stretched out his hand. "It's an honor to be working with you this year."

"It's good to have you. Try not to be late for rehearsals." Mr. Tate stepped back and began handing out the practice schedules.

"Great first impression." Koen mumbled under his breath. He took one of the schedules and leaned against the stage. Mr. Tate came to stand to his right, and Andrea leaned inches from him on his left. He could hear the stage and tech crew talking on the other side of the curtain, but he tuned them out until a laugh from behind the heavy velvet drapes made every hair on his body stand up. It was a voice like his mother's.

He once asked his mother why she sounded different from the other females he knew. She explained it was only the males of their kind who could distinguish any difference.

"Our kind?" he asked.

"We are Vampir," she patted the seat beside her on the porch swing. A note of sadness on her face. "You're growing up so fast, but if you are old enough to hear the echo, you are old enough to know who you are."

At ten, he'd barely understood all she told him that day. Happy stories of mates, blood bonds, and long lives. Then sadder stories of division, control, and hiding when humans misunderstood our rituals.

"We never harmed humans," she brushed the hair from his eyes, ruffling the curls on top of his head. "But the moment they saw our females' fangs, we were feared. So, we've hidden among them for centuries. As neighbors, friends, and co-workers. But there aren't many of us left." She smiled sadly at him. "Unless you are blessed to meet your mate, you may make the choice to take a human wife."

He scrunched his nose. "Eww. I don't want a wife."

She laughed, hugging him close. "Give it time, Ko. You'll change your mind."

His heart launched against his ribcage. He'd never heard another Vampir female, and this one did strange things to his breathing. He closed his eyes to listen and hopefully pick out the emotions in her echo like he learned to with his mother. There was joy, freedom, and a hint of uncertainty, inciting similar feelings in his chest. As he let the echo of her voice roll over him he realized there was more. The freedom ringing in her laugh called to him in a way no other's voice had, bringing him to a startling revelation as hope charged its way through his system.

She's un-bonded!

Whoever she was, she had not yet met her mate.

Without thinking about what his actions must look like, he spun around and hoisted himself onto the stage. Crossing it quickly, he pushed at the heavy folds of the curtain until he found an opening and leaned through the gap. Hoping she was close enough to scent him, he fisted the fabric in his hand as the group of students turned a corner off stage right.

Frustrated that he would have to wait until after class, he whipped the curtain back in place and tried to rein in the desire to chase after her. He turned to see Mr. Tate watching him curiously.

"You okay, Koen?" he said.

Dropping to sit on the edge of the stage, Koen grinned. "Just curious." His mind reeled with the possibilities. "Who's our crew this year? Anyone new?"

"They told me there was one transfer. A makeup artist, I believe." Mr. Tate's eyes narrowed before he looked up, thinking. "There's Aiden, Casey, and Alison working sound and lights. Kim and James for the set. And we have Jessica again for costumes." Everyone groaned. Koen couldn't blame them.

Jessica had only helped him with one outfit for his appearance in the musical, but her body odor was the stuff of legend. When she had helped him get in and out of a shirt and vest while keeping his microphone wires in place, he nearly gagged when she leaned in close to adjust his collar.

"Huh. Well at least we don't have a bunch of rookies," Koen said.

Andrea joined him on the stage. "Jessica shouldn't have a whole lot to do. This year the costumes should be pretty simple." She leaned against his arm. "Taylor wanted the love story to be the focus, not the costumes or props."

She pushed closer to rub her shoulder against his, but this time he hardly noticed. While Mr. Tate laid out the times and expectations for each rehearsal, Koen's mind replayed the mysterious laugh over and over.

An un-bonded Vampir here? How? He tried to pay attention, but instead, his eyes kept watching the clock.

The backstage area was empty by the time Koen got away from Andrea, and his disappointment made concentrating in his next class nearly impossible.

Feeling hopeful for the first time in a long time, he hummed quietly on his way to the dorm. As he bounded up the stairs, a new song wove its way through his mind. The tiny dorm room was empty when Koen pushed the door open.

He and his roommate were almost never in the room at the same time, which was a good thing since the room was more like a closet than a dorm room. With a set of bunk beds, two small desks and chairs, and two narrow closets on either side of the tall window, space was cramped even without people in it.

He dropped his bag next to his bunk and sank onto the thin mattress, picking up the guitar from where it rested in its stand at the foot of his bed. He slipped the strap over his head and after a quick tuning, allowed the words to come. He gave the instrument an open string strum, then let his fingers fret the new song.

A joy that lit my world
You ignited a bonfire in my heart
Just the laughter from your lips
Brought light to a darkened life

I can't stop thinking about the sound
The sound of your sweet voice
You woke something in my soul
You shined a spotlight on my heart

He was so engrossed in the melody that it took him a moment to realize his phone was ringing.

"Hello?" He propped the phone between his shoulder and ear and stood to close the door he'd left open in his hurry to get to the guitar.

"Hey, Koen." His Dad's thick voice made him smile. "How's class?"

"It's going great." Koen laid the guitar across the bed and reached for the bag he'd shoved aside. "I was just writing a song." He pulled a notebook free and jotted down the lyrics before he forgot, only half listening to his dad. "What's going on at home? Anything new?"

His Dad chuckled. "You might say that." Koen heard his mom's nervous laugh as they put the phone on speaker.

He dropped the pen to the bed as his heart picked up speed. His Mom hated talking on the phone. When she did something was wrong.

"Mom? What's going on?" he asked.

"Hi, Koen. Your Dad and I wanted to wait until the next time you were home to tell you, but we couldn't." His mother's voice echoed with confusing emotions. She was excited, scared, and nervous, and his own emotions immediately mirrored hers.

"Mom, Dad, tell me." He held the phone tightly in one hand, the other reflexively going to the charm hanging at his neck. He tensed before he heard the happy sigh from his mother.

"Your mother is pregnant," his dad said quietly.

"That's awesome! How long have you known?" Koen's surprise swelled through him as a relieved grin broke across his face. He released the pendant and glanced at the guitar.

"We're past the dangerous part. It's why we waited to tell you." Her voice coiled calmly around him.

"Eileen and I didn't want to worry you like last time," his dad said.

His mother's previous pregnancies had been difficult for all of them, but hardest on his father. She miscarried four times that he knew of. All near term. Koen was sure there were some earlier on they hadn't told him about. Because it was the male's blood that enabled a Vampir female to conceive and carry a child, his father carried the guilt for each loss.

He pushed his questions about the female from the theater aside for the moment.

"I wish I were there. My practice schedule and rehearsals won't let me get away, but maybe you can come for a visit. What does the midwife think?" he asked.

"She believes the baby is fine. And so do I." The peace in his mother's voice reassured him she agreed.

Ultrasounds and traditional exams were unnecessary. A Vampir mother is always connected to and aware of the condition of her child while in the womb.

"We were planning to come as soon as we got the okay. I think we can convince her that six hours is a trip I can handle." The smile in her voice was obvious even without her echo to tell him she was thrilled.

He drew a breath as it occurred to him how far along she was. His fingers sought out the charm again.

"Mom...do you know?" he asked.

Laughter from both of them brought tears to his eyes. It could only mean one thing.

"It's a girl!" They shouted in unison.

He sank onto the bed again. Tears of relief trailed down his cheeks. "Oh, Dad," he whispered, then repeated louder. "Oh, Dad. You're going to have a daughter!"

He heard the sounds change as his dad switched the speaker off. "I know, son. It's a miracle. Pure and simple." His already rough voice shook with emotion, and he began to cough violently.

Koen closed his eyes and waited for the coughing spell to pass, some of the happiness ebbing with the reminder his father was not well. When his father regained his breath, his voice was barely audible.

"I need to go. We're proud of you, Koen. We'll let you know when we're planning to visit," he rasped.

"I love you, Dad. Take care, and I'll see you soon." Koen hung up, dropped the phone beside him, and reached for his guitar. In seconds he finished the simple melody.

With all my heart
With all I am
I will love you 'til I die
I give my heart
Give it all to you
You are my miracle

He wished his brothers were here to celebrate. Neither of them ever met their mate and married human wives. If he chose to, he could do the same and at least have a family. But his brothers had both died of respiratory diseases before they reached the age of forty, leaving their families without a father. He couldn't find it in himself to do that. He couldn't marry knowing he would never see his kids grow up.

His fingers changed position, and the notes became haunting as the familiar pang of fear edged into his thoughts. He was happy for his parents to be sure, but would he ever get to experience that kind of joy? Harsh notes rose from his guitar as he plucked more violently at the strings. There was nothing he could do but cling to the thinning thread of hope that every day he survived there was still a chance for him to find her. His mother believed his mate was out there. He wanted to believe her, but with every day that passed, it became clearer it would take a miracle for him to find her. Maybe the voice he heard behind the curtain *was* his miracle.

Setting aside the instrument, he finished jotting down the rest of the song he'd written. Staring at the page, Koen fingered the charm at his throat and repeated his father's mantra: *"As long as your heart beats, there is always hope."*

CHAPTER

THREE

LEISEL

L eis swung her messenger bag onto the coffee table in the empty apartment and sank into the couch with a groan.

"Ugh! My shoulders are killing me." She jumped as a door creaked open behind her. Twisting her head toward the sound, she laughed, holding a hand over her chest. "Geez, Kay. I didn't know you were here."

Kay dropped onto the arm of the couch. Leis couldn't help being envious of Kay. She was pre-med and looked like a model with a perfectly spiked pixie haircut and a lithe dancer's body.

"Lab was easy today, and I needed a break. So, I skipped out early. How was your day?" she asked.

"Since the fall production doesn't call for any elaborate makeup, I've been assigned to help with props until we start dress rehearsals." Massaging her upper arm, Leis grimaced. "We had to drag out a living room set that was buried under a couple of years' worth of stuff. Then I got the lucky job of scrubbing it with upholstery cleaner." She blew a wisp of hair out of her face. "I guess when people know you can't smell they give you the nasty jobs. I don't want to know what might have been done on that couch!" Leis shuddered.

"Well, that's gross." Kay tilted her head thoughtfully and ran a hand through her gelled-up hair. "You hungry? I was planning to eat at Osha's. Want to join me?"

"Yeah, I do." Leis glanced at her phone and typed out a quick text. "Baden has class until at least nine. I'll let him know he can meet us there." She dropped it back into her purse and pushed up from the couch. "I need a shower but go ahead if you're hungry. I'll find you."

"I'll wait. We can walk over together." Kay picked up a discarded magazine and glanced at her watch. "You've got half an hour."

Leis grinned, shut the bedroom door behind her, and stepped out of her flats. After showering quickly, she dried her hair straight and let it fall just past her shoulder blades in soft red layers. It was still warm, so she pulled on a black maxi skirt, a white fitted tee, and wrapped a yellow and white scarf around her neck. She slipped into her gray ballet flats, snapped a hair tie around her wrist, snagged her purse, and headed out.

KOEN

WHY DOES music theory have to be so complicated? Koen leaned back in the restaurant booth and pushed the sheet music aside, wondering why he'd ever chosen Music Theory and Composition as his major.

He came to Osha's because on a Friday evening, most people would be out partying, and, as expected, the place was almost deserted.

He glanced around at the chipped and worn booths that lined the walls. Filling the center of the room were square four tops with brown vinyl chairs that looked retro and were probably original. Along the back wall was the kitchen opening and a short bar with four chrome stools covered in the same brown vinyl. Though obviously older, the place was clean, and the food was better by far than the cafeteria across campus.

Ellen, Osha's only full-time waitress, smiled at him when she came through the kitchen door carrying a tray of food. He discovered Osha's early last year and hung out at the diner frequently enough that he became friends with the older woman. He sometimes thought of her as his mom-away-from-mom.

Ellen delivered the food to a couple sitting all the way in the back who were completely focused on the textbooks in front of them.

Like I should be.

Between his frustration with theory, and the laugh still haunting him, he wasn't getting much accomplished.

He absently glanced through the large front window to the congested traffic of Main Street. Swiping a finger across the phone screen, he switched tracks from the concerto he was studying to something a little more his style. His shoulders relaxed as the thrum of a motorcycle gradually blended with a bass guitar through the intro to his favorite song, "The Man Named Hell," by The Showdown.

Turning up the volume, he pulled out the script for the play. He was supposed to have his lines for Act One memorized by Monday, and he was once again behind. Mr. Tate would not be pleased.

He flipped the cover open and skimmed the opening lines. His character, Jackson, was a rich Texas lawyer who returned to his tiny hometown to help his high school sweetheart, Emma, manage the estate of her recently deceased parents.

Koen thumbed through the pages, admitting Taylor Summers was a talented playwright. Taylor's sister Andrea was on his nerves even more than usual though. He shoved the script aside, struggling to balance his thoughts between the girl he couldn't find, the one who wouldn't leave him alone, and the gorgeous red head who haunted his dreams.

He glanced up, and his heart stopped as the redheaded girl walked in. She laughed, then turned wide eyes toward a short haired blonde he hadn't noticed come in with her. Still laughing, the redhead swung her gaze down the line of booths, and he nearly lost his breath along with his heartbeat when her sparkling eyes slid across his. He was closer to her this time, and they were a soft shade of green he'd never seen before.

Trying not to stare, he watched the two of them until they were seated across the restaurant in a corner booth. He forced himself back to his script.

Don't go there, Koen. Cute or not, you know better.

But as he read through the first scene it wasn't Andrea he imagined kissing. It was the green-eyed girl across the room.

As the music screamed in his ears, he wondered what her voice sounded like. She was in the theater building the other day. It *could* have been her voice he heard. With a shake of his head, he quickly discarded the idea.

Get a grip, Lockton. You couldn't be that lucky.

LEISEL

"He said that to you?" Leis looked at Kay in astonishment as they slid into a booth. "What did you do?"

Kay grinned, "I slapped the smile off his face, and told him it would be a cold day in hell before I'd *take him for a ride*." She shuddered as she reached for a menu. "Seriously, why do guys have to be such jerks? It was our first date for goodness sakes!"

Leis shook her head. Every date was a first date for Kay. She could only remember one guy Kay had gone out with more than once, and that had been more coincidence than a planned outing.

Cute and witty, Kay liked to keep her options open and claimed her free time was too precious to spend all on one person. Watching the revolving door of suitors Kay had, Leis was thankful she never had to think about dating.

"I don't know why they act that way. I'm just glad Baden doesn't," Leis replied.

A shiver ran down Leis's neck at the thought of being intimate with Baden the way Kay's last date had suggested. She couldn't imagine it and trying made her blush. Their intimacy wasn't something she was looking forward to, and she had a hard time convincing herself that a ceremony and vows were going to change those feelings. She loved Baden, but every time she tried to think about him as anything more than one of her brothers, her skin crawled.

Kay snorted, drawing Leis's attention back to the present. "Jerks or not, there *are* a couple of guys I might not turn down. One of them is sitting right over there." Her eyes flicked toward a boy across the room, and she almost sighed his name. "Koen Lockton. But he doesn't date. I heard his family is weird."

Leis turned to look. Raven black hair curled softly at the guy's temples and around the back of his neck. His thumbs drummed a rhythm against the table, no doubt along to the song playing through his earbuds. A worn white t-shirt stretched across his muscled shoulders, and a dark, thickly braided necklace surrounded the base of his neck. When the fabric pulled taut across his back as he reached for his drink, Leis swallowed hard and turned away.

"I saw him going into the theater the other day. Is he an actor?" she asked.

Kay nodded and took a sip of water. "He is, and he's also the star of the music program. I heard he's been picked up for a recording contract next year. I went to one of his concerts last year. He's pretty amazing." She lifted the menu, her lips turning down in disappointment. "Too bad he's practically untouchable."

Leis couldn't stop herself from sneaking looks at his handsome face. There *was* something different about him, but she couldn't place it. His cheekbones were high and angular like a model's.

Though intensely focused on the notebook in front of him, he looked like someone who laughed easily. Leis found herself fascinated by the way the muscles in his forearms danced under the skin as he used his thumbs like drum sticks on the table.

While she watched, a grey-haired waitress approached his table. When he didn't acknowledge her, she reached out to touch his shoulder. Startled, he jumped and knocked his water over. Leis giggled as he scrambled to lift his phone and script. Unable to contain it, Leis broke out in a laugh as he tripped and nearly knocked the table over trying to get out of the booth.

FOUR

KOEN

Koen cursed as the water and ice spread. Scrambling to get his things and himself out of the way, he bashed his thigh against the table, further scattering the ice. He muttered another curse and set his script and phone on the table next to his.

He caught Ellen's arm, knowing she hadn't meant to startle him. He pulled one of his earbuds out prepared to apologize to her, but as soon as it slipped out of his ear, a laugh from across the room crashed into him, and he froze.

She's here. Gods, it is *her. The redhead.*

Koen's hand slipped from Ellen's arm, and he closed his eyes as the redhead's emotions swept through his body. He savored each one as they registered: amusement, hunger, embarrassment, *desire*. The moment he sensed her desire, every bone in his body insisted he march over to her. He locked himself in place, his hands tightening into fists at the effort.

"Koen, I am so sorry! I know you didn't hear me." Ellen moved beside him. "I shouldn't have come up behind you." She paused. "Koen. Are you okay?"

He opened his eyes and let out a breath. "I'm all right, El." Hoping she wouldn't notice his sudden nervousness, he tucked the buds into their case and reached behind him for his wallet.

Koen could feel the redhead's eyes still on him, and it made him smile like an idiot. This wasn't exactly the way he'd imagined getting her attention, but he'd take it. Now he just needed to figure out what to say to her when he turned around.

With a shaky breath, he refocused on Ellen. "It was my fault." He unfolded his wallet and laid a couple of bills on the table.

"It's just water." Ellen propped her hands on her hips and watched him with narrowed eyes. "I guess your hearing is okay with all that loud music?"

More laughter sent a thrill of pleasure up his spine, and heat rose up his neck. "My hearing is fine. You surprised me, that's all."

She picked up the cash and handed it back to him, flicking her amused gaze past his shoulder to the table where the girls sat. Her brown eyes sparkled as she leaned a hip against the table edge. "Someone finally catch your eye?"

"Maybe." He patted her shoulder gratefully. "Wish me luck."

LEISEL

Kay gave a short laugh as she continued to watch the exchange between the boy and the waitress. "Serves him right to be embarrassed. He acts like he's so above even looking at a girl." She leaned toward Leis and raised her voice louder than she should. "Do you think he's into guys instead?"

Leis frowned. "Didn't you just tell me he doesn't date because of some family thing?"

A look of panic came over Kay's face as a low voice spoke from the end of the table.

"I'm not into guys, and who said I don't date?"

Leis's mouth went dry, and her thoughts scattered when she looked up into a pair of piercingly light blue eyes alive with humor, and something else.

In the space it took her to draw a breath, something inside her shifted. Something that made her heart kick solidly against her ribs in a way that wasn't at all unpleasant.

Unnerved but refusing to show it, Leis leaned back. "Sorry about that. We didn't mean to laugh." Kay kicked her under the table, but Leis ignored her, instead, she held out her hand, determined not to let him get to her. "And please excuse my friend. My name's Leisel Gottschalk, but everyone calls me Leis. You're Koen Lockton, right? Or so I've been told." Leis tipped her head at the girl sitting in shock across the table. She deliberately broke his intense gaze and lifted her chin toward the bag on his shoulder. "Did your script get wet? You could copy mine if you need to."

"Yes, I'm Koen. Thanks for the offer to copy your script. I might take you up on it." He leaned forward to grasp her hand, sending unexpected chills up her arm. He held her hand a second longer than necessary, then he reached out to Kay, not quite taking his eyes off Leis. "Introduce me to your friend?" he asked.

"Kay Beckett." Apparently recovered from her embarrassment, Kay took his hand and pulled him closer to the table. Leis frowned when she laid a hand on his arm. "Since you do date, are you busy tomorrow night?"

Leis shifted in her seat, suddenly very interested in her menu again, and not sure why it bothered her to see Kay touching him. His amused voice made her hands tighten on the plastic sheet. "No, I'm not busy tomorrow. But I plan to be."

Over the top of her menu Leis watched her friend's face, and from the corner of her eye, she saw Koen look across the table.

"Dinner?" he asked.

Leis lifted her soda to take a drink as Kay's eyes met hers. "What?" Leis managed.

Koen chuckled under his breath, and the roughness of it made her stomach unwind more. She looked up at him as he pushed his hands into his pockets and rocked back on his heels.

"I think I just asked if you would go to dinner with me tomorrow," he said.

Leis choked. "Me? Uh. No. But thank you for asking."

She met his look coolly though her insides were on fire. She conjured thoughts of Baden and his chocolate brown irises, trying to deny how Koen's bright blue ones affected her. He nodded, something like confusion crossing his face.

"Okay. I'll see you at the theater then." He opened an earbud case and slid one in as he half turned away. "Blocking starts Monday, right?"

"I'll be there." She forced a smile. "Rehearsal at 4."

Koen nodded once. "Yep." He spared a glance at Kay and flashed a heartbreakingly handsome smile before his eyes landed on Leis. "Ladies."

Leis held her breath and watched him leave. *What is wrong with me?* Neither of them moved as the door chimed. Kay was the first to break the silence and exhaled loudly as he crossed in front of the window.

"What in the world was *that?*" She fanned herself and looked sideways at Leis. "Did you really turn him down? He couldn't keep his eyes off you. I've never seen him act like that with anyone. He doesn't even look at Andrea that way." Kay huffed and glanced longingly in the direction he'd gone. "You could have at least had dinner with him!"

"Hello! Baden, remember him?" She said with a raised eyebrow.

"Yeah. I guess that would make a difference to you." Kay picked lint from her pant leg. "I'd have at least gotten a free meal out of him."

Leis sighed and did her best to laugh it off, but the encounter shook her. Her heart continued flying in her chest when she realized she would likely be working closely with Koen for the next several weeks. What was she going to tell Baden?

She reached for her water and took a long sip. "Let's talk about something else, okay?"

L eis laughed as Baden slammed his hip into hers, sending her sliding across the bench seat.

"I'm starved!" he whined and swiped a fry from one of the plates a waitress was clearing from their table.

Righting herself, Leis poked him in the shoulder. "How was class?"

"Interesting. The professor showed us how to hack our phones today." He lifted her hand and kissed it.

Though his hand was warm and strong, the kiss he pressed to the back of her knuckles didn't give her chills like Koen's touch had.

Resisting a frown, Leis handed him a menu. "Is that even legal?"

He shrugged. "Probably not. It didn't work on mine, so no harm done."

The gray-haired waitress paused on her way past the table. "Have you decided what you'd like?" she asked.

"A cheeseburger and fries, please," Baden replied.

The woman rested a hand on Baden's shoulder and smiled at Leis. "That was very nice of you to offer to help Koen after his things got wet. He was pretty taken with you."

Baden stiffened, and his head swung toward Leis as she fumbled for words. Guilt slammed into her.

"Was he? I — I didn't notice," she stammered.

"Cheeseburger and fries. I'll have those right out for you." The woman patted Baden's shoulder before walking away.

Leis could feel him watching her but caught Kay's eye instead. Her face was concerned as she slid out of the seat.

"I've got a report due tomorrow. I'll see you at the apartment?" Kay's gaze shifted between them.

Leis bit her lip and nodded. "I'll see you in a little bit. Thanks for dinner." Kay hurried out the door.

Baden moved to the other side of the booth and raised an eyebrow. "Care to explain?"

Blowing out a breath, Leis raised her hands and sat back. "He's the male lead for the play. I thought his script got wet when that waitress startled him, and he spilled water all over the table." She crossed her arms, not sure why she felt defensive. "He came over and introduced himself as he was leaving, and I offered to let him copy my script."

Baden's low chuckle surprised her. He reached across the table and covered her hand with his, stroking her forearm with his thumb. "Leis. Relax. It's no big deal. So, he thinks you're cute." He gave her a fake jealous look, and she laughed with him. "Lockton, huh? Maybe I need to do some digging around about him. You know I can, Leis."

"Yes, B. I know you can." As a computer genius, he had a knack for finding information about nearly anyone or anything. "You know you don't need to. He's just an actor in the play," she said dismissively. Then, remembering her body's response to the blue-eyed charmer, her voice wavered, and she blurted, "I love you, Baden."

"Love you too, Leis." His teasing expression changed for just a second. So quickly she might have missed it if she hadn't known him so well. Then his smile was back, and she wondered if she *had* imagined it. "How are the rest of your classes going?" he asked.

"English Composition is a pain, and European history is killing me. How about you? Learning anything new?"

"Yeah," he said thoughtfully. "The professor for tonight's class has some interesting theories about all the new cell phones. He said mine was as high-tech as they come. Which was why I couldn't hack it. He said it has military grade security." His face took on the distant look that told her he was working something out in his mind. He spun a straw absently in his fingers, then shrugged a shoulder as his food arrived and he dug in.

Leis looked up to give the waitress a dirty look for mentioning Koen earlier, but she was gone before Leis could make eye contact.

Leis reached for her water and squelched her frustration. "Have you talked to my parents lately?"

He swallowed a mouthful of burger. "Last night. Your Mom called to get my opinion on something for the ceremony." Again, something unhappy flickered in his eyes just before a lazy grin spread across his face. "She's got the whole Clan in on the planning I think. Your Mom's having the time of her life, and she's driving Andrew crazy running errands for her. They're planning to come visit next week."

"Yeah," she huffed, "She wants to take me shopping." Her face flushed. "Shopping for dresses and... other things."

He laughed. "Hmmm, I could give you some suggestions." He waggled his eyebrows then sobered when he sensed her hesitation. "Leis, it will all work out, okay? Trust me."

She met his eyes and tears blurred his handsome face. "I do. It just doesn't seem real, you know?"

His phone buzzed, and he leaned sideways to pull it from his pocket. His face darkened, and he tossed a napkin over the half-eaten meal. "Hey, I gotta go. My professor is available right now, and he promised to answer a couple questions for me." He stood, tossing a couple of bills onto the table. His eyes were far away when he spared a smile at her. "Love you, Leis."

"Love you, too, B. Will I see you tomorrow morning?"

"I'm not sure. I'll call if I can meet you for breakfast." He typed something, then leaned forward and placed the phone on the table. His expression was suddenly very focused. "And Leis? Don't be afraid to have fun with your new friends, okay? I'm going to be busy for the next few weeks, and your theater schedule is going to make it hard for us to find time together." A serious tone replaced his casual one, and his chocolate brown eyes were firm. "I mean it. Don't let anything hold you back, especially not us. I'll always be here." He covered her hand with his. "Don't let me hold you back. Get out and have fun. Promise?"

Not sure how to respond, she nodded. "Okay."

"Good." His genuine smile returned, and he winked at her. "Good night, Leis." Then he was gone.

She made sure the bill for his food got paid and headed to the apartment. As she walked the couple blocks, Baden's admonishment rolled over and over through her mind.

From the time they were in middle school, he encouraged her to find ways to get out and have fun without him regardless of what their family expected. But this sudden emphasis on not letting him hold her back puzzled her. Chalking it up to him being distracted by whatever he needed to ask his professor, she decided not to worry about it. They were pledged to bond, and only the Elder could break that.

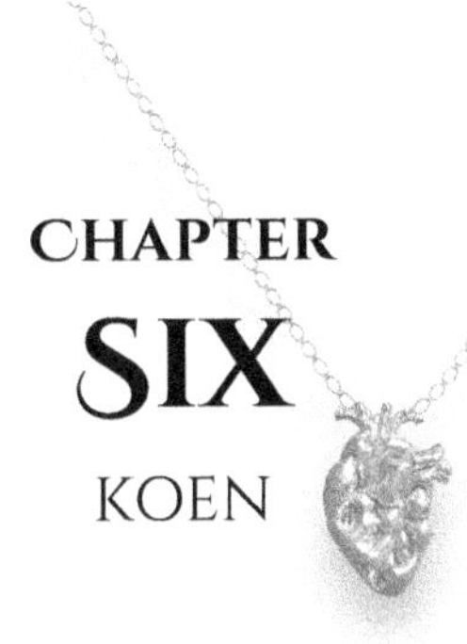

It took Koen a couple of days, but he finally tracked down the apartment Leis lived in. He'd expected her to be in the dorms, but when she wasn't listed in the campus directory, he started asking around.

He was getting frustrated when Ellen mentioned she'd seen Leis and her friend walking in the direction of some pricey off campus apartments.

Standing on the sidewalk and pushing the sunglasses up on his head, Koen spotted the buildings just as Leis stepped outside. Suddenly, he wasn't sure this was such a great idea and turned back to campus.

"Koen?" she paused, shielding her eyes from the sun.

Dressed casually in a pair of skinny jeans that skimmed every inch of her long legs, a pair of flats, and a loose-fitting turquoise top that made her hair color as brilliant as a new copper penny, Leis was the most attractive girl he had ever met.

A curious smile lit up her face. "What are you doing all the way over here?"

"Looking for you?" The nervousness in her voice combined with his, and he felt uncharacteristically hesitant until a shy blush reddened her cheeks. His courage bolstered, he gestured toward the cluster of red brick buildings across the road. "Walk with me?"

"Sure." She cleared her throat as they fell in step. "If we're going to be friends, there's something I should tell you."

He glanced around to ensure no one was close enough to hear them and started to ask her why she was here alone and unbonded. But when his distracted mind registered the effort it was taking her to say what she wanted to tell him, he paused.

"What's that?" he asked.

"I'm engaged. His name is Baden, and we've known each other since we were kids. He's a computer science major." Her confession spilled out quickly, and he tried his best to decipher why she had chosen this tactic to warn him off.

Something wasn't right, but what bothered him most was beneath it all, Koen felt the ripple of her attraction toward him as clearly as if she had just leaned toward him for a kiss.

If she was pledged, and Baden was indeed her mate, they would have already bonded, and the scent of any other male should repulse her. It should be impossible for her to be attracted to him or anyone else. But he'd seen the way she watched him, and even now, he heard the echo of her desire.

There was no one within earshot. If he was wrong about her lack of attachment, she should be able to smell he was a Vampir male and address it directly. Something about her behavior felt very off, so he played along.

"Engaged, huh?" He picked up the pace and tried to sort through the mixed messages she was sending. "When are you getting married?"

"In May, when we get home from school. My Mom is going crazy planning it."

She squared her shoulders as her voice threw a wave of confusion and pain over him. The bright smile on her lips didn't match her tone, but her next words were soft.

"Baden is my best friend." She looked up at him, and the light in her green eyes begged him to understand. "I just thought you should know."

"I appreciate you telling me." Koen pulled the sunglasses down to hide the anger. Trying to understand, he pressed. "You sound nervous about it."

Her head dropped, letting her hair cover her face. "I guess I am. Marriage is a big deal, you know?"

Koen's anger rose toward whoever Baden was. If he was Vampir, he had to know something wasn't right, didn't he?

"Baden must be a pretty cool guy. Is he okay with you hanging out with me?" he asked.

A slight smile curved her lips. "Yeah. He's a great guy. He trusts me."

It was obvious she cared for him, but the intense attraction between a couple intended to be bonded was plainly missing. Koen let it go before his anger got out of control. It wasn't his place to interfere. *Yet.*

"What are your classes today?" He shifted the pack on his shoulder and jerked his chin ahead of them. "I'm heading to the English Department for my weekly dose of Shakespeare."

"Convenient." She patted her messenger bag. "English Composition."

They crossed the campus chatting easily about their professors and the rehearsal schedule, but his mind was still working on a way to ask her what was really going on. Unable to keep up the idle chatter anymore, he reached out to stop her and ask outright, but before he could touch her, the wind blew a whiff of peaches toward him and his nerves stood on end as something one of the stage hands said came back to him.

"Lucky her. She can't smell how bad that couch stinks!"

Almost afraid of the answer, he asked, "What's that perfume you're wearing? You smell like a fruit stand."

Leis laughed and answered casually. "I can't smell anything, so I have no idea." He stumbled, but she didn't seem to notice. "Probably the shampoo. Kay picked it out for me. I think she said it was peaches and cream or something like that." She lifted her face to the sky and inhaled. "I was born without the ability to smell. Weird, huh?"

Koen worked to keep the shock out of his voice and replied evenly. "That is a little weird."

If she can't smell, she has no way to know for certain Baden is her intended. Questions raced through his mind. He didn't know much, but he had never heard of a bonding happening without the female being able to scent her mate. Based on what he knew, it wasn't even *possible.*

And then, like a punch to the gut, it all made sense. She was talking to him like a human because she had no way of knowing he was Vampir.

Koen bit his lip. No matter what was going on, she was promised to someone else, and this wasn't the time to start a conversation about it. With confusion and hope warring inside him, he opened the door and let her go in ahead of him.

"I'm in room 315," Koen said as he watched her sweep her long hair over a shoulder. His fingers tingled with the desire to handle the fiery strands.

"I'm just around the corner here in 110." She turned to go, her expression pained. "Thanks for walking me to class."

"Anytime, Leis." When she disappeared around the corner, he unfurled the death grip on his backpack strap. He made a mental note to talk to his mom as soon as he could.

Shakespeare is going to be a waste of time again today.

Koen slid into his regular booth at Osha's and tugged the rumpled script from his backpack. He laid it open, but his eyes wouldn't focus. All he could think about was Leis and the way she looked at him as she told him about Baden. Her green eyes begged him to understand, but there was no way he could.

How could she possibly be -

He jumped as a book dropped onto the table in front of him, looking up to see a tall, dark-haired guy staring down at him. Clenching his jaw, ready to ask what his problem was, Koen watched incredulously as the guy slid into the seat across from him and crossed his arms.

"We need to talk." Guarded, dark brown eyes bored into his.

"About?" Koen mirrored his pose.

"Leis Gottschalk." Koen's brows shot up, and the other narrowed his lids. "You're Koen."

Koen only inclined his head, not trusting himself to speak if this was who he thought it was.

With an exhale through his nose, the guy dropped his arms and confirmed his suspicions. "I'm Baden, and there are some things we need to discuss."

"Yeah?" Koen tipped his head. "Like your *engagement?* I'm a little confused."

Baden clenched his fists. "That's easy. But I can't figure out how they got you here."

"What?" Koen frowned. Not the response he'd expected.

"It isn't a coincidence you and Leis met." He ran a shaking hand down his face and took a deep breath. "What a mess. I don't even know how to have this conversation..."

"Okay, then let me start." He leaned over the table and lowered his voice. "You're a Vampir?" When he nodded, Koen bit back his anger, reminding himself they were in a public place. "Then how can you miss the fact that she's not yours?"

Baden's eyes hardened to flint. "You have no idea what's going on. So, until you do, lighten up, all right? Leis and I were raised to believe our Clan was all that was left of the Vampir."

"All that's left? How is that..." Koen frowned, remembering a story he'd heard as a boy. "My grandfather told stories about a lost Clan, but none of us ever took him seriously."

Baden huffed. "It seems we have more to talk about than I thought." He swept his eyes around the room before locking on Koen. "Before I say anything else, you need to know that Leis and I are in danger. She cannot know you and I have had this meeting. Not yet." Baden paused as Ellen approached the table.

"Can I get you boys anything?"

"Water would be fine," Baden answered.

Koen shook his head, and she smiled. "I'll be right back then."

Baden leveled his gaze at him. "Look, here's the deal. I know Leis isn't mine, but my grandmother and the rest of the Clan don't give us choices."

Koen flared. "Choices? Either she's yours or she isn't. What does the Clan have to do with it?"

Baden raised a hand. "Being angry at me isn't going to change anything. How about you let me explain, and we go from there?"

"All right." Koen ran a hand through his hair. "Let's hear it."

"I'm going to make this as concise as possible. There are only five families left in the - our - Clan. Three generations ago, the Elder resorted to Vampir law and began choosing who bonded with who. Leis and I are the youngest, and she's one of two females who haven't bonded." Koen flinched, and Baden grimaced. "Yeah."

Koen tried to grasp what he'd said. "You still have an Elder? And what law?"

"The Elder is my grandmother. Simply because at over three hundred years old, she's the oldest of us. The Law, well, that's the messed-up reason Leis and I are here." Baden's face reddened. Ellen set his glass on the table, and he took a quick drink, giving her time to get out of earshot. "I'm going to tell you everything, but you have to promise me not to talk to Leis about it until I do." He bit his lip and made a fist. "I've heard it in her voice, and I can see it in your face. She's yours, Koen, and I'm trying my best to be happy for the both of you." He ground out the words. "But I've been in love with her my whole life, and we've been told it's her fault we haven't bonded. Until recently, I believed it. She still does."

Koen was furious. "Because she can't smell?"

"Yes. I don't even want to know how you know that." His jaw tightened. "You're not going to like hearing the reason why she can't, so I'm asking you to listen before you react." Baden pulled at his neck, looking like a man about to lose everything.

"I'll do my best." Koen folded his hands on the table.

"Because there are so few of us, my grandmother has resorted to what amounts to inbreeding to keep us all alive." Koen's stomach churned, and Baden looked green. "She's been able to disguise what she was doing until now, but defects are starting to show up. Leis's inability to smell is only one of the results. I don't know who else has suspicions, but my father did." His face went from pale to deep red.

"He tried to stop them from forcing Leis and I together. They killed him for it."

Koen stared at the man across the table, afraid to hear more.

Words poured from him as if he had to get them out before he lost his nerve. "Her father and mine were twins. My grandmother separated them when they were babies. She did that with almost every family. She split us up, so no one knows for sure who is related to who. When my father discovered the truth, he confronted her and tried to stop her. Three days later, he and my mother *accidentally* died of carbon monoxide poisoning. She sent me to live with Leis, and here we are." Baden met Koen's shocked eyes. "Leis doesn't know. I will tell her, but not yet. She is incredibly strong, but this will devastate her."

Koen blinked slowly, trying to absorb it all. "How did you find out about all this?"

Baden's smile was sad. "Leis's father told me at the end of last school year." He glanced out the window. "My Dad kept records of everything he learned and hid it in a false bottom built into the crib I would have been given to Leis at our Bonding Ceremony. Hayden found the papers when he was cleaning it." He traced his finger around the rim of the glass. "We were supposed to be bonded last fall, but he managed to get it postponed after he knew the truth."

"Why not just tell her?" Koen challenged. His mind was whirling, and his stomach threatened to return his lunch to the table. "She deserves to know the truth."

Baden's shoulders slumped. "She does, but there's more at stake than just her and I. There are plans in the works to confront my grandmother, but she can't know ahead of time that we're coming. That's the reason we're all in Ohio." He took another drink. "When the time comes, I can't go with Leis. They'll kill me for knowing what I know, and who knows what they'll try with Leis next. Haydn is going along with my grandmother until we can get everything in place." He sighed. "But we've run out of time. We need you to keep her safe until it's time for her to go back and confront my grandmother."

Koen was incensed. "Let me make sure I understand. You and Leis are cousins, your grandmother is willing to kill, and you want me to take Leis back there? What if I say no?"

Baden lifted an eyebrow. "Nothing will happen to Leis. They need her. Every female Vampir is precious." He lifted his chin. "And if my information is correct, the rest of you aren't doing well either? The Vampir are fractured and spread all over the world, right?"

Koen's brows dropped. "Yes, but what do you mean we're not doing well?" He sat back, realization dawning. "My breathing issues. The defects are starting to show up everywhere. Are there similar cases worldwide?"

Baden nodded. "There are also far fewer females born than ever before. Because bonded couples live so long, it's by design that the ratio of males to females is about ten to one. But now, it's twenty or thirty to one." He passed a set of papers across the table. "If we don't reunite our people, none of us will last more than two generations."

Koen pulled the packet toward him. It was filled with names, dates, and locations; each section divided by location. "What's this?"

"What I've been working on since I got here. Everyone thinks I've been in class, but I've been working with computer programmers, hackers, and data mining companies all over the world." He rested his elbows on the table and pressed his fingers to his temples. "But I have to stop. My grandmother has been tracking me, and I'm about to get caught. She's got software and malware on every device Leis and I own, and it's replicated itself onto the school computers somehow. That's the other reason Leis can't know yet. If she lets anything slip, we're done." He indicated the packet still open in front of Koen. "That's a hard copy of all the important information. We're developing a network around the world and storing the data out of the country where my grandmother can't touch it."

Koen straightened the stack of pages. "So, what do you need me to do?"

"We need you to stay close to Leis, and I need you to trust me. She's going to need you." Koen was surprised when tears glistened in the other male's eyes. "And we're all going to need you both."

EIGHT

Koen met Leis outside her apartment building three more times that week. Twice he walked her to class, and tonight they decided to have dinner. Once seated at Osha's, Koen asked several times about her family, but she deflected him by asking how he got so good at music.

"It was my doctor's suggestion. I started singing in high school as a way to strengthen my lungs, and I turned out to have natural talent." He lifted a shoulder. "I fell in love with music, learned how to play guitar, and ended up with an offer from a record company."

His sleeves were pushed up to his elbows, and Leis's eyes frequently snagged on the way the muscle and vein corded his forearms. Tearing her gaze away, she looked up to see amusement dancing like waves in his blue eyes.

She cleared her throat and leaned forward. "That doesn't happen often, does it? How did they find you?"

He took a noisy sip of his milkshake. "I was playing at a local festival between semesters, and a talent scout was in the crowd. He offered to do a four-song demo that summer and my parents used the rest of my college fund to pay for the studio time." His eyes lit up, and Leis couldn't stop staring at the way the blue deepened to midnight as his passion for music animated his face. "I spent about four weeks in Nashville, and they offered me a spot on a tour later this year. They weren't happy when I decided I wanted to finish college before I committed to anything." He shrugged.

They looked up at Ellen when she slid their plates in front of them. "Anything else?"

Leis picked up her fork and smiled. "I don't think so."

The older woman rapped her knuckles on the table. "All right then. Yell if you need anything."

Leis turned her attention to him. "Did they finally agree?"

He sprinkled salt on his fries and grinned. "Not at first, and Mom and Dad couldn't afford it after paying for the studio time. But I'm stubborn and applied for every scholarship I could. Center College offered me a full ride based on my academic scores and the theater program offered to cover my housing and books." He paused, and his tone dropped. "I never questioned it." His piercing eyes swung to hers then to his food, leaving her breathless. "Guess it was just meant to be."

Koen shifted in his seat and suddenly seemed overly interested in his burger. Curious, she said, "Your parents must be proud of you."

His shoulders relaxed. "They are." He looked up, and his eyes were light again. "It's just hard to be away from them sometimes. Especially Mom, she's..." His lips pressed together. "...she misses singing with me."

Leis was certain he was going to say something else but didn't ask. "Is she a musician too?"

"Runs in the family. Mom has a pitch-perfect singing voice, and storytelling is like a family heirloom. Dad and grandpa can sit and tell stories for days." He stretched an arm along the back of the booth. "Sometimes we even write poetry. Add a guitar and bam! Instant song."

"You must be close to her." Leis lowered her eyes and flicked an onion aside. "My Mom and I used to be, but with the...wedding, it's been tense." She took a bite of tomato, horrified she almost called it the Bonding. Koen was so easy to talk to she almost forgot he was human. Chewing carefully, she looked up and caught a glimmer of anger in his eyes.

"Sounds like your wedding is a big deal to them." His voice roughened. He slid a hand down his pant leg as he leaned toward her, the other still outstretched. She swallowed at the question in his stare and the way his body moved. "Why so nervous about it? Most girls can't wait." His eyebrow rose in challenge.

She flinched and regretted bringing it up. "It's a huge deal to my family." She realized how that must sound and huffed a breath trying to make it a laugh. "I mean, it's a huge deal to me too, of course."

Koen snagged the last fry on his plate and pointed it at her. "Then why do I get the impression you're not looking forward to it?"

Her stomach fluttered watching the muscles in his jaw work as he chewed. *Goodness, he even makes eating attractive!* Her heart skipped at the sudden darkness in his bright eyes, and a flicker of defensiveness rose.

"Baden wanted me to pursue my dream of working in the theater before we got married." Spearing another tomato, Leis lifted her shoulder in dismissal. Regret and her unflagging honesty kept her from maintaining the outright lie very long. "Our relationship is - complicated."

Unable to look him in the eye, her gaze fell to the small section of skin at the base of his neck. From the short distance across the table, she could see the charm in the hollow of his throat was an anatom-ical heart. She coughed a little as he swallowed and the charm rose and fell against his tan skin.

"Then un-complicate it." His voice was gruff, and his eyes were sharp. Without another word, he picked up her bill along with his and paid while she sat stunned.

Leis pressed a hand against her racing heart and tried to come up with a response. What could she tell him? The truth? She breathed a quiet laugh at herself. Like he would believe that. Things *were* complicated, and un-complicating them would require her missing sense of smell to suddenly appear.

When he returned to the booth and offered to walk her to her apartment, his lighthearted smile was back. Conversation along the way stayed on safe topics like school and practice schedules until they reached her building. Koen stood in the hallway outside her door with his hands in his pockets. He watched until she unlocked her apartment and stepped inside.

Koen looked over his shoulder before going down the stairs. "See you at rehearsal, Leis." His smile seemed forced, and the gravel in his voice sent a shiver up her back.

CHAPTER
NINE

LEISEL

On Monday, Leis crossed the stage to remove a table before the next rehearsal started and walked up on Koen and Andrea arguing.

"You're not even trying, Koen." Andrea stood in front of him with her hands on his chest. A confusing pang of jealousy rifled through Leis at the sight of them so close. "You never hesitated to kiss me before."

The thought of them kissing twisted something inside her that tightened when the blond stepped into him and wrapped an arm around his waist.

"I told you, I'm tired. Let's not make a big deal out of this." Koen extricated himself and held on to her wrists. His tone hardened. "Besides, I don't play games, Andrea. You know that."

Unable to stand seeing his hands on her, Leis stepped from behind one of the set walls and cleared her throat.

"Sorry, I just need to grab that end table." She moved around them and reached for the small round table beside the couch. "Don't let me interrupt."

Koen's eyes flashed in annoyance, and he dropped Andrea's hands.

"You must be the new makeup artist. I'm Andrea Summers." Andrea turned, stepped in front of Koen, and offered her hand.

After wiping her palms on her jeans, Leis took her hand. The other girl's grip was firmer than necessary.

"I'm Leis. Your brother wrote the play, didn't he?" she asked.

Andrea glanced behind her to Koen, who stood with his arms crossed. Leis's mouth went dry as the muscles in his forearms flexed in agitation. He caught her watching and raised a brow in question, the corner of his lip curving as she blushed. Her blush deepened when she caught the movement of the charm at his throat as he swallowed. Why that fascinated her, she couldn't explain. Her eyes narrowed on Andrea as the actress sidled closer to Koen. When she lifted a palm to rest it on his bicep, Leis wanted to slap it away.

"He did. Taylor wrote it specifically for Koen and me," Andrea beamed.

Koen rolled his eyes, and Leis choked down a laugh as he shook his head quickly.

"Well, that's awesome. It was nice to finally meet you." Carrying the table, she turned to go. "See you around, Koen."

She felt his eyes follow her as she exited the stage and before she reached the side curtain, his voice stopped her.

"Hey, Leis?" he said.

She turned and noted the mischief in his look. She waited and tried to ignore the flutter of excitement his voice always brought.

"I'm playing a concert this weekend at the fairgrounds," he smirked. "I've got extra tickets if you'd like to come."

Leis had tried to get tickets, but the concert had sold out weeks ago. Andrea had gone rigid beside him, but he kept his eyes on her. In his dazzling blue gaze, Leis picked up on the game he was playing. For some crazy reason, she hoped he would keep going.

"I'll think about it." Leis was thankful her voice didn't shake. "My family is coming into town. How many tickets can you get us?"

"I can get as many as you need," he said. Andrea's hand tightened on his arm. He flinched but there was laughter in his tone. "Just let me know."

"Sounds good. See you around." Lifting the table again, Leis walked away. As she passed through the heavy curtain, Leis shook her head and heard Jessica's low laugh.

"You are poking the tiger by messing with the two of them!" Jessica whispered and took the table from her. "She's been *begging* him for tickets, but he won't give her any."

"I have no idea why he felt the need to do that." Leis led the way to the prop staging area and waved to the line of items ready to be moved on and off the set as needed. "Just set it there." She pulled the hair tie on her wrist free and drew her hair into a low ponytail, sweeping it over her shoulder. "I shouldn't have encouraged him, but I couldn't help it."

When he'd caught her staring, the quirk in his lip nearly melted her, and his smooth voice made her heart stop. *He's just a friend and a human.* She chided herself. *A very* attractive *human friend.* She shook her head. Apparently she needed more practice chastising herself.

Jessica threw an arm around her. "Yeah, a handsome face like his can make a woman do crazy things. And lucky for you, Miss I-Can-Do-It-Myself Summers does all her own makeup." Jessica poked her in the shoulder. "You'll only need to worry about Koen for the most part, and I've arranged for you to help him with his wardrobe changes also." She examined her nails with a shrug of her shoulder. "You can thank me later."

"Jess!" Leis covered her face with her hands and groaned. "What have you done?"

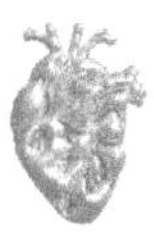

As Leis headed into the theater for a full dress rehearsal, she tried to focus on her duties as a makeup artist. It wasn't easy, especially since she could think about nothing other than Koen's costume changes.

"About time you got here!" Jessica's frustrated voice cut through her thoughts as she crossed the threshold of the staging area. "Get Koen's makeup done, then the two of you need to talk to Casey about his mic placement." She waved to a banged up black door marked 'Dudes.' "Koen is waiting in the dressing room. Go on in. I've got to find Alison. Ms. Sister-to-the-playwright wants a different transmitter pack. She says this one will scratch her designer belts." She strode away still grumbling.

Leis took a deep breath, squared her shoulders, and walked resolutely to the men's dressing room. Reaching the door, she pushed it open, keeping her eyes on the ground. The wheels of her case clacked over the threshold behind her, and she jumped at Koen's bark of laughter.

Her gaze snapped up and found Koen seated in a high back chair in front of a dressing table. He watched her approach in the mirror. Her stomach clenched the moment their eyes met, then the floor fell away when she saw he was already shirtless.

"Seriously?" Koen's voice was incredulous, his eyes wide with mock horror. "Is my face so ugly it's going to take a suitcase full of makeup?"

"Hardly." She replied with a tight smile. "I just happen to have an obsession with it." She grimaced. "With makeup. Not your face, I mean..."

Koen's brows shot up, and he laughed harder. A glossy black guitar hid most of his stomach, but the mirror reflected his upper chest and sharply chiseled shoulders. There was no denying he spent time in the gym like Baden, but Koen's build was broader and more thickly muscled. She swallowed hard and tried to ignore the heat growing in her stomach.

Her gaze trailed away from his shoulder and down the arm that lay casually across the top of the guitar resting across his lap. The rise and fall of his carved bicep and the curve of his forearm slowly pulled the breath out of her lungs. His hand hung loosely over the strings, and his long fingers twitched slightly.

"Leis?" His voice changed from amused to husky. When her eyes whisked themselves up to meet his, he tilted his head and cleared his throat. "Are you all right?"

Composing herself as best she could, she replied, "I'm tired. I must have zoned out for a minute." Averting her eyes, she positioned the case in front of the dressing table.

She was acutely aware of Koen setting the guitar aside and casually leaning back in the chair to watch her. He crossed his arms, and despite the tantalizing view he presented, she refused to let her eyes stray from his face when she turned back. But he had that question in his eyes again, and she had no idea why.

He knows I'm engaged. Be professional.

She cleared her throat and opened the top of the makeup caddy and withdrew a stretchy brown headband. Handing it to him without looking, she instructed, "Pull your hair away from your face, and I'll get started."

He chuckled as she stooped to gather her supplies. She glanced up and matched his smile. The mood lightened at the ridiculous sight of his hair swept back and standing out at all angles.

"Not a good style for me." He turned his head one way then the other. "If my hair was longer, maybe."

Thankful for his humor, Leis rose from a crouch and set the various foundations on the table with the sponges. Trying to relax her hand, she applied the creamy makeup to his throat and down the groove of his sternum, patting the sponge lightly across his skin. As she worked, she swore she could feel the heat of his eyes scorching her skin. He wasn't wearing his necklace, but her throat was too tight to ask about it.

"You have gorgeous skin," she said absently, as the layers of foundation dried to a smooth matte finish just a shade darker than his natural skin tone. As she turned away to pick up the foundation for his face, she noticed his knuckles white on the arms of the chair.

"Thank you." His voice had dropped even lower.

Her eyes cautiously slid up to look at him in the mirror and shivered. His fingers trailed through the ends of her hair so softly she couldn't feel it. Turning back quickly, she flicked it out of his fingers, marveling that had she not seen it, she would never have known.

Anger crept up the back of her neck. He had no right to touch her! "All right, close your eyes and let's finish this."

When his eyes closed, she let herself study the planes of his face. He had impossibly long lashes that brushed lightly against the skin under his eyes. The arch of his brow and his angled cheekbones begged her to touch them. She was thankful she had an excuse to. She smoothed the cream across his forehead, and to her surprise, his body tensed as though he were in pain.

"Are you okay?" She paused.

He nodded but never opened his eyes. His tongue swept across his lower lip before he caught it between his teeth, and her knees nearly buckled. She couldn't stop herself from wondering what it would be like to kiss him.

Shaking herself out of the thought, she reminded herself she was a professional and hurriedly finished smoothing out the tones of his skin. Then she brushed a hint of bronze across his sharp cheekbones and under his jaw line. After sealing it with a matte powder, Leis steeled herself to apply the mascara.

"Open your eyes and look up," she said.

Leis thought she was prepared for the blue under those thick black lashes, but she wasn't. Her breath hitched when Koen's pupil narrowed then widened as he focused his gaze on hers. From this close, she noted his gorgeous eyes weren't pure blue. The fathomless black of his pupil was ringed with gold and the outer edge of his iris was as gray as a storm cloud. In between, they were striated with too many shades of blue to count.

Her voice choked. "Look up."

He did, but not before his attention flicked to her lips. With a jolt, she realized she was biting her lip in a mirror image of him.

Releasing her bite and taking a breath, she hoped her shaking hands wouldn't jab his stunning eyes out with the mascara brush. As quickly and carefully as she could, she coated his lashes with short, practiced strokes of the tiny brush.

When she was done, she admired her work. The liner and mascara did their job, making his eyes stand out like gems and his sharp features were even more defined. She told herself she was making sure she hadn't missed anything, but her fluttering stomach knew better.

After a few seconds, Koen cleared his throat. "Can I move now?"

She became aware of something hot against the side of her hip and jumped away when she realized she was leaning against his open palm.

"Yes." She whirled away so he wouldn't see her flushed face and packed up her things with trembling hands as he rose.

Leis looked into the mirror and watched him stride away. The lines of the vinyl chair were imprinted in his skin but did nothing to hide the incredible definition of the perfectly formed and tapered back that disappeared into the top of his dress pants. In one hand he held the guitar, in the other his white shirt and a tie.

Over the thunder of blood in her ears, she barely heard what he said as he exited the dressing room.

"I'll go change in the bathroom and meet you stage right to talk to Casey about the mic," he said.

She collapsed into the chair after he was out of sight. How could she possibly do this five nights in a row? Taking a deep breath, she stood and walked over to Koen's rack of shirts. The air seeped from her lungs when she saw the neatly folded pair of men's jeans hanging at the end. It sent a swarm of butterflies through her stom-ach. She was going to be helping Koen change more than just his shirts.

Embarrassment heated her cheeks, and she pressed her palms against them. Baden was the one who should be causing her heart to race, not some guy she met weeks ago. Tears stung as the anger turned swiftly to confusion.

Why didn't Baden make her feel this way?

Baden was just as handsome, equally as fun and talented, but she couldn't deny that the pull she felt for the blue-eyed actor was incredibly different. Her inability to keep Koen at arm's length frustrated her no matter how much Baden trusted her. She let the frustration strengthen her determination to be professional and rolled the rack into place near where Koen would exit and make his change between scenes.

Straightening her back, she tried to convince herself that a weekend talking about the dreaded ceremony with her mother was exactly what she needed.

All she had to do was get through this rehearsal.

K oen left the bathroom and met Casey at the side of the stage. He could still feel the point of Leis's hip against his palm and tension lingered in his arm from the effort it had taken to keep from wrapping it around her and pulling her closer. When her gentle fingers caressed his face, it was all he could do to control himself. Then, when he opened his eyes to see her close enough to kiss, he'd nearly done it.

Her lips were inches from him, and the sweetness of her breath made him ache for a taste of her. He ran a hand down his face in frustration, then hoped he hadn't wrecked his makeup. After those last few minutes, there was no way he could deny her attraction to him. He didn't even need to hear it in her voice. He could feel it in the way her whole body trembled when she was near him.

When he'd left her in the dressing room, frustration was building in her. In the time between the makeup application to the moment he saw her again at the edge of the curtain, her eyes changed from confused to hard. Her face was set in harsh lines, and she must have made the determination that being angry was her best course of action. He would have to tread carefully during the rest of rehearsal.

"Don't pull on the tie." Casey readjusted the mic. "Do that on stage, and it will sound like you're sanding the floor!" Casey was a hefty guy, and his girth was not helped by the screen print on the front of his black t-shirt; a soundboard with the words 'I control you' spread across his broad stomach.

Casey turned to Leis and pointed to the small black microphone attached to Koen's tie. "Here's what you need to know, sweetheart."

"Leis. My name is Leis." Koen almost laughed at her bristling tone but covered it with a cough when she pegged him in a glare.

"Whatever." Casey waved his other hand, pointing again to the mic then Koen's face. "When he takes that shirt off," her face paled, "you make sure the wires are still taped to his skin and then make sure the mic is secured to the new shirt. No closer than eight inches and no further than nine from those pretty lips. Got it?"

Leis swallowed thickly and tore her eyes from his mouth to stare at the floor. She mumbled in answer, "Keep the wires taped, secure the mic between eight and nine inches from his mouth."

"I can take care of it, Casey." Koen patted the tech's shoulder.

The tech lightened up but pointed at Leis. "You still check it, and keep the makeup off my gear, got it?"

Keeping a tight smile, she nodded. "Got it."

With a last pat on Casey's shoulder, Koen headed for the stage.

He stood behind the curtain, the sound of Leis's harsh breathing carrying from where she waited next to the clothing rack. When she cleared her throat, all kinds of frustration rushed through him. He didn't want to leave her like this. The curtain was going up in front of the small group of family and friends invited to attend, but Koen looked at Leis in question.

He was greeted with a stony glare, and a tick of her chin redirected his attention to the stage.

He heard the cue from Andrea and stepped into the glaring stage lighting. As he stepped onstage his gaze crossed the sparse audience, landing briefly on the group of people sitting second row from center stage. There was no denying the redhead in the middle was Leis's mother. Even through the flare of the lights, he could see how much they looked alike.

Pushing away the distractions, he fell into character and reached out to touch Andrea on the shoulder.

"Emma, I am so sorry for your loss," he said.

She turned to face him, wiping a fake tear from her eye.

"Why are *you* here, Jackson?" she drawled.

"I heard about your parents and came home to help you." Their cheesy southern accents made him want to cringe. "I told you I would always be here for you."

They spoke their lines and moved around one another as the scene unfolded until Koen was on the opposite side of the stage looking toward where Leis still stood in the shadows of the stage wing. She stood stiffly, arms crossed, with anger and something else burning in her eyes. Koen refocused on his part and sank onto the hideous brown plaid couch next to Andrea. He reached for her, but she backed away.

"Emma, I do believe you are still the most beautiful woman I have ever seen." He took her hand, leaning toward her and forcing himself to smile.

Turning away, she spoke in obvious fake denial. "I don't believe you, Jackson."

Pushing down his disgust at what he was supposed to do next, Koen reached for her chin and pulled her to face him.

"Then let me show you." Swallowing his body's resistance, he leaned in and kissed Andrea on the lips.

She was supposed to immediately slap him, but she kept their lips against one another much longer than necessary. He squeezed her hand. *Hard.* At that, she reared back and landed a genuine slap to his cheek.

"Of all the nerve!" She stood and exited. The lights fell.

Shaking his head, Koen hurried off stage as the orchestra played and the narrator's voice continued the story. He kicked off the dress shoes as he reached the edge of the curtain and loosened his pants.

Hands pulled at his tie and unbuttoned the top of his shirt. Leis refused to meet his eyes. When he started to ask what was wrong, she stopped him cold.

"Not a word, Koen." Her anger and frustration had grown, and to his surprise, she was wrestling with more than a touch of jealousy. The corner of his mouth quirked.

She pushed the small mic between the buttons on his shirt and pulled the tie from around his neck, touching him as little as possible. He let the pants fall to the floor, dutifully ignoring Leis's gasp. While holding the microphone's pack in one hand, he reached for the jeans that hung on the end of the rack, but she stopped him again.

"Shirt first," she said.

Her struggle tore him to shreds. Baden needed to tell her what was going on soon. This wasn't fair to any of them.

He reached behind his neck and tugged the shirt over his head, careful not to pull the mic pack through his sleeve. When her warm hand pressed against the bottom of his ribcage to check the wires he swore and nearly dropped the pack. He sucked in a breath, making his abs clench just under the heel of her hand. Their eyes slammed into each other.

"Please, don't make this harder, Koen. Just. Don't." Frustrated desire and uneasiness laced through her anger, and he caught her wrist before her touch caused another problem. Her eyes were a dark emerald. A matching response flared in his chest.

Too late.

"I've got it." Koen broke their stare and brushed her hand away. He turned his back to pull on the jeans, then stepped into his boots and snagged the first shirt on the rack. He yanked the new shirt over his head, clipped the mic where it belonged, and hooked the pack to his back pocket. By then the lights were up and the narrator's voice faded through the auditorium.

Koen reminded himself *again* they were supposed to be professionals and strode into the stage lights again. He forced himself to shut out Leis' strangled breathing and barely stifled tears. Determined to make things right after, Koen relaxed his shoulders and took his place on stage.

Koen kept his word and distance by taking care of his own mic and shirt changes between the next scene changes. She leaned against an unused backdrop and watched silently.

When the lights went down after the final scene, Koen wasn't surprised to find she was already gone.

As the lights went out on stage, Leis pushed open the building's rear door and stepped into the fresh air. She didn't know or care if she needed to check in before leaving. She could come back for her makeup case once everyone was gone. Her pulse thudded in her ears, and a headache blossomed at the base of her skull. Her only goal was to get as far away from Koen as possible. The door thunked shut, and she shoved her hands into her pockets against the chill.

Gaining distance from the stage, her anger subsided. Her attraction wasn't Koen's fault, but being angry with him was easier than admitting her feelings were real. It was like her body functioned on instinct when he was around.

She reached the end of the building and took the sidewalk toward her apartment.

I need a shower, a cup of coffee, and a long talk with Baden. She grimaced and guilt lanced through her. *Baden. Why can't I feel this way about him? If I did, I wouldn't be in this mess!*

Lowering her head against the breeze and tightening her jacket, she hurried her footsteps. She was so focused on covering the ground she nearly ran into the tall man blocking the sidewalk.

Strong hands caught her shoulders and a familiar voice questioned her. "Where are you going in such a hurry?"

"Daddy!" Leis leaped into her father's arms, vaguely aware of the rest of her family behind him. "You're early." Leis buried her face into his shoulder and willed the tears away, then leaned back to look into his smiling eyes. The others gathered around them. Andrew and Carol to her right, and her mother hovering to the left.

"How's my girl?" Her Dad stood her on her feet, resting his hands on her upper arms. "You look beautiful."

Her heart slowed as his familiar comfort washed over her. "I'm good. Just tired. It's been a long day." He looked tired too, and she reached up to touch his cheek. "It's better now that you're here."

Her Dad wore a pair of light-colored slacks and a close-fitting blue sweater over a gray oxford. Glancing to her right, she grinned when she saw several girls staring at her brother Andrew.

Dark and brooding perfectly described her brother. In his navy slacks and snug gray sweater, he looked like a model with all his long lines and sharp angles.

He was spinning Carol's long blond braid around his finger. "Hey, Leis."

She moved out of her father's embrace and reached for a hug from her brother and sister-in-law. They pulled her close, and Andrew kissed the top of her head. "Missed you, Red."

"Missed you, too." A couple months away from her family hadn't seemed all that long until now. Behind Carol, she spotted her mom waiting her turn.

"Your Dad is right. You do look beautiful." Her mom's hug was tight and fierce. Something like pain flashed across her mother's face, and then the pride was back. She ticked her head backward. "We found this one wandering the campus. Does he belong to you?"

Behind her, Baden was leaning casually against a tree. His eyes were locked on hers, a quirky smile curving his lips. Slim fit jeans were tucked into low lace-up boots, and a black dress shirt hugged his upper body and accentuated his narrow waist. His hands were tucked into the front pockets of his jeans slightly rucking up the untucked hem of his shirt. He was painfully handsome with his piercing stare and playful grin. Although seeing him made her happy, she was disappointed when there was no rush of desire like there was with Koen.

Angrily shaking off the thought, Leis broke into a run. "You came! I thought you had class."

Baden laughed and pushed away from the tree to pull her in for a bear hug. She wrapped her arms around him and pressed her face into his chest.

"They couldn't keep me away another day." He rested his chin on her head and cupped her face. "I had to see you. We need to talk," he said quietly.

She leaned back. "Is everything okay?"

He looked up as the rest of the family joined them.

"Everything is fine." She frowned when Baden shot Andrew a challenging stare. "Nothing to worry about."

Leis spent the evening at the hotel restaurant catching up with Baden and her family. He was unusually quiet and apologized, saying he had a lot of schoolwork on his mind. When they dropped her off at her apartment, he walked her to the door, promising to be more attentive tomorrow.

Early the next morning, Baden called, claiming he needed to work on a school project and said he would need most of the morning to finish it up. At noon he sent a text saying it was taking longer than he expected and would meet her at the hotel later.

Leis had skipped class to spend time with Baden, but since he was busy, she, her mom, and Carol spent the day shopping instead.

Their trip through a lingerie store made Leis blush from head to toe.

"Really, Leis," her mother scoffed. She held up a skimpy pink and white negligee that was little more than three pieces of thread. She handed it to Leis to try on. "You and Baden have had to wait all your lives. This should be a relief. You don't have to pretend you aren't looking forward to it."

Leis tried to hide her cringe, but her mother was right. She *should* be looking forward to spending her life with Baden. The problem was, she wasn't. At least not this part of it.

Closing her eyes and taking the sheer outfit from her, Leis tried to convince herself she was only nervous because her whole life she had been coached not to think about him that way. Maybe they had worked so hard to be chaste it would simply take time to mentally make the transition.

Leis opened her eyes to see her mother and Carol watching her. "It's just hard to talk about *this*," she shook the outfit slightly, "with my *mom*."

Carol laughed. "You'll get over that quickly enough."

She and Andrew were always pawing at each other, and while Leis sincerely hoped things between her and Baden would change, she didn't think she ever wanted to be quite that open about it.

"I hope so," she conceded.

They bought the outfit and moved on to the next store to find a dress for the party that would follow the ceremony. The dress didn't need to be overly formal, but her mother would expect her to choose from the designer labels.

Leis sorted through racks of sale dresses until her mother's condescending voice cut her search short.

"Leave the markdowns, Leisel. Really." Green eyes the same color as hers rolled with disappointment. "Buy something *new* for goodness sake, not a display that's been worn by half a dozen other women."

"Yes, Mother." She obediently followed her mother and Carol, allowing them to point out the racks she should choose from, but every white sundress she looked at made her palms sweat.

Leis reluctantly pulled out another as Carol and her mother murmured behind her. The dress was strapless, its satin bodice and knee length skirt overlaid with fine lace and trimmed at the waist with a narrow satin sash dotted with small crystals. The designer label would satisfy her mother, and Baden would love it.

As she held it, she envisioned herself standing in the circle of the Clan, surrounded by her friends and family. Closing her eyes, she inhaled, wondering what Baden's scent would be like.

Imagining the comfort and love that would wash through her, she pictured looking up into a playful smile and sky-blue eyes. She was surprised to find she welcomed the idea of the pain she would feel as her fangs pushed down. Koen leaned forward and pressed his lips to hers.

Her eyes flew open, and she covered an audible gasp with the back of her hand. *Koen?!* She shoved the dress back on the rack as shame rushed through her. Turning to her mother and hoping her cheeks weren't as red as she knew they had to be, she announced, "I'm done. There's nothing here I want."

Her Mother's brows creased in concern. "Are you all right?"

Leis hitched her purse higher on her shoulder and forced a smile. "I'm fine. I think I'm just hungry."

The three of them turned to go, and Leis sighed in relief as Carol's stomach growled loudly. Laughter broke the tension, and her mother lead the way out of the mall. She sighed; thankful she hadn't pushed for answers. As they exited the building, she did her best to remind herself how much she loved Baden.

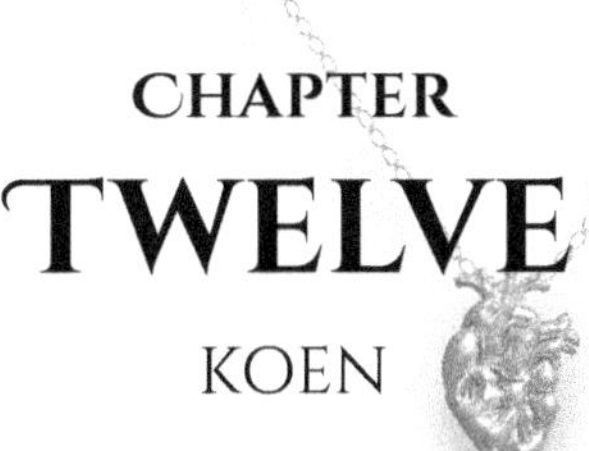

CHAPTER

TWELVE

KOEN

Andrea pounced on him the moment he exited the dressing room.

"That went perfectly! You are such a natural," she gushed.

"Thank you. You did a great job, too." With a polite squeeze, he disentangled himself and took a step back, shifting toward the exit door. "I'm starved, and I need a shower."

The makeup Leis's careful fingers had smoothed over his skin had melted into a gooey paste, and he couldn't wait to wash it off. When the memory of her hands on his skin sent a shiver through him, he grimaced knowing Andrea would interpret it as encouragement.

She smiled coyly at him. "We could meet at Osha's for dinner." Her fingers traced his arm when he opened his mouth to decline. "Come on. It's just food, not a date!"

Koen pushed the door open and stepped into the darkness. Andrea matched him stride for stride, and he sighed. All he wanted was to get to his dorm to shower and relax. He glanced at Andrea then trailed his eyes across the street.

"Maybe another time. I'm just not..." He froze when he saw Leis tucked under Baden's arm. Jealousy kicked him low and hard.

Andrea got a few strides ahead before realizing he had stopped. Her gaze followed his to the group across the street.

"Koen?" Andrea moved closer, pulling on his arm to break his stare. "Dinner?"

He looked down at her, his eyes unable to focus as the reality of Leis's situation sank in. She had no idea what was really going on between them. Her anger was more than justified. Andrea waved her hand in front of his face, and he flinched before he refocused on her.

"Dinner?" she said again.

He looked up in time to see Baden place a kiss on top of Leis's head. As they walked the opposite direction, he stared after them and willed her head to turn his way, but the group disappeared behind a building without a look back. His chest tightened painfully, and he blew out a breath.

"All right. I'll meet you at Osha's in half an hour."

Andrea rose on her tiptoes and kissed his cheek. "Don't be late." She cooed, then strode off toward her apartment.

The bright echo of Leis's laughter taunted him on the night air. He pinched his eyes shut as feelings of happiness and safety carried to his ears. Willing himself to move, he headed to his dorm to shower and meet Andrea for dinner.

Though an asthma attack sounded more fun.

THIRTEEN

After dinner, her Mom couldn't take the humidity anymore, so she and her dad returned to the hotel, suggesting the rest of them enjoy a night out together.

"Where to, Leis?" Andrew asked as he started the car.

"Anywhere but Osha's," Baden said. "I'm tired of that place."

Laughing, Leis poked him in the ribs. "You said you love it there!"

"I'm in the mood for something different." He pushed her back. "There's a nice outdoor mall not far from here. They should have live music." He pointed over Andrew's shoulder. "Turn left, and it's just up the road."

Andrew followed his instructions. "Maybe we can catch a movie. Isn't that new sci-fi flick out you wanted to see, B?"

Leis rested against Baden as he answered, "Yeah. That one would be good."

"As long as you buy me the super-size popcorn!" Leis lifted Baden's arm and wrapped it around her shoulders.

Laying her head on his chest and pulling the edge of his jacket over her face, she inhaled as quietly as possible. Baden tightened his arm.

"I love that you keep trying," he whispered in her ear. "And I love you."

She tucked closer. "I love you, too."

Baden did buy her the huge tub of popcorn, and the movie was actually pretty good. Since it was still early in the evening, Andrew and Carol lead the way toward the square where a guitarist was playing. They wandered through the crowd and listened as a woman sang.

Baden stiffened as the woman's clear voice rose and fell across the crowd. The singer's voice was strong and controlled, clearly a talented musician, but the sound made both Baden and Andrew stare tensely toward the sound.

She was about to ask what was wrong when Andrew turned away suddenly. "Carol isn't feeling well. I think we need to get her back to the hotel."

Carol did look a little green, so they headed toward the car. As they walked, Leis caught Baden and Andrew exchanging glares.

"What is up with you two?" She glanced between them. "Are you fighting?"

"No. But we shouldn't have come here," Andrew growled, and glanced over his shoulder as the woman's voice continued to float through the night air.

"They're just worried about you." Baden kissed her forehead while Andrew unlocked the car doors.

Andrew grunted and climbed into the driver's seat. The ride back to campus was silent. Baden tucked her against him, running his fingers through her hair. The feel of his gentle fingers on her scalp eased the tension until she nearly fell asleep. A soft kiss to her temple woke her.

"I'll walk you in." Baden pushed open the door and helped her out. Andrew started to follow. "I don't need your help, Drew."

"Stay where I can see you," Andrew warned.

Baden walked her quickly to the outside door of the building.

"What was that all about?" Leis gestured toward the car. "Why is he being such a jerk to you?"

"I'm going to say this quick." Baden turned her to face him. "Your family is not here for a casual visit. I need you to trust me."

She paused in confusion with the door halfway open. "What? Why?"

Baden positioned himself in front of her and pulled a lumpy envelope from a pocket inside his jacket and handed it to her. When she reached for it, he closed his hands over hers, keeping his body between her and the car to hide it from view.

"You'll need this. I'll explain why tomorrow. Trust me?" he asked.

She nodded and he cupped her cheek in his palm.

He pressed his lips to the corner of her mouth, and then he was down the stairs and onto the sidewalk before she could respond.

"He is just beautiful." Kay's dreamy voice cut through her shock. "I can totally understand why you keep turning Koen down."

Leis stepped all the way into the building and turned to see Kay standing in the apartment doorway. Her friend was staring out the window above the door, shamelessly watching Baden get into the car.

"Yeah. He is." Leis climbed the stairs and pushed the apartment door shut behind them. She sighed inwardly, once again wishing she reacted to him with the enthusiasm her friends did.

"What's in the envelope?" Kay followed her across the room and sat down with her at the tiny table in the breakfast nook.

Tearing open the seal, Leis's brows creased as a new cell phone and charger slid out. Hoping for some explanation, Leis peered inside the envelope and found a folded piece of paper stuck inside.

"What in the world?" She unfolded the page, and in his perfect script, Baden had written:

Meet me tomorrow, 6:30AM behind the apartment. Look for the path.

DO NOT turn this phone on until then.
Leave your current phone at the apartment
and bring only this one.
Tell No One

"What does it say?" Kay asked. "He bought you a new phone?"

Leis slowly picked up the new phone, turning it in her hand. "He's a tech head. He likes to make sure we have the latest and greatest." She tucked the phone into her pocket along with the note and stood. "I'm exhausted. See you in the morning?"

Kay rose with her. "I was going to ask if you wanted to go out with us tonight. There's a new music club across town, and a group of us are going to check it out. I was actually just leaving when Baden dropped you off."

"I'm going to pass." Leis faked a yawn. "Have fun and don't get into too much trouble."

"You know better than that!" Kay snorted as Leis waved her out the door, leaving her alone with her scattered thoughts.

She sat down at the table, staring at the note as her stomach tied in knots. Setting the phones side by side, they looked identical.

She scrubbed the heel of her hand into her eyes as dread crept up her spine. It was true she and her mother had their differences, but Baden's words seemed to prickle something deeper. Was there really a reason she shouldn't trust them? Baden had been even more protective in the weeks before they left for school. Did he know something she didn't? Maybe. But why did she need a new phone?

FOURTEEN

KOEN

Fending off Andrea's hands all evening wore Koen's nerves thin, and unsurprisingly, she protested when he said he was tired and wanted to turn in early. Eventually she conceded, but only after he agreed to walk her to her dorm.

Before they left Osha's, Andrea went to the restroom. As soon as she was out of sight, Ellen appeared at his shoulder and slid a large bulky envelope across the table.

"Hang on to this until later. It has to do with Leis." With no more explanation than a smile, she walked away untying her apron strings. Pushing the diner door open, Ellen looked back with a wink. "Take care of her."

Anxiety tightened his chest, making him cough. He took a quick puff of his inhaler, his eyes dropping to the envelope lying ominously on the table.

Andrea's arm wound around him as Ellen passed the front window and turned a corner out of sight.

"Are you all right?" Andrea asked.

Koen stepped out of her embrace and dodged her wandering hands as he slipped the envelope under his arm.

"Fine." Taking her elbow, he directed her out of the restaurant. "Let's get you home."

He practically dragged her to her dorm and managed to evade her attempt at a good night kiss before escaping to the bus stop.

Hopping on the next bus to the outdoor mall, he smiled in anticipation. His Mom was in town and scheduled to play acoustically in the square tonight before joining him for his concert tomorrow. They were looking forward to singing a song or two. It had been a long time since they had performed together.

As the bus rolled away from campus, he absently slid the contents out of the envelope. A cell phone and a neatly organized packet of documents landed in his lap. Glancing around, he slid all but the phone back into the envelope. A sticky note attached to the glass front read:

Turn on immediately

He did, then withdrew some of the paperwork to flip through the first few pages. He thumbed through a car rental agreement, directions to a hotel in Chicago, and fake IDs for both him and Leis. Their departure was already planned. The false documents kicked his heart rate up, and he slid it all into the envelope, glancing around to see if anyone noticed.

They had never discussed a specific date, but Baden also never made it sound like it was imminent. He opened the envelope again and blew out a breath. He was in deep now, but he would do whatever it took to keep Leis safe.

The ride seemed to take forever, and as he exited the bus, he could hear his mother's guitar as she tuned. He was still reeling from the contents of the envelope in his hand when he approached the small shelter. He followed the movements of his very pregnant Mother as she unplugged her guitar and looked up.

"Granddad was right. The lost Vampir Clan isn't a story," he said. Just then, the phone in his hand vibrated with a text.

Call this number tomorrow, 6:45 AM

He looked into his mother's wide eyes. Her hands were still on the guitar.

"You found them?" she asked. He nodded, and she looked out over the crowd. "So, all the stories *Papa* told are true and not just a legend."

He shook his head and followed her gaze, "It's not. They're Leis's family, and I'm being asked to get her away from them." He held up the envelope. "They've got it all laid out, and according to this, I'm leaving with her tomorrow."

His Mom set the guitar aside and led him toward a bench, her face pinched and worried. She could scent his fear and doubt, and he wanted to be honest and tell her about the danger they were in, but he couldn't. He wouldn't risk her worrying about him and putting the baby in jeopardy.

Pasting on a smile, he gripped her hand and gave her the good news instead, hoping she would read his nervousness as excitement.

"But - I'm convinced she truly is my intended, Mom," he said.

She absently rubbed her growing belly. "It's one miracle after another." She laid her hand on his arm, pride shining from her eyes. "*Papa* always told you there was hope."

FIFTEEN

When her alarm went off at six AM the next morning, she did as Baden had instructed her. She turned the new phone on at exactly six thirty and headed out, leaving her original phone on the bedside table. With the new one in her front pocket, she quietly let herself out of the apartment, careful not to wake Kay.

She breathed a sigh of relief when she turned the corner behind the building and spotted the path Baden mentioned. She stepped past the first line of trees as the phone in her pocket vibrated. The text was short.

Look left

Leaning against a massive oak tree, Baden stood watching her. He wore tight black running pants, and judging by the way the material of his dark gray shirt lay wet across his muscled chest, he had run hard from his apartment on the other side of campus.

As soon as she spotted him, he tucked his phone into the zipper pocket at the back of his shirt. A sad smile played on his face.

"Come here." He opened his arms, and she fell against him, wrapping hers around his neck despite his sweaty skin. He tightened his grip when she tried to push away.

"Are you going to tell me what's going on?" Leis asked.

When he didn't let go, she pushed at him, wanting to look him in the eyes but he held her tighter. Suddenly, he spun around to pin her against the tree. His strong, toned body pressed her from knee to chest, holding her immobile.

"What are you doing?" Bile rose in her throat as she pushed at his shoulders.

His eyes were hard but not angry. "Haven't you ever wondered why this was never a temptation for us?" His head dipped, and he pressed kisses to her neck. "Haven't you ever wondered why I never even *tried* to kiss you?"

"Because it's forbidden until after the ceremony. Please!" she choked. "Stop!"

"Forbidden? No. It's not." His voice was thick with disgust she didn't understand.

He finally put space between them but kept his arms braced on the tree leaving her caged. He looked down and away.

"It's because we're family and our genetics won't *let* us be attracted to each other." His voice lowered. "No matter how hard some expect us to force it."

Trying to catch her breath, she ducked out from between his arms, mildly surprised he let her go.

"What do you mean *family*?" A sudden chill ran up her spine. "How?"

He kicked a fallen branch and pushed off the tree. "Ever wonder why my grandmother insists it's the female's last name that's kept after a bonding?"

Confused, she shook her head. "I guess I never thought about it. It's just the way of the Clan." She tentatively reached out and touched his arm. "Tell me what's going on."

He swung around, his fists tight at his sides. She didn't back away even though she was shaken by his aggressiveness. She instinctively knew he wasn't angry with her.

"It's not the way of *the* Vampir. Just our Clan." His voice quieted on the last word. Compassion filled his eyes at the confusion that was growing on her face. He took her hand as he blew out a breath, then spoke so quietly she almost couldn't hear. "Hundreds of years ago, something happened. I couldn't track down when or why, but a *long* time ago our Clan hid from the others. Our family's ancestors basically disappeared."

She tried to grasp what he said. "*Others?* As in other Vampir? You know that's not possible!"

He laced his fingers with hers and pushed the hair out of her face. "It's true. Remember what my professor said about the phones?" Trying her best to follow, she nodded, and he continued. "The phone you left at the apartment, and the ones we've been carrying, are not only extremely high-tech, but they're also one hundred percent off the normal cellular grid." His eyes went far away. "They contain technology to track us, control what we can see, who we can talk to. Even the laptop you brought with you runs the same software. It's virtually undetectable. I've been in contact with other Vampir around the world, and they're working on breaking the code for me."

She stared, trying to absorb what he was telling her, but nothing made sense.

"I was close to getting us out, but I had to quit doing the hacking myself because Grandmother was too close to figuring out what I've been doing." He shook his head, and his attention fell to her. "I've been careful, but I can't risk your safety anymore." He tapped the phone in her pocket. "This is the first step toward getting you free from what our twisted family has planned."

"What?" She looked at him sideways. "You're not making sense!" Her head spun, and she tried to track with him. "You keep saying *our* family? What does that have to do with anything?"

His look went away again. "My father's name was Heinrich."

"I know. He and your mom died when you were just a baby." Leis softened. "It's why you lived with us."

"They didn't just *die,* Leis." Tears filled his eyes, but he quickly blinked them away. His voice grew rougher as he spoke. "I believe they were murdered because my dad refused to cooperate." Sadness washed the strength from him. "He tried to stop our bonding, because Haydn is..." He swallowed hard. "Because your *dad* is my *uncle.* Haydn and my dad are brothers. They were twins." Pain filled eyes met hers. "Leis, we're first cousins, practically siblings."

Her knees gave way, and he caught her before she fell to the ground. He held her as they sat in the leaves. She choked at the implications of what had almost happened between them.

"How did they hide this from everyone?" she asked.

He pulled her close. "They hid the truth by using our mothers' last names instead of our fathers'." His breath was hot on her cheek. "My Grandmother is involved. She's been orchestrating the whole thing."

"My Mom and Dad know about this? They agreed to it?" she asked.

"Your Mom did. Haydn found out not long ago and told me," he said softly.

"What are we supposed to do?"

"We don't have much time, and that's not all of it. You're going to have to trust me until I can explain." He lifted her chin. "Can you do that?"

Unable to answer, she nodded. He stood and pulled her up with him. He glanced toward her apartment.

"Your family will be looking for you soon, and you can't let on that anything is wrong. I wasn't sure I should even tell you before getting you out of here, but you've been lied to enough." He rested his hands on her shoulders. "The only reason for their visit is to bring you back and force a bonding. We can't let that happen. I *won't* let that happen." He growled then softened. His face tightened as he slid his fingers behind her neck and into her hair. "Do you trust me?"

"Yes. Of course, I trust you," she said. His eyes fell to her lips, and she drew an unsteady breath. "Why does this feel like goodbye?" she whispered.

He lowered his head toward hers and his warm breath feathered across her lips.

"Because it is, and I won't have time to say it properly later." A tear rolled slowly down his cheek as he pulled her face to his, chastely kissing her mouth. "I love you, Leis." He stepped back. "Remember to keep the new phone with you. I'll still see you tonight for the concert." Baden released her and let his hands drop to his sides. The phone in his pocket began to ring. "Until it's time for you to leave we have to act like nothing is different, okay?"

Pressing one last kiss to her forehead, he turned and disappeared into the trees as he answered the call. How could anything he said be true?

Yet, despite the confusion, she felt the honesty of it. Even in the face of her family's possible deceit, the knot of constant dread had been untied deep inside her.

Then, so faintly it almost wasn't noticeable, Leis tasted a sweetness in her mouth. Inhaling deeply, she realized the taste wasn't a taste at all.

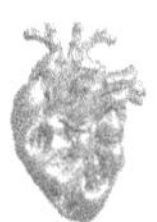

KAY STUMBLED out of her bedroom to the sight of Leis's face pressed into a box of dish-washing powder.

"Uh, Leis?" She rubbed her eyes. "I know I just woke up, but could you please tell me why you're huffing dish soap?"

Leis swung around to face Kay, her eyes wide. "Lemon! It smells like the lemons I found in the fridge." She reached for half of the lemon lying freshly sliced on the counter. "Kay, I love the smell of lemon!"

Kay walked toward her, hands out to take the fruit. "Are you telling me suddenly you can *smell?*"

She bobbed her head, unable to control her excitement. "It's a miracle!" She turned to the bag of coffee on the counter. "And *this.*" She set the box of soap in the sink and held the bag of grounds up to her face. "*This* is heaven in a bag."

Laughing, Kay shook her head and took the coffee from her hands. "Let's slow down. When did this happen?"

Leis looked out the window and spotted the tree Baden hid behind. Her excitement fled as she realized she couldn't tell Kay the truth.

"I - I don't know exactly." She focused on her roommate leaning against the refrigerator. "I woke up, and when I came into the kitchen, I could *taste* something." Leis picked up the lemon. "But it wasn't a taste." She pointed to the box still in the sink. "It was that. It said lemon scented on the front, and I knew you had lemons in the fridge."

Kay's smile was sleepy but genuine. "Well, good for you." She pushed away from the fridge and started to her room with a yawn. "I'm getting in the shower. For the record, coffee smells even better when it's brewing."

Leis waited until the bedroom door shut behind her before pulling the new phone out of her pocket. Quickly she typed out a reply to the text Baden sent earlier.

L - I can smell!

A reply came instantly.

Number Unknown Message Not Sent

She tried again and got the same response. Staring at the phone in her hand, tears welled and she ground her teeth as her question to Baden replayed in her head.

"Why does this feel like goodbye?"

"Because it is."

Her hand tightened around the phone. *What is going on?*

CHAPTER

SIXTEEN

KOEN

Though it was still early and load in for the show wasn't until three, Koen nervously packed and repacked his bags and totes. He sorted through his gear choosing the cables, guitar pedals, and the one guitar he could live without. He did his best to minimize the items on stage for the concert because everything would be abandoned after the show. His Mom watched quietly as he stacked the cases they would transfer to her van.

"You are so much like your father." The pride in her voice helped dispel at least some of his nerves.

He set aside a tub of cables he didn't need and opened the pedal case again.

"I wish he could be here." Koen looked up to meet her eyes. "How are you feeling? Are you sure you feel well enough to close out the set?"

Her hands gently swept over her pregnant stomach. "I haven't felt this good since I carried you." She took the case from him after he removed what he needed. "It's my honor to help you and your Leis." Her brows dropped. "But be patient with her. She's going to be very confused. Especially if she doesn't know who or what we are yet."

"She's smart, Mom. It won't take her long to figure it out once Baden makes his move."

Satisfied he had his gear sorted; he reached for the duffel bag with fresh clothes and a variety of toiletries. Unzipping it, he unpacked one of his changes of clothes to make room for the neatly folded sets his mother had brought. Sliding the extra t-shirts and sweats underneath his own, his hand brushed against the folders tucked in the bottom of the bag.

"Baden gave me a letter for her." He looked up again, uncertainty filling him with dread. "What if she doesn't want to go?"

She took his face in her hands. "If she's as smart as you say, then she'll know he is telling her the truth."

He inhaled, thankful his breathing was clear today, and especially thankful for his mother's encouraging presence. Despite all the odds against him, his parents always believed he would find the one he was intended for.

"I know she'll believe what he says, but how can she know for sure if she can't smell?" He worried his bottom lip between his teeth.

She laid his hand on her stomach. "Little miracles, remember?"

He pressed his forehead to hers, lost in wonder as his baby sister kicked repeatedly under his palm.

"Little miracles," he whispered.

SEVENTEEN

Leis stood on the stairs and watched her dad park the SUV at the curb outside her apartment. Her heart raced as she tried to assimilate all the smells assaulting her. She couldn't identify any of them, but the moment the car door opened and Baden stepped out, the breeze carried a warm spicy scent she instantly associated with him. Unable to contain her smile, she waved him toward her. Because he had told her not to trust her family, she wasn't sure she should share her new ability with them.

"Hey, beautiful," he called.

As he approached, his eyes swept across her in a way that made her uncomfortable. She was wearing black skinny jeans tucked into tall riding boots, a gray v-neck shirt and a long multi-colored cardigan. He took her hand and pulled her tightly against him.

"You look incredible." He pressed his lips against her bare neck, and she shivered at the contact. At his closeness, she could smell him strongly, and the emotions that swept through her made no sense.

He hates this as much as I do. She tried not to twist away as he pressed even closer.

"Baden, stop. I can smell you," she said.

Though he didn't pull back much, his body stiffened, and he leaned back to lock eyes with her. Shock and then relief registered on his face.

She quickly continued. "When you left this morning, I could smell. How did that happen?"

He turned his back completely to the vehicle and spoke quickly. "Put your arms around my neck." When she obeyed, he whispered in her ear. "I don't know how it happened, but it will help us. I don't have time to explain much but pay attention to what other people's emotions are telling you." He looked her in the eye again, kissing her lightly on the cheek. "Follow my lead." He cupped her face. "Trust me?"

"Always." She stepped back, unable to bear being so close to him.

Baden's expression hardened as he took her hand and led her to the car. He opened the door for her.

"Do you have the tickets?" her mother asked.

Andrew and Carol were in the rear seats, and though they were smiling, the moment she breathed the air inside the vehicle she was hit with a pungent smell. There was anger riding the biting odor and she forced a smile she hoped would hide her surprise.

"I have them." She patted the purse at her side. "And a parking pass. Should put us close to the gate."

From the front passenger seat, her mother laid a hand on her father's arm and turned to look at her. "It was very nice of that human boy to give us tickets. It will be a nice night out for all of us before we leave tomorrow."

She fought hard to quell the bitterness rising in her chest, swallowing reflexively against the bile burning the back of her throat.

She knew her expression had to be more stunned than relaxed. Then, when Baden pulled the door closed and shut her in, smells and emotions she couldn't separate overwhelmed her, forcing tears to her eyes.

Her Mother's brows rose. From where she sat behind her mother, Leis looked to her father. Concern was not only etched into his face, but it was rolling off him in waves. Glad to have at least one person's emotions tagged and labeled, she looked at Baden for reassurance.

He took her hand and squeezed it as she inhaled. His biting scent was filled with sharply edged emotion. *He's sad, and angry, and very determined.* She stared at him, battling down the tears threatening to overwhelm her.

"Are you all right?" her mother asked.

Her mother knew all along what was going on. Leis' own anger rose.

"Fine, Mom," Leis managed. "I just wish we had more time to visit, that's all."

Baden squeezed her hand again, and she leaned toward him, trying to inhale his courage. She picked up that he was doing his best to communicate something to her, but nothing made sense. Baden's eyes met her father's in the mirror, and he nodded.

I have to trust Baden.

The SUV pulled away from the curb and merged into traffic. She slid closer to Baden in an effort to let his strength and confidence override the anger coming from the rear and the confusion and bitterness from the front.

His arm tightened around her shoulders, and he pulled her close enough to whisper, "You're doing great, Leis. Hang in there."

Aside from her father taking direction from the parking attendant, the rest of the drive was quiet. At the gate, Leis handed over the tickets and they filed through the opening to mingle with the rest of the crowd.

The moment they merged with the crowd, Leis was thankful for Baden's steady arm around her waist. When the foot traffic became too heavy and they were forced to stop, she did her best to smile as Andrew angled his way toward them.

"Don't let go," Baden whispered.

She leaned closer to him and inhaled. The truth of his affectionate love for her swept her immediate fears away. She trusted him. She would always trust him.

"I love you, B."

"Love you, too, Leis. Always," he said.

Andrew and Carol reached their side as anger hit her in a wave.

"You're making this harder," Andrew snarled.

"I know what I'm doing." Baden pushed him aside.

Leis's father stepped between them.

"Hey, kids." He held his hands up. "Let's enjoy the concert, okay? There's no need to fight tonight."

"There are a lot of people here." Her Mother focused her calculating green eyes on Leis. "I know you don't like crowds. We can go back to the hotel if you want."

"I'm fine." Leis took Baden's hand and turned away before anyone could respond. Furious, she wanted to get as far from her as possible.

Her body shook, and she clung to Baden's arm to steady her as they pushed into the group of people in the line for the barricaded area around the stage.

Baden's thumb traced circles on the back of her hand as he parted the crowd for her. She tried to focus on his touch, desperate for something to distract her from the chaos of emotion and smells assaulting her. Baden was familiar, and his emotions were the only ones that made sense. Her mom was right. She hated crowds. Desperate to leave, she leaned closer to him. Baden's sadness swept over her.

"Can we go now? Just us?" she pleaded.

"Let's head to the stage, okay?" He tugged her alongside then kissed her forehead. "Enjoy the concert then we can leave. Trust me, I want to get away from here as badly as you do. Just a little longer." She looked up, and his warm eyes swallowed her.

"Okay." She followed him closer to the stage.

Most of the fairgoers were kept outside the steel barricades, but the six of them quickly joined a loose and excited crowd gathered inside waiting for the headliner. Looking around, Leis saw many of her classmates and recognized Jessica close to the stairs at the side of the stage. Heading in that direction, she and Baden worked their way through the throng of people.

As they broke through the final group of students milling around the stairs, the lights went down, and a guitar began to play a rich, haunting sound. Leis and Baden reached the stairs, and Jessica opened her mouth to say something just as the rest of the band hit in hard and drowned out her words. The band's sound was incredible, and Leis looked up to see Koen striding out to take center stage.

In light colored clothing, he stood out like a beacon, the crowd following his every move. He wore stylishly worn and ripped jeans and scuffed leather boots. A bright blue shirt was unbuttoned at the neck and exposed the top of his chest while the sleeves of a thin, white leather jacket were pushed up past his elbows. His wrists were encircled by leather bracelets and a blue bandanna the same color as his shirt. She watched his hands in awe as they flew across the strings of the guitar.

Breathtakingly gorgeous, Koen's every move radiating confidence. The guitar slung over his shoulder looked like an extension of his body, and he expertly brought it to life with his music. Unable to tear her eyes from him, the music rose to a near deafening crescendo until her breath was stolen as the band fell out and he began to sing. The rest of the world stopped as his silky voice wrapped around her. She moved closer to get a clearer view.

Baden's arm tightened briefly around her waist, and she glanced back to see calm resignation on his face. His confidence wavered for a moment, and in his normally happy brown eyes, she recognized the sadness she sensed earlier. He held her gaze for a moment longer, then broke eye contact to sweep his eyes across the crowd.

She wasn't sure how to react to his expression. There was no anger and no disappointment at her obvious enchantment with Koen, and the resolve she picked up from him earlier was still steely strong. Shaking off her worry, she returned her attention to the stage.

A jolt of surprise went through her when she found herself

looking up into Koen's piercing blue eyes. The shocking difference between his light-colored irises and Baden's dark ones made her breath catch.

Still singing, he grinned down cockily, and the rest of the air was sucked out of her. Around her, the girls swooned. Leis blushed and Baden's arm loosened.

Even more energized, Koen stepped back to swing his guitar high then down to end the first song. He welcomed the crowd and stalked across the stage as if he had been born on it. When he struck the chord for the next song, the people erupted in cheers and pressed even closer to the stage. She stared in awe, seeing a side of him she never imagined existed.

After four or five high energy songs, someone brought him a stool. The lights dimmed until a single spotlight shone on his tousled black hair.

> You ignited a bonfire in my heart
> The laughter from your lips
> Brought light to a darkened life
> I can't stop thinking about the sound
> The sound of your sweet voice
> You awoke something in my soul
> You shined a spotlight into my heart
> With all my heart
> With all I am
> I will love you 'til I die
> I give my heart
> Give it all to you
> You are my miracle.

The crowd stilled, and he repeated the simple melody again, this time joined by a female voice that blended so seamlessly with his Leis almost didn't notice until a second spotlight gradually illuminated a beautiful pregnant woman on a stool next to him.

With her matching crystal blue eyes and singing voice, it was obvious this was Koen's Mother. She looked impossibly young and beautiful.

The woman's eyes were locked on Koen, and there was no denying the pride on her face as he played and sang.

As the last note rang out, Koen leaned over and hugged the woman. Then he stood, let the guitar swing around to his back, and introduced Eileen as his mother.

Baden leaned close and near shouted into Leis's ear as Koen edged toward the stairs while the intro to the next song began.

Baden turned her toward him, and his eyes searched hers. "Remember when I said I need you to trust me?"

EIGHTEEN

"Leis, you need to run when I tell you to run, okay?" Baden brows creased as he gestured with his chin toward the side of the stage. "Get backstage and go with Lockton. He'll be waiting for you."

Leis laid her hands flat on his chest. "Lockton? You mean Koen? Aren't you going with me?"

Baden looked over her shoulder, and his eyes darkened. "I don't have time to explain. You are going to run backstage, and he is going to get you away from here." Baden's hands moved. One landed on her right butt cheek, and the other slid up to nearly palm the side of her left breast. His eyes were tortured. "I love you, Leis." He pulled her tight against him and crushed a kiss to her mouth.

Shocked for a second, Leis froze in place. Then revulsion took over, and she flung herself backward, a slap connecting with Baden's cheek.

He caught himself then glared at her. "Nice. Now run!"

A red handprint appeared on Baden's cheek, and Leis reached out to touch it, but he brushed her hand away.

"Go backstage!" He growled.

With a last look into his velvet brown eyes, she took three steps toward the stairs, but Jessica was blocking the way. Leis dodged to the side and ran behind the metal staircase. When she turned to look over her shoulder, she ran into someone and found herself wrapped in familiar arms.

"Daddy?" Leis froze. He held her tightly, but confusion swelled around him. He eased his grip when she resisted. Behind him stood her mother.

Her eyes were blazing green fire. "We thought you might try to run. Where is Baden?"

Determination rolled from her father, but a flicker of doubt crossed his face as her mother reached for her arm. Leis yanked away then relaxed when her father wedged his tall frame between them.

His chin lowered, and he spoke softly. "Stefanie." He rested a hand on Leis's forearm. "Is this really what you want?" He inched Leis slowly to the right, his tone even. "Do you really want to force her into the same life we've endured?"

Taking a small step in the direction of her Father's pressure, Leis spotted Koen behind her mother. He watched her father's face, his hands clenching and unclenching in agitation.

A decision registered between the two men and the breeze grew thick with a sharply protective scent. She glanced between them in confusion.

Unaware of Koen's presence, her mother went toe to toe with her Father and reached around him for Leis. "It was your family that brought this on us all! Now get her and let's go home."

Behind them, the crowd let out a cheer, causing her mother to look up in surprise. In that instant, two things happened simultaneously. Her Father pushed Leis and Koen surged forward, pulling her into the shadows surrounding the raised stage. The lights on the platform faded out and if possible, the crowd noise rose further, calling out for an encore.

Koen's arms wrapped around her, and one breath told her he was determined to protect her at any cost. He caught her hand and led her through the mass of technicians and stagehands. He took off in a sprint across the rear parking lot full of vans, trailers, and dually trucks that pulled the food trailers filling the fairgrounds. He didn't slow until they reached a rear corner gate.

From the moment he grabbed her, his presence infused her with such confidence, she was instantly unafraid. She matched her steps to his, their breaths and running feet rising and falling in rhythm. The more she inhaled the trail his body left in the cooling air, the richer the smell of him grew in her lungs.

They wove between the large vehicles, heading in as straight a line as possible for the fence opening. Outside the chain link, he headed for a dark blue compact car.

Koen hit the remote to unlock the car. "Get in. We've got to move before they figure out where we went," he said.

Leis raced around to the other side, jumped in, and slammed the door behind her. Koen already had the car started and shifted into gear. He accelerated away from the fairgrounds, careful not to draw attention.

Once they merged with traffic, he relaxed, and Leis drew a deep breath. Her heart rate began to settle, but her nerves were rattled. She looked over her shoulder.

Where is Baden? She had expected him to meet up with them, but he was nowhere in sight.

"Are you all right?" Koen concentrated on the road, still breathing heavily. His hands gripped the steering wheel so hard his knuckles turned white. "I can't believe he let you go."

Leis huffed a breath. "Me either. I don't understand anything." She clenched her teeth, determined not to cry, not to break down.

Koen reached for her. "I'm just glad we made it this far safely."

The moment his hand touched hers, it registered that the undercurrent of protection hadn't been coming from her father. She stared at Koen's profile as he maneuvered the streets leading away from the fairgrounds.

She didn't understand why the simple contact of his fingers on the back of her hand rushed intense affection through her pores in a way Baden's never had. She knew she should move away from him but couldn't.

Within seconds the air in the car shifted like it had at the dinner the first time they met. As his touch lingered, her world began to change. She knew beyond a shadow of a doubt that she needed this man more than her next breath, though she could not have explained how she knew it or why.

He's human! What she was feeling for Koen was dangerous. Forbidden. Impossible.

Koen's shoulders dropped, and his scent evolved from survival to a complex mix of feelings and impulses that she shouldn't be able to understand. She'd never been told her sense of smell would allow her to read human emotions. Yet instinctively she knew Koen cared for her as much, and possibly more than Baden did.

As he continued to stroke the skin of her hand, she tried to detangle her own jumbled emotions from what she was getting from him.

"Koen?" She asked tentatively.

He glanced away from the road. "Leis?" He chuckled a little, easing the tension.

"Can you please tell me what's going on? One minute I'm in school, the next my family is — crazy, and now I'm on the road with you. You're taking me who knows where, and I have no idea where Baden is." She rubbed her forehead with her thumb and forefinger. "Please tell me what's going on. Where is Baden?"

He cleared his throat, obviously trying to figure out how to tell her something that made him uncomfortable. Fear crept up on her, and she went very still.

"Koen. Where are you taking me?"

NINETEEN

KOEN

The pleading in her voice was Koen's undoing. Instead of answering, he glanced at her and sighed. Though he wanted to stop the car and tell her the truth himself, he knew she wouldn't believe him.

Pulling his eyes back to the road he quietly asked, "Can you reach the bag behind my seat?"

She leaned between the seats to look behind him. When she did, her hair slid down his arm like satin, and he shivered. Glancing over, he saw the front of her thin shirt had slipped to the side. As the gray fabric shifted, exposing a sliver of her lacey pale pink bra strap, fire shot down his torso. He jerked his eyes to the road, hoping it wasn't too late to stop the thoughts from filtering through his body.

She froze, picking up on his sudden arousal instantly.

"What's in the bag, Koen? What are you thinking about?" Her voice shook with confusion and desire.

Having her this close was torture, especially when he knew her body recognized him as her mate though she still believed him to be a human. He wrestled down his desire to claim her and finally understood what it meant when his Father said his blood would cry out when he met his mate.

His veins sang with need. If her voice ignited the fire in his blood, her presence added gasoline. The fire raging in his veins needed cooling, or he was going to do or say something they would both regret.

He pushed those thoughts aside. His initial fears about the content of Baden's letter returned, effectively icing his rushing blood.

"It's a letter from Baden," he said. "He wanted to explain things face to face, but he ran out of time. It's at the bottom in a white envelope." He refocused all his attention on the road. "We have about two hours until we stop. Go ahead and read. We can talk when we get to the hotel."

In his peripheral vision, he watched her carefully unzip the bag and reach to the bottom. She pulled out the large brown envelope stuffed with their travel documents. Clipped to the outside was Baden's letter, her name carefully written on the front.

His stomach lurched as her breath hitched. Pulling it free, she put the other items back in the bag and placed it on the floor behind him. For a long time, she held the envelope in her hands, sliding her thumbs back and forth across her name before she turned it over and broke open the seal.

Leis carefully broke the seal and opened the envelope, afraid of what she would find. Her hands shook as she pulled loose and unfolded several neatly folded pages of lined paper. Baden's tidy handwriting covered the pages both front and back.

She tried to read but the words blurred. She wiped hastily at her eyes. When they wouldn't clear, she looked up to the roof of the car and drew a deep breath. Koen's worry and doubt softened. Leis released a slow breath and heard him do the same.

Holding the papers tightly in her hands, she looked over. Koen's jet-black hair was gelled to hold the natural curls even under the heat of the lights, and she frowned at the lingering tension in the tick of the muscle in his jaw. For no reason she could easily define, she ached to reach over and smooth the bunched muscles. As though sensing her stare, he glanced over. His lip curled up in a sexy half smile.

"Read, Leis." He turned back as his smile faded. "Looks like Baden had a lot to tell you."

Not sure if it was her own need for comfort, or a desire to offer it to him, Leis reached for his hand.

We're friends, she reasoned. *And obviously Baden trusts him.*

He moved their hands to rest on the shifter, then turned his palm up to lace his fingers through hers. Wearing a full smile, he gave her hand a gentle squeeze, and she turned her attention to the pages in her lap.

> Leisel,
>
> If you're reading this, then you are safely away from our Clan, and I am on my way out of the country. Once I know it is safe, I'll contact you. For now, trust that I am safe just as I trust you are.

She pulled away from Koen to grip the pages with both hands.

> You probably have so many questions and no idea which to ask first, so I'm going to do my best to explain.
>
> First, I want you to know who and what we truly are. Not what we've become, or what you've been told we are, but who we were created to be.
>
> You know we are the Vampir, sometimes called The Lasting Ones. Our ancestors were protectors, advisors, and leaders in the communities they lived in until our numbers increased, and the humans became jealous and suspicious.

Why the history lesson? She just wanted to know where he was!

> You also know females like yourself live extraor-

dinarily long lives. Three to four hundred years is normal now, but it used to be closer to thousands of years.

I found recorded histories of our people living more than two thousand years. These men and women lived and served their villages, clans, and towns as advisors and healers because of the knowledge they gained from their long lives. But the more they learned and the wiser they grew, the more suspicious humans became.

In the end, it was our bonding ceremony that drove the wedge between us and the humans. The ceremony was once celebrated together by Vampir and humans. But one day the humans began to distrust the mating Blood Exchange.

You already know this much, but please keep reading. It relates to us directly.

The exchange that allows the male to live as long as his mate. He becomes her protector, her lover, her provider until death takes them both. It was the male's sudden long life and apparent instant dedication to his mate that spawned the legend of the vampire.

The humans began to believe the females enchanted men and enslaved them. When the humans began to kill us, we went into hiding.

Gradually, we were able to re-integrate into towns and villages, but we kept our identity secret.

We became nomads, hiding our long lives by moving frequently. For a century or more, our people thrived in relative peace, but after decades of being careful, the Bonding Ceremony was again discovered by those who didn't understand, and our people were labeled witches and pagans.

The humans who saw the presentation of the crib believed we were sacrificing children and drinking their blood to stay young.

In fear, they tracked down entire Vampir families and wiped them out. Their efforts to eliminate us almost succeeded. Within a century, our people were nearly extinct.

Only eight families survived, and they went into hiding in the hills and mountains of what is now Germany and Austria. As our numbers increased again, our people split up and spread in every direction.

Gaps in Leis's knowledge began to fill, and her feelings of betrayal grew. All her life she'd been told her Clan was all that was left of her people. After reading this, she realized how foolish she had been to believe that.

Exactly what happened next, I've never been able to discover. The only clue I found was a reference to one of the families being recordkeepers or Historians. Though we all carry a strong German heritage, there is a reference to a Clan that settled much further north with the name Loxton who may have kept the written and oral stories of our people.

But, since our Clan was driven into the mountains, the histories we have been taught are incomplete.

I believe Koen is a descendant of theirs. If they are who I believe they are, his family might be able to help us piece together what happened to drive our Clan away from the others.

Trembling, Leis read the last paragraph again, and reality crashed in on her.

Koen isn't human.

"Stop the car," she whispered.

Koen slowed but didn't pull over. "Leis? What's wrong?"

Anxiety crept up her neck with cold fingers, and she reached for the door handle.

"Stop the car, Koen!" As soon as he complied, she flung the door open and jumped out.

"Leisel! Stop!" She heard Koen throw the car in park, then his footfalls as he followed her up the steep bank next to the highway and into a thick tree line. They were near an airport, and a jet screamed overhead, drowning out his call.

Ducking around a tree, and still clutching the letter in her fist, Leis fell to her knees. She read the last lines again, the ones that told her Baden thought Koen belonged to another Vampir Clan - something she had been told her whole life wasn't possible. If his words were true, everyone she knew had lied to her.

Including Koen.

Koen crashed through the underbrush, his breathing rapid and hard. His movements stirred the musty ground, and she coughed against the smell of decaying leaves. The jet's engines faded, and Leis looked up to follow its path across the inky blackness.

Sensing Koen's scent closing in behind her, Leis's back stiffened. "Stop. Please don't come any closer."

"Okay." Koen paused. "Leis, talk to me."

"You knew?" she asked.

"Yes." He took a tiny step forward. "I knew the moment I heard your voice."

She looked over her shoulder. "How?"

His eyes were soft and glistened in the dim light. "A Vampir female's voice sounds...different to us males."

She flicked her eyes to his, and he continued.

"The moment I heard your voice I knew what you were. When I figured out you had no idea who - or what - I was, I didn't know what to do."

Anger and hurt choked her. "Why didn't you tell me? Why didn't you ask me?"

"You were promised to someone else." Koen's jaw sawed back and forth. "I didn't understand how or why, but I couldn't interfere until I knew what was going on. And honestly, how would you have reacted to knowing I knew?" He lifted an eyebrow. "You would never have believed me."

He took another tentative step, bringing him close enough that she could scent the truth of what he told her. He gestured at the pages still clutched in her fists.

"I don't know how much or what Baden has told you in that letter, but he knows the truth of our situation." Koen was nearly over her, and his anguish at her pain and confusion was evident not only in the wafts of his body's scent but in his shimmering blue eyes. His voice was laced with awe. "I've never met an un-bonded Vampir female, Leis. You are more precious and rarer than you realize. Our kind is dying all around the world, and we need you. We've been searching for your Clan for centuries. We've all heard the legends, but now...we know they aren't just stories." She watched warily when he knelt next to her. "But not only is your Clan precious to our kind, *you* are very special to me."

Covering her mouth, Leis stifled a cry. The honesty of his words and the intensity of his emotions were undeniable. Despite it all, she instinctively trusted the man kneeling in front of her.

"What do I do?" she whispered. "What do I do with all this?"

He tenderly thumbed the tears from her cheek, then pulled her into his arms. "How about you let me help you?"

He shifted slightly, and she was in his lap. One strong arm encircled her waist, while the palm of his other hand cupped her cheek as tears overwhelmed her. His thumb stroked her jaw just under her ear, and she sank further into him, her sobs lessening as he held her.

Safety wrapped her like a blanket, and for a few minutes, she marveled at the feel of his heartbeat in time with her own. She pressed her face into the fabric of his shirt and drank in his earthy smell, his scent imprinting itself on her heart.

When she was finally able to draw a deep breath, an emotion she couldn't identify surged through her. She felt the reality of its implication through to her bones.

Koen is mine.

As the thought took hold, his arms tensed, and he whispered in her ear using a language she didn't understand. The stillness was broken as another jet crossed overhead. Its fading roar muddled his voice, but somehow, his indecipherable words wove together with the knowledge that he was hers and settled something firmly inside her.

Inhaling deeply, Leis leaned away from him calmer but still confused. "What did you say? Was that another language?"

He was very still and didn't answer right away. There was something different in his eyes, and more noticeably, in his scent. It was sharper, crisper, but sweeter. Whatever had changed slowed his racing emotions and quieted his doubts.

"We should keep moving." He ignored her question and stood,

helping her to her feet. "Let's get to the hotel. I think you have more reading to do on the way." His jaw tightened, and his eyes flashed silvery in the moonlight. "Then we'll talk about what I said."

TWENTY-ONE

KOEN

As they trekked back to the car, Koen's mind raced back to his father's explanation of what it would be like when he finally met his intended.

He'd been in high school when he asked his dad what it was like when he met his mother. His Father's eyes went distant, and a wistful smile lightened his normally somber expression.

"It was like the whole world stopped." His Dad ran a hand through his hair. "We were at her parents' farmhouse, sitting on the porch with her brothers after a bonfire. Eileen sat down next to me, and everything around me just *stopped*." His brows rose in emphasis. "I knew at that moment she was the one. I knew she was *my mate*, the one I was meant to take care of, the one I was intended for." His grin grew. "And that was before I even looked her in the eye. When I did, she was staring at me with this stunned look on her face." He laughed. "It was the cutest thing I'd ever seen. But when she introduced herself, and I heard her voice," his eyes drifted closed, "Koen, I knew she felt the same thing. So, I did the only honorable thing and pledged my blood to her on the spot."

"But Mom talks all the time about the Bonding ceremony you

had!" Koen had exclaimed. "She never told me you completed the Blood Exchange before then."

Dad's blue eyes twinkled. "Believe me, I wanted to kiss your mother that instant, and I don't think she would have stopped me. But her brothers saw what was happening and made sure we did things the right way." He stood and clapped Koen on the shoulder. "It's about time you learned the Pledge. Every male needs to be prepared for the moment that will change his life."

From that day on his Father taught him the traditions and stories of the Clan even though everyone knew Koen had little hope of ever meeting his mate.

Kneeling in the grass with Leis curled into him, he knew exactly what his father meant. When she was lying relaxed and trusting in his arms, there was no longer any doubt she was his. The formal words of the Pledge rolled from his tongue before he could stop them. He knew she was crying too hard to recognize it, and the plane overhead drowned out his voice, but he felt the moment her body acknowledged him as her mate, even if her mind hadn't caught up yet.

Leis's hand in his steadied his emotions. Her touch assured him she was physically close. Though that gave him strength, he was still reeling from the need to kiss her and complete the bond.

They were almost to the car, and the words of the Pledge wound through his mind again. He felt guilty for denying her the answer to her question. She had no idea what he said, and that knowledge rocked him.

He was barely able to keep himself from kissing her, claiming her, and it appeared she was completely unaware of what had happened to him.

There was a very good reason the Clan rarely allowed their young sons and daughters to date or spend unsupervised time together. When a male meets his mate, his sole focus becomes making her his. Permanently.

Leis needed him to explain, but the driving need under his skin to complete the bonding and prevent her from being taken from him was nearly overwhelming. The danger he knew she was in only increased his need.

He was certain she wouldn't resist him, but he couldn't allow himself to take advantage of her vulnerability. She needed time to come to grips with all that had happened to her. It would be a brutal test of his resolve to keep his distance until they were safely among his Clan, but it was the only way.

The highway was deserted, and though he had planned to wait until they were inside the car, safely separated by the center console, he wasn't ready to let her get that far from him.

Instead, he gently turned her to face him, letting her back rest against the passenger door. When he placed his hands on the roof above her shoulders, her red-rimmed eyes looked up in worry and almost undid all the control he worked so hard for. He kept space between them, but the craving to taste her made him shake.

"Please help me understand." Her voice cracked.

He took a deep breath and lowered his chin. "How much do you know about the Blood Pledge?"

Leis shook her head in confusion. "You mean the Blood *Exchange?*"

"No." He tilted his head, his voice low. "The Exchange is what bonds us. The Pledge comes first." His eyes narrowed as he began to comprehend just how little she'd been told. "Baden never spoke the Pledge to you?"

At Baden's name, she flinched. "No. Why would he? The Clan makes the Pledge. It's part of the law. It just *is*. I don't understand why that matters now." The letter crinkled as her fists clenched against his chest. "Baden and I can't be together…"

Afraid she was going to push him away; Koen caught her face in his hands. When she refused to look him in the eye he whispered, "Leisel, look at me. Please." At his quiet request, she met his eyes. "The Blood Pledge isn't *law*, it's a promise. It's the promise that my blood belongs to you - and you alone. The Pledge might sound formal, but it is the way we males offer our lives to the one we are meant for. It gives you the choice to accept me, or not." His gaze slipped to her softly parted lips then up to meet her shimmering eyes. "Though not kissing you is the hardest thing I've ever done," he whispered.

A single car drove past, illuminating her face. Shaking with need and hanging on by a thread, he bent and allowed himself to taste the tears glimmering on her cheeks.

TWENTY-TWO

Koen's strong hands trembled against her jaw, and when his warm lips met her cheeks, a searing pressure built in the roof of her mouth. Her fangs! A whimper escaped her throat, and she leaned toward him as pain lanced through the bones of her cheeks.

Koen sucked in a breath and pulled away.

Gasping for breath, she closed her eyes wondering why she so desperately needed him closer. It had never been like this with Baden. Holding his letter in her hand, made what she felt for the man in front of her seem a hundred kinds of wrong. Though she understood the horror of her near bonding with Baden, letting go of a lifetime of dreams and expectations was hard. Her instincts told her there was an undeniable connection to Koen, but her mind refused to let go of Baden.

"Baden asked for my help, and I promised him I would protect you." Koen cleared his throat. "What I said back there was the formal offering of my blood to you. That Pledge is only spoken when a male *knows* he has met the one." His thumb smoothed over her cheek, the pulse in his throat was pounding under the black leather of his necklace. "Please tell me you understand. Do you even want what I'm offering you?"

She rested her cheek against his palm and fell helplessly into his searching eyes.

"I don't know how I know it," she whispered, her brow creasing as she forced herself to admit the truth. "But I know I - belong with you." Her voice faded as a fierce reality poured out. "You are mine."

He lifted his free hand to smooth the skin between her eyes, and his lips curved in the half smile she was beginning to crave.

He swiped his chin on his jacket to wipe his tears. "I never thought this moment would come for me. You've changed my whole world."

Willingly, she went into his arms when he pulled her against him. He whispered softly, his breath warm against her scalp.

"Leisel Gottschalk, I pledge my blood to you. I will not offer it to any other because you alone are uniquely created to receive it. Though you have not yet taken my blood, it is pledged to you until I die. I am yours, and you are mine."

The heavy thud of his heart sang in her ear as she pressed her cheek into his chest. His fingers slid over and over through her hair, and as the moment wore on, she sensed he was waiting for something from her. The silence stretched as another lone car cruised past. She searched her mind for what he was expecting her to say but came up with nothing.

His blue shirt was unbuttoned at the top, and she couldn't resist pressing her nose against his skin. He was still sweaty from his onstage performance and their hasty escape, filling her nose with his unique scent.

He was hers, but not because he spoke ancient words that were written centuries ago. He was hers because his scent told her he was the only one who could give her what she needed. He willingly offered his very life's essence to support and protect her, and she ached to know how to respond to him properly.

Soon their breaths evened out, and he softened his stance. His arms relaxed into a comfortable embrace. He rubbed his cheek atop her head.

Leis stepped back. He gave her space, resting his hands on her upper shoulders, but she felt bereft without his arms around her.

"If there is something formal I'm supposed to say back to you, I don't know what it is." She bit her lip. "I'm sorry."

Frustration edged his voice. "I know you don't. It isn't your fault no one told you."

She shook her head while looking at the crumpled and creased pages in her shaking hands.

"Baden wrote this letter to fill me in on a lot of things I wasn't told." Her eyes lifted to his. "Can you tell me what I'm supposed to say to you?"

He exhaled and slid his palms down her arms to grasp her hands. "I can tell you the formal response, but honestly," he softly kissed the back of her knuckles, and his lips sent fire up her arm. "I don't need the words." He let their hands and the letter dangle between them. "Seeing the answer in your eyes and hearing it in your voice is enough. We can discuss formalities later."

She sighed. "I feel so...lost."

Koen released her and reached around to open the car door. "You're not lost." His smile warmed her through to the core. "We can't stay here. Did you finish the letter?"

She sat down and smoothed the pages across her lap. "No." He brushed his knuckles down her cheek before closing the car door.

He climbed in and started the car. She stared out the windshield until Koen reached for her hand.

"Hey. Read," he encouraged. "You'll feel better after you hear it all."

Leis nodded and concentrated on Baden's words.

I know this is a lot to absorb, and I hope

that what I can't take time to explain, Koen and his family will.

I've known from the moment you mentioned his name Koen was a fellow Vampir, and he would have recognized your voice instantly.

From the time we were old enough to understand what we were meant to be to one another, I knew you loved me enough to go through with the bonding even if you knew, like I did, there was something wrong about it.

Even beyond discovering we are related, it's become clear we've been lied to about so many things. Our lack of connection was never your fault, no matter what our family or the Clan told us. Our bodies are uniquely created to recognize the one we are to spend our lives with.

We were all told that it is the female's sense of smell that is the catalyst for the Blood Exchange. It is not. Our lack of connection was never your fault and there is nothing wrong with you.

I'm learning that there are a lot of scientific things that come into play, but at the basic level, my instincts knew we were related. They prevented my body from responding to you, in turn preventing your response to me.

Something in a male's body chemistry changes the moment we meet our mate. It's said that our blood calls out for her. This makes our attraction to and instinct to protect so strong we are driven to give her our blood. When the female senses the pheromones in our blood have changed, her body recognizes it, and her fangs make the Blood Exchange possible.

I've been told that when you meet your intended mate, it is unmistakable. If the attraction between you and Koen is as strong as I think it is, I am certain you are intended for one another.

Koen will be the catalyst. Trust him to know.

Above everything else, trust what you and Koen have. Refuse to let anyone come between you. You will always be my best friend, and not knowing if I will ever see you again is hard. Knowing for certain that the next time I do, you'll be bonded to him, is both the happiest and saddest moment of my life.

I love you more than I can begin to put in words, but you are not mine, and I am not yours. If you truly belong to Koen, let him claim you.

If anyone challenges his Pledge to do so because of me, show them this letter as proof that I have released you. This may not make sense because it is one more thing that was never explained to us.

I will leave it to Koen, it's his right.

I hope your daughters are as beautiful as you are, and that your sons live long lives as providers and protectors for the generations to come.

I love you, my sister in heart.
Baden Allen Dietrich

I love you, my sister in heart.
Baden Allen Dietrich

TWENTY-THREE

KOEN

The directions sent them to a hotel just west of Columbus. The outside of the yellowing building looked tired and in need of a serious upgrade. Koen eased the car into the lot and cut the engine.

Leis exited the car and leaned against it heavily. She'd finished Baden's letter with tears streaming down her face but remained silent the rest of the drive.

He stepped out and watched her as he reached into the back seat for the bag containing their changes of clothing and the rest of the documents from Baden.

His instructions were clear enough. Get out of Ohio, don't let Leis use her old cell phone, and wait at his parents' house until contacted. Everything they would need for the journey had been provided under false names.

"Leis, before we go in you'll need to swap the IDs in your wallet with these." He opened the bag and withdrew the fake identification, then handed her a new driver's license and a credit card.

Her eyes were distant, but she took them. She set her purse on the hood of the car and pulled out her wallet. After slipping the new cards inside, she handed him the valid ones without looking up.

He put everything back and shouldered the duffel. The parking lot lights cast her face in shadow, while sadness hunched her shoulders. He resisted the urge to wrap her in his arms and never let go. She looked so fragile and lost, but he didn't want to push her. The letter from Baden clearly pained her.

"Are you all right?" He rounded the car to where she stood.

"I will be." She looked toward the main doors of the hotel.

He nodded and held his hand out to her. She stared at it. He turned his palm up. "No more heavy conversation tonight. I promise."

A weak smile crept across her lips, and she placed her hand in his. He squeezed her fingers lightly and tilted his head.

"Tonight, we're Owen and Denise Jackson." He bumped her playfully as he reached down to pick up his guitar case. "Owen would like to practice some guitar. What would Denise like to do?"

She smiled tiredly. "Denise would really like a shower and room service." Glancing at the condition of the hotel, she snorted. "Though walking next door for a sandwich and chips is probably a better idea."

TWENTY-FOUR

Koen checked them in under false names, and they were relieved when the interior of the hotel was in better shape than the outside. The room turned out to be a small suite with two queen beds and a sitting area.

Koen laid his guitar on the bed closest to the door and dropped their bag on the dresser.

She surveyed the room as the implications of their situation settled on her. She and Koen would be all alone for an entire night.

In a hotel room.

She turned toward him as he lowered himself onto the orange and tan loveseat, causally stretching his arm along the back of it. He crossed one long leg over the other and chewed his lower lip thoughtfully.

She shifted nervously from one foot to the other. "Do you want to shower first or should I?" She flinched and stepped back when he stood.

"Go ahead," he said. "I'll walk over to the sandwich shop next door and bring us some dinner." He paused at the door. "You have all the space you need."

When the door closed behind him, she sagged against the wall.

In a matter of three days, her entire life had been turned upside down. Though the tension from their earlier encounter beside the highway had eased considerably, it was only going to get harder. She wasn't afraid of *him*, but the way he made her *feel* terrified her.

Every moment of her life with Baden had been carefully structured with rules in place for any and every situation. Going to the movies, a dance, or a party required a chaperone.

It was only in the last year that the two of them were permitted to be completely alone for any real length of time. Permission to come to Ohio together had more to do with their heavy study schedules than allowing them any freedom. It had left her completely unprepared for the rush of desire she felt for Koen.

Just being near him was like a drug she couldn't get enough of, and trusting her instincts didn't sound like a very good idea, despite what Baden said.

Tense and tired, she rubbed her aching shoulders and glanced into the bathroom, glad to see it contained a jacuzzi tub.

A relaxing bath is just what I need.

Inside the duffel bag, she found sweatpants, a couple of hoodies, and several clean t-shirts. Carrying a pair of sweats and a green hoodie into the bathroom, she locked the door and started the bath water.

She wound her hair into a loose knot atop her head and stepped into the tub. As the water closed around her, the strain of the day's events began to fade. Turning the knob to activate the jets, she almost moaned as the pulsing jets of air brought relief to her aching muscles. She closed her eyes and hummed. The tune was familiar, but she couldn't remember the words.

While her body relaxed, she let the melody roll through her mind and her tension seep into the water.

TWENTY-FIVE

KOEN

With no idea what she would prefer, Koen bought four different sandwiches, two bags of chips, and two large bottles of water. Pushing the keycard into the door and stepping inside the room, he heard the jets of a jacuzzi running in the bathroom.

He toed off his boots. The only light in the room came from a lamp between the beds, so he flipped the rest of them on to make the room as non-threatening as possible when she came out.

Shrugging out of his jacket, he hung it on the back of a chair. He looked back at the bathroom door. He desperately wanted to peel the shirt off since the sweat from being on stage and their sprint across the parking lot had dried uncomfortably on his chest and back. The jets shut off and a blow dryer started.

Suspecting it was going to take her some time to dry her hair, he unbuttoned the sticky shirt and slipped out of it. He stuffed it into the bag and reached for the clean hoodie. Just as he slid his arms inside, the bathroom door opened, and a rush of warm air swept the smell of shampoo and soap toward him.

Leis's sharp intake of breath lanced through him as if she had traced her hands down his bare spine. Rushing to pull the sweatshirt over his head, he apologized without turning.

"I'm sorry." His voice was strained even to his own ears. "I heard the blow dryer and thought you'd..." He turned while still pulling the shirt into place, intending to hurry into the bathroom for his own shower. But the sight of her wearing his clothes stopped him cold.

His sweatpants were far too long, puddling at her ankles, and his shirt hung nearly to her knees. His eyes slowly traveled from her tiny feet to the words printed across the front of the green hoodie. Her hands gripped the material so hard he suspected her nails had punched holes in the fabric. Her coppery hair was pulled away from her freshly washed face and braided down her back. Even in over-sized clothes, she was breathtaking.

He forced his eyes up to meet hers and found them glowing with a heat that fanned the ache already burning low in his stomach. He cleared his throat and quickly decided the only way out of this was to deflect, or he was going to be in danger of doing more than kissing her. Glancing at the sandwiches on the table, he drew a quick breath, speaking before he acted on the thoughts racing through his mind.

"Chicken, turkey, ham, and roast beef. I hope you're not a vegetarian. If so, I'll take the sandwiches, and you can have all the chips."

He lifted an eyebrow and was glad to see the tension slowly release from her hands as a soft smile made her lips curve upward.

"Thank you," she whispered.

Timid as a mouse, she hugged the wall as she moved from the bathroom door to the couch. Her eyes met his, their green depths dancing with gratitude, and he was relieved to see that the blazing desire had cooled to a smolder.

"You're welcome." He swiped the other pair of sweatpants from the bed and hurried toward the bathroom.

Once safely on the other side of the locked door, he leaned heavily against the counter and reached for the shower controls.

Turning the temperature to full cold, he scrubbed his hands down his face. "I sure hope this works like they say it does, or this is going to be the longest shower in history."

TWENTY-SIX

KOEN

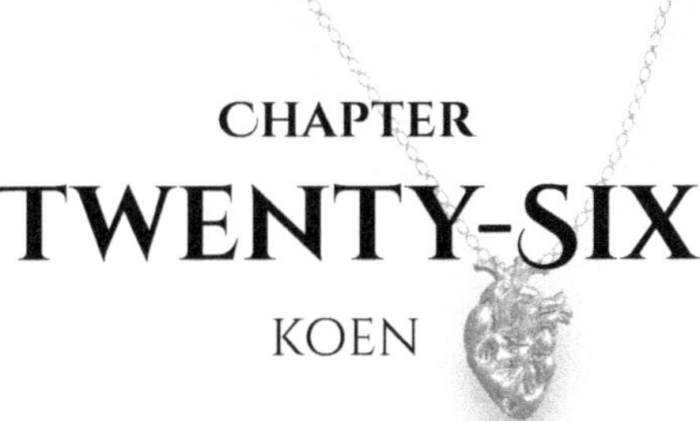

After letting the frigid shower literally chill his blood, Koen shut it off and hurriedly pulled on the sweats. Taking a deep breath, he opened the bathroom door.

Most of the lights were out, throwing the room into near darkness. The fixture above the door was still on, casting a soft glow that gave him just enough light to see Leis curled up in the bed near the far wall.

He lifted the guitar from his bed and set it beside the sofa. For a moment, he allowed himself to watch the gentle rise and fall of her breaths. It didn't surprise him that she was already asleep, but his mind was too full and his body too tense to allow sleep.

Stepping between the beds and averting his eyes, he folded the comforter down on the empty bed and shifted the extra pillows aside. He turned to sit, and his eyes landed on the graceful outline of her sleeping body.

Blowing out a breath, he leaned forward to watch her sleep. When he did, his eyes caught on her softly parted lips. Groaning inwardly, he let his head fall into his hands to stare at the floor instead.

All his life he guarded his heart and emotions so carefully, yet one word from her broke down every wall he'd built in seconds. As a popular musician, even if only locally, he always had his share of opportunities for relationships. Once or twice, he allowed himself to be talked into a date, but they never made it to a second one. Being near a girl always made him uncomfortable. Until *her*.

In a few days, she had become the sole reason for his existence. The intensity it tore through him every time he looked at her. It was so much more than a physical attraction. Though he wasn't ready to call it love, devotion was accurate. He tightened his fingers in his hair and reminded himself he vowed to protect her. Even from himself.

She mumbled in her sleep and rolled over with agitated movements. Confusion and doubt echoed in her voice as she dreamt, stirring his emotions in ways he couldn't control and didn't fully understand.

He released the tension in his hands and lifted his shoulders. He had to get himself together. For her sake. She was the one whose life had been turned upside down.

In the space of a few hours, she found out her family had been lying to her, the man she thought she was going to spend the rest of her life with was practically her brother, and she was adjusting to being able to smell the world around her.

They had two more days before they would be among his family, and he would be able to rely on the safety and accountability of his Clan. Until then, he had to find a way to control the gnawing need inside him. Sitting so close to her was not helping, and it raged when she whimpered again.

He pushed to his feet and carried the duffel into the seating area. Clicking on the lamp next to the chair, he withdrew the heavy envelope. Baden was thorough, that was for sure.

He had managed to get them not only false IDs and Social Security numbers, but phones, hotel reservations, and credit cards in the fake names.

Koen shook his head. Either Baden was a genius or the whole

system was a setup. Figuring it was probably a little of both, he spread the itinerary across the coffee table.

He sorted through the car rental agreements and hotel reservations. Scribbling on the hotel notepad, he laid out their next steps.

Tomorrow they would leave Columbus and make their way to Chicago.

Once there, they would drop off the car they were currently driving and pick up a new one. The rental they would pick up in Chicago would be dropped off at a mall in O'Fallon near his parents' house.

If they could safely make it that far, he knew his family and Clan would be able to protect them.

Koen sifted through everything one last time, and a white envelope with his name on it fell out. He leaned back and tore it open.

Neat handwriting filled the pages, and Koen frowned.

Koen,

These documents should provide everything you need to get you and Leis to your family.

At some point, you will be contacted by the person who will escort you and Leis back to Arizona. I haven't been told who that is or when they will meet you, but they will identify themselves to you.

I've talked to Leis's father, and things in Arizona are not going to be easy.

The only thing I can be sure of is that they won't hurt HER.

My grandmother knows about my betrayal and is plotting to get Leis back. I sincerely hope I am right about the connection being so strong between the two of you, because the consequences to Leis are the only thing that will prevent my grandmother from killing you on sight.

But I'm not going to lie. She will do anything short of it. I highly recommend keeping your breathing issues from her for as long as possible.

Hayden tells me she is contacting two other males my grandmother wants bonded, and she is setting up a challenge.

I understand it will be along the lines of the ancient practice when there were more of us, and it was believed there could be multiple potential bondmates.

According to custom, the female has the final say, but my grandmother will not let that happen. If one of them shows the slightest indication he could bond with Leis, she'll make it happen.

I don't need to tell you what that would mean for you.

The good news is the network we've established around the world is committed to reuniting the Clan again. I am leaving the country to meet with a large group in Europe. I will be out of contact until I know exactly what the plans are, but we will be in Arizona with you in less than ten days.

Let the challenge happen. We need all the time we can get.

Take care, Lockton, and love Leis the way she

deserves.

I hope your daughters are as beautiful as Leisel and that your sons live long lives as protectors and providers for the generations to come.

Baden Allen Dietrich

Koen read the letter twice. Everything in him wanted to take Leis and run far away. All he ever wanted was to find her and raise a family. Instead, they were thrown into a civil war that could not only take her from him but potentially cost both their lives.

TWENTY-SEVEN

Sunlight filtered through a crack in the drapes beside the bed, and when Leis opened her eyes, it took her a few seconds to orient herself. Pulling the blanket tight around her neck, she rolled over and found the bed next to her roughly made but empty.

She sat up. "Koen?"

Rubbing sleep from her eyes, she pushed out of the covers and stood. The hallway outside was quiet, and with a yawn, she glanced at the clock on the nightstand.

A red glow soaked through a piece of paper leaning against it. Scribbled on the hotel stationery was a note from Koen letting her know he had gone to the gym and would be back in an hour. A time of six fifty was added as an afterthought at the bottom. The clock read seven thirty.

The bag of clothing was open and laying on the floor. Crossing the room, she snagged the tiny coffee pot from the counter beside the desk and carried it to the bathroom with her. The lock on the bathroom door clicked just as she heard Koen re-enter the suite. He paused on the other side of the door. He knocked gently, making her jump.

"Leis? Are you okay?" he asked.

"Fine. I'll be out in a few." She set the coffee pot next to the sink and unwound her hair.

Under the door, she watched the shadow of his feet. He stood there a moment longer before moving away. Realizing she had his clothes with her, she changed quickly. The braid left her hair with soft waves, so she ran her fingers through it to arrange it loose down her back.

She tore open the free toothbrush and minty paste provided, scrunching her nose at the smell.

Mint. Not sure how I feel about the smell of mint.

After she filled the coffee pot with water, she glanced at her reflection and sighed. Pale cheeks and tired eyes stared back at her. Though she was a makeup artist, she rarely wore it herself. Frowning at her weary face, she wished she at least had some mascara. Shrugging, she opened the door.

"Thank you for the clean shirt." She'd put the jeans and boots from yesterday on, thankful Koen had packed an extra t-shirt for her. It was maroon with another band logo across the front.

"This shirt seems a little small to be yours." She tugged at the hem.

Quiet rustling and a short hiss came from his direction as he took a puff of his inhaler before responding.

"It was the last concert that band ever had, and the last t-shirt at the table." She finished getting the coffee started. Her nervousness grew as the sound of his feet moved closer. "It was too small for me, but I wanted it anyway."

Satisfied the tiny machine was working, she turned. He was leaning against the wall; his feet casually crossed at the ankles. Though she told herself she wasn't going to, her eyes moved slowly from the dark running shoes and shiny track pants up his body on their way to his face.

One hand clasped his wrist while the other slowly spun the inhaler between his deft fingers. The black pants rode low on his hips, and the shirt fit close to his flat stomach. The red material was wet in a v pattern that started at his sternum and widened across the front of his shoulders. She found herself jealous of the beads of sweat still lingering on his neck and shivered at the faint scruff of hair that darkened his cheeks and chin, wondering if it would scratch her if she pressed her face to his.

Finally making eye contact, Leis was surprised to see amusement in his gaze. He smirked.

"The workout was all right. A treadmill and a few nautilus machines, but good enough until we get home." He pushed off the wall and angled past her. "I'll get my shower, and then we'll grab breakfast downstairs before we leave."

As he crossed in front of her, he reached up to stroke her cheek softly with the back of his knuckles.

"I like your hair that way," he said.

She braced herself to be overwhelmed by his desire but instead found herself wrapped in the strong scent of safety.

She closed her eyes and breathed in the reality that Koen cherished her.

The intensity of his feelings stole what little breath she had and held her feet frozen to the carpet as the bathroom door closed behind him.

TWENTY-EIGHT

K oen watched in amusement as Leis approached the breakfast bar in the lobby.

He set their bag and his guitar case beside one of the tan and orange tables and watched her face scrunch and stretch as she walked past each of the breakfast offerings. The eggs and sausage got an extra sniff and a smile, while the waffle iron someone had just filled caused her to freeze in place. Her eyes closed as she inhaled, and he chuckled at the look of bliss on her face. He walked up behind her and leaned down to whisper in her ear.

"If waffles can put that look on your face, I might have to make sure you get them every morning." She groaned and he laughed out loud.

She tipped her head backwards to rest it on his chest as her face blushed crimson, and he relished the feel of her hair sliding down his bare arms. After her hesitation last night, he was glad she didn't pull away from him.

"Was I that obvious?" She huffed.

"A little bit. Yes." He kissed her upside-down forehead and

reached for an apple. "I'm going to enjoy watching you figure things out."

Crossing to the other side of the buffet, he loaded a plate with eggs and bacon and snagged a cup of yogurt from the cooler. He carried his plate to the table and waited for Leis to make her waffle and pour herself a cup of coffee. She still looked a little tired but seemed in good spirits as she dug into her breakfast.

"Did you say we were heading to Chicago?" She inhaled the steam coming from her cup and quirked a shy smile, clearly enjoying the smell of the coffee.

"Yes. We'll pick up another car, then drive to my parent's house. Once we get there we can figure out what's next."

"Do you think they'll find us?" She pushed bits of her food around the plate.

Chewing slowly and swallowing, Koen covered her hand with his. "We've done all we can to make sure they don't."

He had no idea when the person Baden mentioned would contact them, and he knew once they did, time alone with Leis would be over. He pushed those thoughts aside.

"It's about a six-hour drive today and four hours tomorrow. We'll have plenty of time to talk at least," he said.

Leis wiped her mouth and laid her hands in her lap. When her eyes met his, there was a new strength in her gaze that left him breathless.

"I have lots of questions. Especially about you," she said.

He couldn't stop the slow grin that spread across his face. "Then what do you say we get moving?"

She nodded as he stood. Leis had the duffel bag over her shoulder when he returned to the table. He lifted his guitar and reached for her hand.

Slipping her fingers between his, she squeezed. "No laughing at me if I make funny faces. This whole smell thing is weird. Nothing smells like I expected it to." She tugged him closer. "Except you."

Her breath whispered across his neck, and he stilled when a look of rapture took over her face. Joy brightened the emerald depths of her eyes, and her voice was soft. "You smell like I expected home to smell."

This woman is going to be the death of me, but at least I'll die happy.

He regretted knowing her joy wouldn't last when she found out the danger he was in, and he determined he would keep it from her as possible. He wrapped his arm around her shoulders and guided them toward the exit.

TWENTY-NINE

They nodded at the clerk behind the desk as the doors swished open and the cool air chilled Leis's skin. As they stepped off the curb, Koen stiffened and positioned himself a fraction of a step ahead of her. His eyes were locked on something across the parking lot, and she followed his gaze.

Their car was parked under a light pole, and in the circle of light they could make out the dark form of someone leaning against the driver's side fender.

He looked about fifty and wore a light brown, long sleeved shirt, blue jeans, and dark non-athletic sneakers. Koen's arm dropped from her shoulders to catch her hand.

"What's he doing here?" he muttered.

As if hearing Koen's quiet question, the man looked up. The open expression on his kind face was familiar, but she couldn't remember his name. His eyes met theirs then fell to their clasped hands. He smiled widely and waited for them to approach.

"Stay behind me. I've no idea what's going on here." Koen leaned toward her, his eyes never leaving the other man's.

She nodded and slowed her steps as Koen offered his free hand.

"Mr. Tate? What are you doing here?" Koen asked.

"That's a fairly long story." Mr. Tate released him and extended his hand to Leis. "It's good to see you again, Leis. Emerick Tate. Call me Eric."

"Nice to see you, too sir." Immediately at ease, she smiled back, finally recognizing him as Director Tate from the school.

Koen watched them carefully. "What are you doing here?"

"I'm your chaperone." Eric raised an eyebrow and chuckled lightly. "Though it looks like we underestimated you two."

Koen crossed his arms. "Who is we, and what do you mean you underestimated us? How did you even know we were here?"

"The *we* will be harder to explain, so I'll save that for the rest of the trip, but you two are to be commended. It was a calculated risk sending you here alone for the night." His eyes danced with amusement and respect. "You are a strong young man. I fully expected to arrive and find the two of you already bonded."

Indignation rose as Leis's face flamed. "You think I would run away with Koen and..." Her arms were stiff as she gestured at Koen then the hotel. Koen stepped in front of her, his neck flushing red in anger.

Eric stopped them both with a raised hand. "I would never think such a thing of you." He looked at Koen with a tortured smile. "But the drive to claim the one we know is ours can be..."

"Overwhelming." Koen finished his sentence and Leis stared in shock. "You're one of us?"

"A Vampir? Yes," he replied.

"How is this possible?" Koen frowned.

"I told you the *we* would be harder to explain." Eric gestured toward the keys hanging from Koen's hand. "We should be going. The rental agency in Chicago closes at six. Open the trunk, and I'll get our things loaded."

Leis could scent Koen's distrust, but one inhale of the wind blowing past Eric told her he wasn't being deceitful. He intended to help them.

After loading the bags, Eric settled himself in the seat behind Koen.

"Do you need fresh clothes?" He gestured toward the trunk. "It doesn't look like you were able to bring much with you."

"Leis could probably use some. I'm good until we get to my house," Koen replied sharply.

Eric shifted in the seat as they pulled out of the hotel. "We probably need to do some shopping once we get to Chicago then. You'll both need more clothes than what's in that bag."

Koen shook his head. "Leis left everything behind, but my parents will still have the rest of my clothes."

"We're not going to your house, Koen." Eric's voice held a warning, and Leis's breath caught, knowing what he was about to say. "We're going to Leis's."

Koen slammed on the brakes and whipped the car into an empty restaurant parking lot. Shoving the car in park, his knuckles went white on the steering wheel, his blue eyes glittering in warning as he glared into the back seat.

"Explain," he barked.

Leis laid her hand on Koen's tense arm. He was terrified, but her instincts were telling her Eric could be trusted.

Baden's words reverberated in her ears. *Pay attention to what other people's emotions are telling you.*

"Hear him out, Koen. I believe he's here to help," she said. Koen covered her hand with his and searched her eyes. She answered without thinking. "I can smell he doesn't mean us any harm."

Koen relaxed slightly but glared again at Eric's reflection in the rear-view mirror. "I still expect you to explain before we go anywhere."

Eric appeared completely unruffled by the whole exchange. "You've learned to rely on the ability quickly, Leis. I'm impressed."

Leis grimaced and glanced at Koen. "It was...a friend. He told me to pay attention to what other people's emotions were telling me. So far, he's been right."

"That's because Baden is a smart kid. Koen, you should have been expecting me." When she snapped her head toward Koen, he flinched. Eric leaned forward and rested his hand over theirs, drawing her attention back to him. "It's going to take all four of us working together to confront Res."

Leis's heart stuttered, but before she could ask a question, Eric continued.

"Running away is what created the division of our people in the first place. I don't have time to convince you." He met Leis's stare evenly. "Either you trust me, or you don't."

Koen looked at her for confirmation.

"I believe him. I can't explain why, but I do."

THIRTY

KOEN

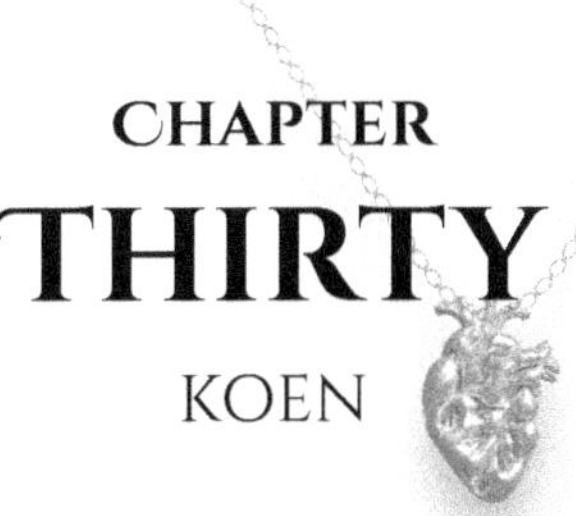

"If you trust him, then so do I." Koen reluctantly admitted.

He restarted the car and eased into the early morning traffic, baffled that Mr. Tate – Eric - was the contact. "I would really like to hear more about this plan though."

Eric crossed his legs, his knee bumping the back of Koen's seat. "We've had plans to confront Res with members from the other Clans for quite a while. Circumstances forced us to change plans when she was tipped off to what Baden was doing." He sighed. "A few months ago, he copied a couple lines of code from Res's network to build the new one, and we didn't catch it until it pinged one of the towers in Arizona. As soon as it happened, she sent Leis's parents to check on them. She thought Baden was doing it on his own." Koen glanced up to see a satisfied smile on his face. "She never suspected he had so much help."

Leis pulled her hair over her shoulder and began to braid it. "So, what happens when we get there?"

Eric pursed his lips. "As you can imagine, Res and the family are not happy we were able to get you away last night. They've locked us out of all the systems we hacked, and it's making it hard to predict what she will do." His smirk was back. "But I think Baden and his new friend will make quick work of her efforts to keep us out."

"Is...is he safe?" she asked.

The ache in her echo threatened to blind him with jealousy.

She's in love with him. Even knowing the truth, she loves him.

Koen looked sideways at her, reminding himself again Baden was very much like a brother to her.

Eric replied quietly, "He's perfectly safe. If all goes as planned, he'll meet us in Arizona soon."

The car fell silent, and Leis closed her eyes. From the sound of her steady breathing, Koen could tell she had drifted to sleep. He rested his hand possessively on her thigh, needing the contact to reassure him she was near, safe, and *his*.

She mumbled, twisting in the seat so her back was against the door. The braid she had woven was falling loosely around her face, and he couldn't imagine anything more beautiful. Hours and miles passed as she slept.

Koen and Eric talked little, content in the quiet. Koen's mind rolled through the events that had brought them to this point.

Yesterday, he was unwilling to admit he had fallen in love with her. Today, he knew he was fooling himself. There was no denying she stole his heart that first day at Osha's, and every time they walked to class or shared lunch he fell a little further.

Koen's thoughts drifted back to the day he first heard her voice from behind the curtain, and a thought occurred to him.

"Mr. Tate? Sorry, Eric. What's happening at school? With the three of us gone, what are they doing about the production?"

"My attorney shut the whole production down yesterday." A genuine chuckle escaped him. "Copyright infringement. Taylor Summers has been stealing other writer's stories for years, but none of them were ever willing to do anything about it. I arranged for him to have access to some of my early work knowing he wouldn't be able to resist. I write under several family pen names to hide how long I've been in the business. Just before I left, I issued a cease-and-desist order on behalf of my dear deceased grandfather." Eric sighed. "He copied one of my plays almost word for word."

Koen nodded, amazed by the foresight involved to get them to their current situation. The false ID's, rental cars, cell phones... It had all been planned so far in advance that even the school's theater schedule had been involved. It was hard to wrap his mind around it all.

Eric spoke quietly, "We've been orchestrating this since before you were born." His voice carried a note of sadness and regret. "We made contact with Baden's parents when Leis and Baden were born. It was a huge miscalculation. We underestimated the lengths Res would go to in order to maintain her bitterness. When we lost Baden's parents, Heinrich and Gretchen, we almost decided to wait another generation." Eric slid forward to lean between the seats. "But another Vampir offered to help us get someone on the inside. When they were successful, we knew we couldn't let their sacrifice be wasted."

Not sure if he was referring to the death of Baden's parents or the person on the inside, Koen glanced at Eric's profile. "What happened to his parents?"

"The Dietrichs?" Eric sighed when Koen nodded. "Heinrich went to Res and told her he wasn't going to let her force the two of them together. He knew we were planning to get them out but didn't know when. He threatened to tell the kids who they really were." He settled back once again. "Res has it in her mind she can cure *her* Clan of the increasing birth defects by what she calls 'strengthening the blood lines.' Heinrich stood firm, and Res was furious. It was carbon monoxide poisoning. Baden was staying with Leis's family for the night, and someone tampered with Heinrich's furnace. "

"You mean she was inbreeding her own family?" Koen couldn't keep the disgust out of his voice.

"She's very confused and bitter for a lot of reasons. That kind of bitterness can make people believe some foolish things." Eric's tone was full of compassion. "Her sister and I hurt her severely when we bonded. Because of it, Res and her group of followers disappeared. When they did, they took a chunk of our genetic code with them. Not only that, but the whole situation also caused a lot of anger and division that eventually led to the rest of the Vampir being split into multiple...clans, for lack of a better word. We are a very rare people and guarding our genetic diversity has always been our only hope for survival. Now," he sighed, "we're divided, weak, and dying. Until we are one Clan again, the birth defects and genetic degradation will continue until we are no more."

"How could this happen so quickly? I mean, I know it's been generations, but it seems it would take longer than your lifetime for it to happen," Koen said.

Eric's phone vibrated, the sound loud in the quiet car. He quickly typed out a reply, then met Koen's questioning gaze in the mirror.

"To say that I am older than you think I would be an understatement." He nodded to Leis who was beginning to stir. "There are eight generations between us."

"But that's..." He did quick math in his head. Eight generations of people who lived on average four hundred years. "...over three thousand years!"

Eric smiled, "Are you calling me old?"

Koen shook his head. "Ancient would be closer to the truth."

They both laughed as he exited the highway somewhere just before the Illinois state line and pulled into a convenience store to fill up. He shut the car off and leaned over to brush the tangled hair out of Leis's face.

"Hey, beautiful. We're almost there." He glanced back as Eric opened his door and stepped out. A blast of cold air shot through the car, and she shivered. "Why don't you go inside with Eric and grab us some coffee?"

"Mmmhmm." She rubbed the heels of her hands against her eyes and yawned. "Sorry I was asleep. Coffee does sound good."

The breeze shifted as she opened her door, and the smell of pigs washed all the color out of her face. Koen stifled a laugh as she nearly gagged. He pointed toward the side of the building.

"Hauler over there." He chuckled as her face turned red, then green. "Back home, my folks would call that fresh country air."

She covered her nose and mouth with the back of her hand, her eyes watering. "I take it all back. I don't want to be able to smell!"

Eric had gotten a few strides away from the car and gestured to her. "Come on. It'll be better inside."

THIRTY-ONE

Less than an hour later they arrived at the mall. The lot bustled with cars and people as Koen parked outside the rental agency. Leis opened her door and was immediately greeted by another blast of icy air. Shivering, she hurried to follow Koen inside and was thankful to feel the warm gush of air that blew down on them as the building door opened.

While he returned the car and finished the necessary paperwork, Leis picked up a map of the attached mall. It was huge, and the layout looked confusing, but at least they would be able to enter the mall proper through the department store that operated the rental agency without having to go back outside.

Through the window she watched Eric transfer their bags into a bright red luxury sedan. She jumped when Koen's hand landed on her shoulder. His handsome face creased into a huge smile and his eyes sparkled with mischief.

"Ready to spend some money?" He gestured to Eric who was heading their way. "I think it's going to be his treat."

She raised an eyebrow and grinned up at Koen. "In that case, I think I need a whole new wardrobe."

Eric approached and slanted his eyes at them. "What am I buying?"

Koen's chuckle sent shivers through her as he took her hand and pulled her close.

"I want to take you to the center court first. If you think the waffles were amazing, wait until you smell the cinnamon rolls." His blue eyes went dark, and the fluttering in her stomach was back. He whispered huskily, "I'm betting you go weak in the knees over them."

Letting go of his hand, she let the tie loose from her still partially braided hair and hid her blush behind a curtain of red waves. "I'm glad I entertain you."

Koen brushed her hair aside and leaned close. She looked up into his sapphire eyes. The crisp smell of his cologne blended with his natural earthy scent and her thoughts scattered. His mood went from playful to something more intense.

His breath whispered across her cheek. "No Leis, you excite me."

Her heart launched into a frenzy and the ache in her jaw caught her by surprise.

Eric cleared his throat. "Okay kids." There was laughter in his voice at Koen's unashamed smirk. "Let's find something to eat and get you both some clothes." He rested an arm on each of their shoulders, wedging himself between them. "Flirt away, but remember the risks."

He slipped through them and took the lead toward the center of the mall. Koen recaught and tugged her hand, following Eric through the crowd.

For these next few hours, they could enjoy being a regular couple hanging out at the mall. The tension and stress that had been pushing at them from the moment they left the fairgrounds seemed to fall away when he gave her his signature lopsided smile.

"Can you smell it yet?" he asked.

"I don't know." She wrinkled her nose. "I'm still trying to figure out how to tell everything apart."

She stopped at a kiosk selling carved multicolored candles and picked up a pastel blue and purple pillar with intricate flowers in the layers of wax.

"This one says lavender." She took a sniff and grimaced. "Mmmm. Don't think I like lavender any more than I like mint."

Koen reached around her and lifted a wide red and black one with two wicks in the top. "I kinda like this one."

Her eyes closed and she inhaled again. A girlish smile crept onto her face. It reminded her of the way Koen smelled when he got out of the shower, fresh and distinctly masculine. Opening her eyes, she saw Koen had taken out his phone and snapped a picture of her.

"Why did you do that?" she smacked his shoulder.

"Because you look happy." He showed her the picture, but as he was turning it away, she stopped him.

"Hold on." She pulled it back and laughed, turning to look behind her.

In the photo, Eric's wide eyes and blank face were eerily positioned over her shoulder. Koen was unable to hold back any longer and laughed with them.

"He was behind you the whole time with this creepy look on his face." He took the phone and saved the picture. "Who knew old guys could be so funny?"

"Hey!" Eric feigned indignation. "I'm not old, remember? The word is ancient. And we ancient guys have had years to perfect our comedic timing."

THIRTY-TWO

KOEN

Koen hadn't been wrong when he said she would love the smell of cinnamon rolls, but it was the fresh baked pretzels that ended up being her favorite. Leis dipped her pretzel bite in the cup of mustard they shared.

"Why didn't you want the cinnamon rolls?" he asked.

"Too sweet and sugary," she replied. "Makes my teeth ache just thinking about it."

"Fair enough." He brushed the salt from his fingers and swept his eyes around the mall.

Eric took the trash and tossed it. "You've got the card, right?" When Koen nodded, he hooked a thumb over his shoulder. "I need to take care of something at the wireless store. Can you two behave for an hour or so then meet me back here?"

Leis stood and pushed her chair under the table. "I think we can do that."

Wanting to have her in his arms, Koen grabbed her from behind and lifted her off the ground. She screeched and swatted at him.

"We'll be back here at nine." He set her down but kept one arm around her waist and wrapped the other high around her shoulders.

Pulling her warm back flush against him, he pretended he couldn't see his watch without pressing his cheek to hers. "It's about seven thirty. Will that give you enough time?" When he dipped his head to sneak a kiss to her exposed neck, Eric gave him a warning glare.

"Take it easy, Romeo." Eric lifted an eyebrow, his voice serious.

Relenting, Koen loosened his hold and stepped to the side. "We'll be fine. I promise to be careful."

"I may be old, but I still know how you think." Eric sighed and turned to go. "Have fun."

Leis elbowed him lightly in the ribs. "Come on. I saw the perfect outfit for you a couple of stores down from here."

She turned in his arms, and his breath was stolen by the depth of her moss-colored eyes.

He kissed her forehead. "And I saw the perfect coat for you." He held out his arm for her. "Let's go, my love." The words were out of his mouth before he realized what he said.

She hesitated, and surprise drained the color from her face. It was clear she wasn't expecting his declaration. He lowered his arm and watched her face carefully.

"I do, you know," he said.

Taking his hand, she recovered from her surprise. "I do know it. I believe you, I'm just - just not ready to..."

He pressed a finger to her lips. He did wish she would say the words, but Koen heard it in her echo.

"It's okay." He was rewarded by the relief on her face. "We've got our whole lives, right?" She nodded. "Then let's shop!"

In the first several stores they purchased the basics they needed, and Koen quickly discovered making her laugh was his new favorite thing. While she was trying several pairs of shoes on, he wandered to the back of the store and picked up a pair of tall black wedges. He asked a young salesgirl to bring him the largest size they had. The girl gave him a suspicious look but did what he asked.

Koen slipped them on and made his way to where Leis was

putting her choices back in the boxes. Pausing in front of her, he stuck out a toe and wobbled.

"What do you think?"

"Oh my gosh, Koen!" Her eyes flew wide, and she covered her mouth, then hissed. "Take those off before you break your ankle!" She looked up and around the store to see the faces of other shoppers watching them.

"Seriously?" In her voice was both embarrassment and admiration.

He stood there until the laugh he had fallen in love with seeped through her fingers, and he grinned in success. Then, unable to stay on his feet any longer, he fell into the chair next to her and groaned loudly.

"As a guy, I want to apologize to every woman who wears these things." He pulled off one of the wedges and held it up like a trophy. "You are my heroes!"

Leis covered her face in her hands as those around them snickered.

"You are crazy." Peeking between her fingers, she watched him inspect the offending shoes.

He waggled his eyebrows. "They are kinda hot though, right?"

Giggles took over as they gathered the pairs she had chosen, and he put his socks and sneakers back on. The saleswoman behind the counter was not amused by his antics, but Koen was unperturbed. He politely paid for Leis's purchases and thanked her for having such an accommodating staff. She seemed to accept his statement as an apology and shook her head. A fraction of a smile lifted the corner of her lip.

"You might try a stiletto next time. Those babies are the real killers," she quipped.

"I'll keep that in mind." He lifted the bags and inclined his head to her. "Thank you."

Leis was waiting near the door with an exasperated smile. "Is there anyone you can't charm?"

He shrugged. "Probably not." He settled the bags in one hand and guided her out of the store with his palm resting on the small of her back. "Your family will be the real test, eh?"

Her shoulders dropped a fraction, and he regretted bringing it up.

"I hope they'll come around." She lifted her eyes to his and her voice was sure. "They'll have to. We're intended for each other. They have to accept that."

On the way back to the center court to meet Eric when they both received a text.

> Meet me at the car.

After purchasing the requested suitcases, they met in the parking lot and loaded everything into Eric's rental car. This time, Leis rode in the back, choosing to sit behind Koen. Eric drove to a large hotel and helped Koen unload the shopping bags while Leis guided their empty suitcases and the guitar case inside.

The lobby's ceiling rose five stories overhead and several floors of balconies looked down on them. To their left was a small indoor cafe with tables covered in white linen and place settings of fine china and crystal. A large, colorful chandelier hung in the center of the space casting an orangish glow on the silvery glass tiles of the wall above the elevators. To the right was a cozy seating area where an ivory-colored grand piano sat in the middle of a circular carpeted area. Past the piano and stretching along the entire right wall was the hotel desk and concierge.

The employees were all attired in suits, ties, and tailored dresses. Even the wait staff and room service employees were dressed in classy, well fitted pants and sharply pressed white shirts and bowties.

Koen stuffed his hands in his pockets, suddenly uncomfortable in a t-shirt and jeans.

Leis touched his arm. "Have you ever stayed somewhere like this?"

Shaking his head wryly, he said, "No. Not even close." He trailed a hand down the back of her head, threading his fingers through her hair. "Have you?"

"Once or twice." She leaned her cheek against his shoulder. "The only time I really remember was when my brother Josh and his wife Gina got married. It was their wedding gift and going away present from the Compound." She righted herself as Eric approached. Koen's arm felt cold. "I think my parents rented the whole hotel that night."

"That must have been some party." He did his best to hide the rising insecurity. His Clan didn't have this kind of resources.

"Are you okay?" Her fingers brushed lightly across his forearm again as concern deepened on her face.

He inhaled and lifted his chin. "I'm fine. A little overwhelmed is all."

"It will all be fine, you'll see." Rising on her toes, she planted a quick peck on his cheek then turned to follow Eric who was waving them into the elevator.

After maneuvering the packages inside, they made it to the top floor and Koen was stunned again when the doors opened to the penthouse.

The penthouse doors opened into a large living room facing a wall of floor to ceiling glass looking out over the suburbs. In the dim space, the lights of Chicago were a faint glow on the horizon.

The carpet was a soft cream, and two large, black leather sofas, one facing the windows and the other turned toward a softly burning fireplace made a sitting area.

Leis set her purse on a round, glass topped coffee table and admired the semi abstract black and white photos on the walls that appeared to be close-up shots of the Chicago landmarks. The glossy, modern fireplace released warmth into the room. Flat grey stones covered the hearth and stacked to the ceiling with a large flat screen TV mounted above the flickering of the fire.

Adding color to the space were red velvet pillows on the couch and upholstery. Six chairs surrounded a sleek black table near a silver bar that stood just outside what looked like a large bathroom.

"There are two bedrooms and one master suite." Eric lifted the bags and placed them on the dining table. "The Vampir Clan maintains a contract with this chain that allows us access to the penthouse when we need it."

Though Leis had stayed in hotels like this, she had never been inside a penthouse and felt a little of what Koen must have experienced downstairs. Leaving the suitcases and guitar in the sitting area, she walked into the closest of the rooms.

Double doors swung wide to welcome her with a view of soothing cream-colored linens and silvery grey carpet. She turned as Koen lounged against the doorway behind her.

She slipped an arm around his waist. "What's wrong?"

His lip curved upward, but the smile didn't make it to his eyes as they traveled the room. "Just thinking about how beautiful you look in a place like this."

She huffed a dismissive laugh. "It's a hotel. A place to sleep." Sensing it was more than that, she placed a palm against his cheek and turned him to look at her. "Talk to me. Tell me what you're thinking."

"I've only seen rooms like this in the movies." He wrapped his arms loosely around her shoulders. "Being here is a little surreal for me. You look like you belong here." She stiffened, and he shook his head. "I know you're going to tell me it doesn't matter, but I can't give you this." He looked around again. "I wish I could."

"I won't say it doesn't matter because it does. It matters because it's where I came from." Koen tensed, and she tightened her arms. "But it's just stuff, and it doesn't change anything." She swallowed and her eyes burned. "This might be what my life *was* like, but *you* are my future." Her voice faltered and fell to a whisper as emotion tightened her throat. "As long as I have you, I know I'll have all I could ever need."

He relaxed and pulled her close, resting his cheek on her head with a sigh. "I do love you, Leis."

"Enjoy the evening." Eric's eyes were warm as he met each of their gazes. He gestured toward the table and couches holding their purchases. "Our flight to Arizona leaves at eight AM, and you still need to pack." He picked up a key card and stepped inside the elevator. "Order some room service and relax. I'll be back in a couple of hours."

Was he leaving them alone again?

Her stomach fluttered as mischief leaped into Koen's eyes.

"Pack first, then a movie?" he suggested.

She nodded, and they quickly sorted through the clothing and set the suitcases inside their respective rooms so they would be ready to go first thing in the morning.

Leis did a quick inventory of the bar and snagged a soda water and cola from the refrigerator under the counter.

Koen lounged on the couch tuning his guitar. The clear notes he drew from it filled the room with a sweet sound that both relaxed her and heightened her awareness of Koen's strong presence. A thrill went through her at the opportunity to hear him play just for her. She settled on the opposite couch watching in fascination as his hands moved deftly on the strings.

After a few minutes, a sly smile crossed his face. He looked up, and her lungs seized mid breath. Shining from the depths of his vivid blue eyes was every desire of his heart, and when they swept down her, the rhythmic motions of his hands on the guitar made her tingle all over. She shuddered, wanting his hands on her instead of the beautiful instrument.

Koen began to sing softly in his incredible low register, and his intensity drew her in even though his words were in that haunting language she didn't understand. She moved closer, curled her feet under her, and rested in the corner of the couch beside him. His eyes saturated to a deep midnight blue as they followed her. His open expression and gravelly voice asked again the question wasn't ready to answer.

"What song is that?" Hunger thickened her voice as Koen's gaze slid over her again, moving more slowly this time.

Without answering, he finished the song and moved on to something she'd heard on the radio recently. He looked away, but not before she saw the sliver of disappointment on his face. He ran through several more seconds of the song, then palmed the strings to silence them. Setting the instrument aside, he opened his arm and beckoned her closer.

"It's something my Dad taught me after he helped me memorize the Blood Pledge." Once she was settled against his shoulder, he kissed the top of her head. "He said it used to be sung at the Bonding ceremony, but the translation was lost."

She knew he wasn't telling the truth. She might not recognize the words, but her heart knew what the song meant. Koen was asking her to accept his offer, asking if she was ready to admit her feelings. Though they both knew she loved him, she wasn't ready to admit the truth out loud.

He reached for her knees and pulled her legs across his lap as he shifted back into the cushions. The v-neck t-shirt he was wearing left the silver heart in the hollow of his throat at eye level.

She reached out to touch it. "Why an anatomical heart? Isn't that a little morbid?"

He leaned away and reached behind him to unclasp the leather choker. "My father gave it to me when I was fifteen." He held it out to her. The heavy pendant was still warm from his skin. "It was about the time Mom lost her third pregnancy, and we realized my breathing issues were getting worse." His hand fell to rest on her bent knee. "He gave it to me to remind me that as long as my heart was beating, there would always be hope."

She wrapped it in her hand, wanting to hold the heat his body had given it. "Your family sounds like they love you very much."

"I like to think they do, and they'll love you just as much. When this is all over, I can't wait to take you to meet them." He leaned back and pulled her with him until her head rested on his hard chest.

She drank in the sound of his heartbeat and rubbed her cheek against the smooth skin above the v of his shirt. His warm earthy scent filled her senses, and she drew a welcome breath as his arms tightened around her. Content to be in each other's arms, they sat in the quiet as Koen's thumb traced a lazy circle on her kneecap.

She tucked her hand behind him as he shifted to get more comfortable. When she did, her palm slid against the bare skin of his lower back. The taunt muscles on either side of his spine flexed at the contact, and the air in the room changed from content to charged instantly.

Embarrassed by his reaction, she tried to withdraw, but he tightened his hold. His hand slid up her leg to draw her further into his lap.

She tucked further under his chin, and felt his heart rate jump, and his breaths shorten. The heady smell of him grew stronger, and she pressed her nose against him to inhale the scent that was distinctly Koen. She was helpless to resist the intoxicating mix of his protectiveness of her and his desire for her. She sucked it in, her breath hitching loudly in her throat.

She was suddenly desperate to taste the blood he promised her. As pressure built in the roof of her mouth, she fought to keep a groan of need from escaping.

She burrowed further against him, and the movement slid the v of his shirt down. When her lips met his smooth skin, she was unable to help herself. She parted her lips, tracing her tongue across his collar bone.

He jolted at the contact, and his scent deepened. A harsh cry of pain and want escaped as without further warning, her fangs ripped down from the roof of her mouth and snapped into place.

His entire body went rigid before he suddenly pushed her away as though she'd burned him. The fear in his eyes sent her scrambling to her feet.

Chest heaving, he looked up at her from where he was still pressed into the couch. She gasped at the streaks of blood just below the spot his pendant normally rested.

Koen's brilliant blue eyes locked on her mouth, his raspy breaths loud in the quiet room. He gripped the edges of the couch, visibly struggling to keep himself seated as intense longing raged across his face and through her body in response.

He slowly stood, covered his mouth, and drew his hand down his face. Pulling his lower lip between his teeth, he closed his eyes and clenched his hands at his sides.

Her fangs were still down, and she desperately wanted to sink them into his lip. The smear of blood on his neck made her shudder.

"Did I..." She pointed to the blood as his breaths became shallow and irregular.

He shook his head as he reached to cup her jaw. He leaned in, closing the distance between them when the elevator doors opened.

Koen's eyes flew to meet Eric's. He covered his mouth again, shame on his face. He growled. "It's my fault."

Eric crossed the room in long strides. "Did you...?"

When Leis and Koen shook their heads, a strange expression crossed the older man's face. He swore then turned to Koen.

"Are you all right?" he asked.

"I'm okay." Koen's hands fisted at his sides again and his eyes closed. When they opened he looked at her through his dark lashes. "Are you?"

She touched her lip and was shocked to find that as quickly as they dropped, her fangs had retracted. She forced herself to let out a steady breath.

"I'm fine," she said and looked down at her hand.

A thin line of crimson blood dripped down her index finger. She looked up to as Koen disappeared, pushing his bedroom doors closed. Eric's gentle hand on her shoulder stopped her from trying to follow.

"Might be best to give him a few minutes." He cupped her elbow and guided her toward the bathroom. "Why don't you get cleaned up, then you can tell me what happened."

With a glance at the silent doors across the room, she flipped on the bathroom light and shut the door behind her. The bathroom was as elegant as the rest of the penthouse, with cream tile on the floor and a dark gray stone counter surrounding a matching double sink and brushed nickel faucets.

She gasped at the reflection of blood still covering her bottom lip and smeared along her chin. Soaking a washcloth, she wiped her face as shock settled in.

She had known her fangs would come through when she scented Koen during the ceremony, but after experiencing it, she couldn't imagine it being as sterile as the ceremonial act she'd been conditioned to expect. Koen's nearness completely overrode any control she thought she had.

It was a good thing he pushed her away, but her body wasn't convinced. Her sinuses ached as his scent remained, and her muscles strained with need. Forcing herself to relax, she ran the cloth under the water until the blood stain was only a faint pink hue on the white terry cloth and then laid it across the faucet to dry.

As she ran her tongue over her teeth and clearly understood the driving need Koen and Eric talked about when they thought she was asleep. The desire to complete the Blood Exchange was very real, the reality of how strong it was terrified and thrilled her at the same time.

Against Koen's chest, with his powerful scent filling her lungs, every fiber of her body craved having a part of him in her veins.

She swallowed against a faint metallic aftertaste and touched her tongue to the long slits in the roof of her mouth. There were two rough slashes where the fangs had cut through, viper like. The skin was healing quickly, and even as she pulled her lip down to inspect the corner of her mouth where her fang had sliced the thin skin, it closed as she watched.

A soft knock on the door made her jump. Eric's concerned voice was gruff. "Leis, are you all right?"

"Yes." She glanced in the mirror to make sure the blood was gone and noticed a drip of red on the neck of her t-shirt.

The last few minutes crashed in, and afraid she must have done something horribly wrong, tears stung her eyes. She lifted her head to the ceiling and pushed them back before opening the door.

Eric stood beside the table, one arm across his chest as he chewed on the thumb of his other hand. He dropped his arms and met her at the couch. Offering her a bottle of water, he sat next to her.

"Can you tell me what happened?" he asked.

She took a long swallow of the cool liquid before trying to put it into words. "I'm not sure. One minute we were sitting here," she gestured toward the couch opposite them, "the next I'm bleeding, and he's pushing me away."

Her eyes slid down and spotted Koen's necklace on the floor. She picked it up, but the pendant was cold against her fingers, and she shivered.

"He was holding me, and I..." She closed her hand around the heart, remembering the feel of his skin under her tongue. "I wanted him to kiss me. As soon as I thought it, my fangs came through."

Eric made an agreeable noise. "That's what is supposed to happen." He smiled easily and rested an ankle on his knee. "It means Koen's blood has already changed. When you were that close to him, you could smell it, and your body responded exactly the way it should." He swiped invisible dust from the back of the couch. "The question is, how does your heart feel about it?"

"I don't know." She leaned forward and stared sightlessly at the carpet as Eric sat very still beside her. "Everything has happened so fast. I have no idea what to expect, and the feelings I have for Koen confuse me." Her eyes strayed to his bedroom doors. "I believe we're intended to be together. I can feel it. I can *smell* it. My mind is just having a hard time catching up." She clutched the pendant tighter, and her voice fell to a whisper. "How can I possibly fall in love with someone when everything else is falling apart?"

When Eric reached for the leather strap trailing out of her fist, she released it to him. He held the heart up to the light, examining it.

"Are you in love with him?" he asked

All the air left her lungs and Eric gently touched her back. She bobbed her head once, unable and afraid to speak. She couldn't deny she loved him, but it felt so wrong! Baden, her family, the Clan, Koen's addictive presence, Eric's past — all of it pressed in on her and expected something from her.

The instinctive response she'd had to Koen went against everything she knew about the ceremony, and the Blood Pledge was still something she didn't understand. No one ever told her anything more than she and Baden were pledged to one another. Growing up with her parent's constant guidance and instruction always frustrated her, but the full reality of their deception set in.

They were going to force *me to bond with Baden!*

They weren't protecting her; they were controlling her, and she suspected she wasn't the only one.

Eric interrupted her thoughts. "Leis, you and Koen have an opportunity to change things. To make things right again."

The weight of his words sliced through her, and she shook her head. It was too much.

"I can't," she whispered.

"Yes, you can." He lifted her chin until she met his eyes. "But the only way is to beat them at their own game." He handed Koen's necklace back and held her hands in his. The strength of his conviction soaked into her, and she drew a ragged breath. "The two of you have a connection that is stronger than any I've ever seen. And I've seen a lot in all my years. There is no question you and Koen are intended for each other. Do you truly believe that?"

Still unable to speak, she nodded. That was one thing she was sure of. Even without completing the bond, he was part of her.

Eric let go and rested his elbows on his knees to rub his temples before looking up at her. "In my day, the two of you would have completed the Blood Exchange tonight, and everyone would have celebrated tomorrow."

She blushed at the implications. "But what about family? What about the ceremony?" She shook her head. "That can't be how it's done!"

If she and Koen completed the bonding without her family's support, she couldn't imagine what the Clan would do. But did it really matter anymore what they thought?

She had no answer to that, and until she did, she wouldn't go against her family. Everything in her told her what they had created was wrong, but outright rebellion wasn't in her. Eric was right, she had to play their game until she could convince them to see the truth.

Eric huffed a sad laugh. "You're right. That's *not* how your Clan does things. They have a rule for this and a ceremony for that." He pushed to his feet in frustration and paced the seating area. "It was never meant to be this way. None of it." He pointed at her and she flinched. "Your generation can change it. *You* can change it. But you're going to have to trust your heart, and even more, you're going to have to trust what you have with that young male in there." Eric tipped his chin toward Koen's room. The intensity of his conviction frightened her, but his words rang true, almost verbatim what Baden told her.

"Ceremonies and traditions are good, but they were meant to *protect* people, never to control them," he said. He raked a hand through his hair and leaned his hip against the table. "Under the Vampir law, a bond requires two things to be official." He ticked them off on his fingers. "The obvious connection between the couple, and an authorized member of each family to agree. The individual Clan should have no say so in it." His jaw hardened. "But I suppose that is partly my fault."

"How could it be your fault?" she asked.

A muscle ticked in his jaw before he spoke again. "I was young, and I didn't follow rules very well. When I met my mate, I had already pledged myself to Res." His expression went far away, but Leis was arrested by his admission.

Baden's grandmother? A chill coursed up her spine.

"Res and I hadn't told anyone we were pledged. Her parents were traders and were gone on a long trip. We planned to wait until they got back. One night I was supposed to meet Res at her home, but I got there before she was able to return from the market, and I met her twin sister, Ellen. It was instantly obvious she was the one." He glanced wryly at Koen's door. "As you've just experienced, it's impossible to hide. I didn't think with my real brain and took Ellen home to meet my parents. They gave us their blessing to complete the bonding. Ellen asked one of her brothers to be our witness. He didn't know that Res and I were already pledged, and he gave his blessing." He gripped the table behind him and crossed his ankles in front of him. "We completed the Blood Exchange the moment we had her brother's permission. I never sought out Res for release from my original pledge to her. I was too wrapped up in my own needs. And desire." His voice lowered. "As you can imagine, Res was devastated.

But there was nothing anyone could do. Ellen and I were united forever."

"You said Res. You were pledged to Baden's grandmother?" He nodded. "I didn't know she even had a sister..." Leis's heart stopped when she heard Koen's voice behind her.

"Ellen. From the diner is your mate?" he asked. Eric nodded. "I should have suspected that's how she had the packet from Baden."

Koen's tone was tight, and his pent-up frustration hit her like waves crashing against a beach. With every word, the intensity of his desire pushed at her. Her heart raced faster as Koen continued to speak. She felt like they were hurtling toward a cliff.

"You are here as more than a chaperone. You're the family representative here to ensure the rules are followed," Koen said.

"It's both, but yes. I am legally able to validate a pledge to Leis," Eric replied.

With deadly calm and forced formality, Koen addressed Eric. "I've pledged Leis my blood and my life, and she has accepted me." He stood in the doorway, the dim lights casting him deep in shadow.

Eric nodded, then looked to Leis for confirmation. That was the question Koen kept asking. It was the question the Pledge itself begged her to answer.

Will you accept me? Do you love me?

Koen knew she did. He wrote that song to let her know he knew without pressuring her. Baden's words echoed again.

Trust Koen to know.

She squared her shoulders and nodded.

Koen stepped into the sitting area, watching Eric closely as he crossed the room. "I would imagine Ellen is traveling with Baden?"

Eric chuckled. "She is. I'm the one bringing Leis back because I'm the one that broke Res's heart." He sighed. "My Ellen is with Baden to verify the release for him should he need it, and because he might need a translator. Ellen always was better with languages than I am."

Leis's heart clawed at her throat when Koen stalked toward her. His gaze met hers, and his voice was raw but gentle.

"Whatever we are walking into tomorrow, know that my blood is yours when you're ready to take it. You are and always will be my mate." he said.

She wanted to surrender to Koen, wanted to bond herself to him, but she was desperately afraid of how the Clan would react to her betrayal. As he knelt in front of her, fear tightened her shoulders.

"When you're ready, Leis." Koen's scent swept over her in a wash of patience and understanding.

Leis relaxed and the shaking subsided when it was clear he wasn't expecting anything from her tonight. He softly brushed his hand over hers and tugged the leather strip from her tightly clasped fingers. With careful hands he tied it around her neck.

"As long as my heart beats it belongs to you. When you're ready to complete the Blood Exchange, give this back to me." He kissed her forehead, and his gentle lips lingered against her skin.

Tears rolled down her cheeks as he stood and quietly closed himself inside his bedroom.

Leis heard Koen return from his workout and sighed with relief. Some part of her had known he wasn't in the suite, and that depth of need for him frightened her. Outside her room was quiet, and she relaxed as the ache subsided a little.

How did I fall for him so fast?

Later today, she would be back home with Koen by her side. Tension rose inside her at the thought of facing her family. What would they do?

How was she going to look her mother in the face knowing she agreed to Res's plan all along?

What happened to her father after he helped her get away?

She rubbed her temples.

And what about Baden? Where was he? Was he okay?

So much happened in three short days, she needed time to stop and think.

A knock sounded on her door followed by Eric's steady voice.

"Leis, we need to leave in ten minutes. We'll get breakfast at the airport," he said.

"I'm ready. I'll be right out," she said and glanced at herself in the floor length mirror.

It was cold here in Chicago but would be much warmer when they arrived in Phoenix. She layered a gray button up blouse under a kelly green sweater and tossed her new camel colored leather jacket over her arm. The loose-fitting dark jeans would be comfortable for the long flight, and the tan leather heels would be easy to slip in and out of when they went through security. Wanting the warmth of her hair on her neck, she had left it down but clipped it out of her face with a few pins.

She took a deep breath and reached for her suitcase, trying not to instantly search our Koen the moment she opened her door. But she did.

Koen was exiting his room with his case in tow, and she was once again caught by his classic rock star looks.

His dark hair was still damp from the shower and lay in shiny curls around his handsome face. He was also wearing new dark wash jeans, and his brown lace up boots. A white leather belt crossed his narrow hips, and the rich brown leather jacket she picked out for him hugged his wide shoulders and skimmed his upper body. Underneath it, he wore a simple white t-shirt.

He was the perfect picture of a musician with the guitar case in his hand and cocky grin on his face.

"Good morning." The tired roughness of his voice sent shivers through her. "Did you get any sleep?"

She cleared her throat, "A little."

Her stomach fluttered as she got a whiff of the soap and shampoo that mixed perfectly with his musky scent. The moment stretched as she stared, and he stared back.

Amused, Eric stepped into their line of sight and gestured to the elevator.

"Shall we?" he said.

She shook her head to clear it and then followed him through the silver doors as they slid open. Eric stepped aside to allow Koen to stand next to her.

He shifted his guitar and placed a hand on the back of her head. She sighed and leaned into his touch as his fingers curled in the hair at the back of her neck. His touch reminded her of how much they stood to lose by confronting Res. She instinctively pressed closer.

"Everything will be fine." He pulled her toward him to place a kiss on her temple. "I've never flown before," he said.

"It's not so bad. First class makes it nicer." Leis frowned. His scent carried a tang of uncertainty, but he was amused more than anything and holding it back.

Strangely enough, the same amusement was coming from Eric. As the doors opened into the parking garage, the two men were stifling laughter.

"Okay. Spill it you two." She stepped out and turned to face them.

Koen bit his lips and tilted his head while Eric walked to the car. Koen's sky-blue eyes sparkled.

"Are those the new jeans we bought?" he asked.

She looked down. "Yes, why?"

He stepped into her, wrapping his arms around her so she couldn't back away.

"Koen?" she asked, then jumped when his fingers slid up the back of her thigh. At the sound of peeling tape, she realized she hadn't checked the pants for tags.

"Thanks for the excuse." Koen dangled the clear piece of tape between them. His warm breath against her cheek sent her heart skittering.

"You're welcome," she rasped and backed away.

When he laughed at the heat suffusing her cheeks, she swiped the offending label from him and pushed him with her elbow.

His deep laugh echoed through the garage. It was her new favorite sound.

The airport was un-surprisingly busy for a Monday morning, but they made it through security quickly and were able to eat a quick breakfast before boarding the jet.

Once on-board Leis settled into the comfortable seat and waited for the steward to secure their carry-ons in the overhead bins. Koen's uncertainty was back as he dropped into the seat next to her.

"First class, huh?" He glanced around nervously as passengers filed past.

"Sure." She pulled the magazine from the seat pocket in front of her. "The seats are more comfortable, and you don't have to wait to get on or off the plane."

As an event planner, her mother traveled all over the world and whenever possible, Leis and her father went with her. She never gave a thought to where they stayed or how they traveled.

Flying and staying in pricey hotels had advantages Leis appreciated, but she wasn't like her mother who insisted on designer labels and fancy clothes for status. She was more like her father, enjoying the comfort money could buy. The way her mother sometimes flashed their wealth never sat well with her father, but he always went along with her whims.

The only time she ever remembered him trying to talk her mother out of such a show was Josh's wedding. She was eleven, and alone at the house when her parents came in from meeting with Josh's mate's parents.

The two of them paused in the kitchen while Leis stood in the hallway. Memories flooded back, and what hadn't made sense then fell into place.

"Stefanie, we can't afford to draw so much attention to ourselves like this." Her father's voice was uncharacteristically hard.

"It's a wedding, Haydn." Her Mother snapped back. "It's supposed to be extravagant."

"These rituals are overdone." Her father's voice softened as he tried to reason with her. "Josh and Gina clearly love each other, and I'm glad we can give them the wedding of their dreams, but a ceremony doesn't make a marriage. We of all people know that."

Cabinet doors opened and closed, and Leis leaned closer to the doorway to catch her mother's response.

"Josh is leaving us, and I want to give my son the best before he dies." Her voice was sad. "After watching five sons leave the Vampir with human wives, knowing they will live such short lives, is it so wrong to want to spend a little money on my last son?"

"You still have Andrew." Haydn argued.

"It isn't the same. The Clan pledged Andrew to Carol's family. He is their responsibility now." Glasses clinked and a wine bottle popped as it was opened. "Baden and Leis have been entrusted to us. Once Josh's wedding is over, the Elder will expect us to make sure the two of them are able to complete the Blood Exchange."

It was quiet for a moment before her father spoke.

"Heinrich tried to stop it, Stef. Maybe he knew something we don't," he said carefully.

A glass hit the counter sharply. "Heinrich thought he could go against the Clan's decision. Baden's blood is ours. *My* family will do what *yours* was unwilling to do. Nothing good comes from breaking the rules, Hadyn."

With a bump, the plane moved away from the terminal, and Leis's mind swirled through the memories of the days following Josh's wedding. Her Mother had chastised her with the same warning every time she and Baden got into trouble.

"*Nothing good ever comes from breaking the rules, Leis.*"

Though her constant reprimands chafed, Leis always believed her mother was protecting her by enforcing the Clan's rules.

Leis hated to disappoint anyone and did everything asked of her to try to gain her mother's approval. It was never enough. At the slightest mistake, her mother was quick to remind her the Clan was watching and expecting great things from her and Baden. She would then remind Leis that Baden was already at a disadvantage because of her handicap.

Baden's sharp retort to her mother's condescension the night before Andrew's ceremony made it clear in hindsight he had known for a while something wasn't right.

Koen reached for his phone and earbuds, offering one to her. "Want to share?"

She glanced at the screen and saw that the band was a little crunchier than her preferences. She shook her head, and he grinned.

"Suit yourself." He slipped the earbuds in and leaned back in his seat.

Leis smiled and drew a deep breath of Koen's smell. Warmth filled her when she breathed him in, soothing her nerves and sending them into a frenzy at the same time. In a very short time, he had become someone she could never live without.

Koen's breathing was steady, but as the plane lifted from the ground, he tensed, and she reached out to lay her hand over his. He relaxed as the connection washed contentment through them both.

He lifted his hand and brought her knuckles to his lips. Just as his breath skated across her skin, his eyes drifted open, and her belly clenched. He held her eyes as his lips parted and his tongue touched her skin as she had done to him the night before. Her insides somersaulted, and a slight curve lifted his mouth as his eyes closed again.

His self-assurance assaulted her senses. Eric and Baden said she needed to trust what she and Koen had, even insisting she refuse to let anyone come between them. Trusting Koen was easy. Trusting what they had would mean breaking every rule she had ever been taught.

THIRTY-SIX

LEISEL

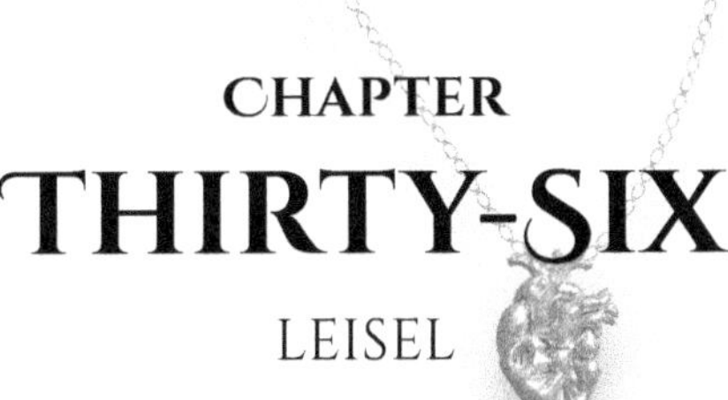

The moment Leis's feet touched the carpet inside the terminal, dread settled in the pit of her stomach. In less than an hour, they would be at the compound, and the only thing they knew for sure was that the Elder would be waiting for them.

Koen pulled their bags, his eyes watching everyone as though he expected to be apprehended at any moment. The unease rolling off him only made her more jittery.

Eric's shoulders were set as he led the way to the trams. He had been especially quiet the entire flight and only spoke to let them know they could now use their true names. He took the false IDs and cards once they were past security and stashed them in his bags.

When they stepped outside, the warm, dry air was a welcome change from the bitter cold of Chicago, and they all shed their jackets. The car was another sleek luxury vehicle with angles and sharp lines, the paint a deep blue that reminded her of Koen's eyes. He helped Eric load the bags into the trunk, then turned to open the car door for her.

"Why don't the two of you ride in the back?" Eric's concern rode through the air, tightening her throat. "A few more minutes of quiet will be all you get for a while."

She did as he suggested, and Koen slid in beside her.

"What are you expecting when we get to the compound?" Leis asked.

"Res will separate you two." He steered the car out of the garage and into the exit lane.

Koen's eyes narrowed, and Leis's sinuses ached as his anger rose. "I've claimed the Blood Pledge; can she do that?"

"For a time." Eric sighed. "We have a plan, but it's going to take at least a few days. Res will know immediately how close the two of you are to being bonded. It's obvious your blood has changed in response to one another, but she believes it's possible to reverse it. She will have set up a challenge." His knuckles were white on the steering wheel. "She thinks there can be more than one potential bond mate. She believes that's what happened between her sister and me." He growled. "Ellen changed my blood, not Res."

Leis looked between the two men. "So, she knows Koen is Vampir?"

"She will be able to smell him." Eric reminded her. "And if she finds out you can smell, she won't hesitate to let the challenger get closer to you than he should." He shook his head. "Honestly, she probably will anyway. It won't change your connection to Koen, but that won't stop her from trying."

"How am I supposed to just let that happen?" Koen growled.

"If it won't change anything, why worry about it? You know they won't hurt me." Leis asked.

Koen went rigid. "No way," he snapped. "If anyone touches you..."

"There's more to it than your bond at the moment." Eric raised his voice. "Baden needs time. The challenge is a farce, but it will buy us the time we need." Koen glared, but Eric didn't budge. "There's more at stake than just the two of you. We need to delay as long as possible."

Koen crossed his arms. "I don't like it."

"Neither do I!" Eric slammed his hand on the steering wheel and took a deep breath. "But I also know if we don't do something our people will cease to exist. Someone has to be willing to stand up and do whatever it takes to save all of us. We don't always get to choose who that someone will be. Sometimes timing chooses you, and you two are it." His eyes were stony as he glared at them in the mirror. "If you want out, say it now, but there are a lot of people counting on the two of you to do the right thing." They stopped at a light, and Eric turned to look at them. "What do you want to do?"

Stunned, she glanced at Koen. His jaw ticked but he nodded.

"We're in," he said tightly.

Eric's eyes met hers and new determination coursed through her.

"I'll do it. I'll go along with this, but that doesn't mean I won't fight for Koen." She knew what they had to do, but she would do it on her terms. "I'm not going back and let them treat me like this is my fault. Not anymore."

The light changed, and Eric turned back with a satisfied chuckle. "You two are stronger than you think. Res has no idea what she's in for."

Three large guards greeted them at the car when they arrived at the top of the long driveway. Eric looked back at Leis and Koen, then cracked his door open.

"Let me get out first. I am the last person Res will be expecting. Let's get her off balance early," he said.

As soon as he was out of the car, the taller of the three men narrowed his eyes. "The female will come with us. You and the boy will leave."

Ignoring his order, Emerick gestured at the front door. "Tell Res that Emerick Tate is here to see her. I'm sure she'll recognize the name."

There was a flurry of motion in the expansive widows on the second floor. Leis looked up in time to see Res freeze when her eyes landed on Eric leaning against the car. He didn't acknowledge her presence at the window.

"Leis's mate and I will accompany her inside," Eric said.

Koen's hand tightened on hers as the guard moved toward the car. The man paused and glanced at the house before responding.

"Mr. Tate," he said tightly. "You are welcome to join the female, but the boy will not come inside."

"Then we all leave." Eric opened the driver's door and sat inside. As he was pulling the door closed, the man's large hand caught the top of it.

"Res would like to offer all of you lunch before you and the boy go on your way." His voice was frigid, and the smell of violence burned Leis's throat.

Without further warning, Koen's door was yanked open, and he was dragged out the other side. His eyes were clear and determined when they met hers through the back window, and she scrambled to follow.

"Koen!" she shrieked. Her door opened and a strong hand wrapped around her upper arm.

"It's all right! I love you." Koen said before one of the guards pushed him toward the house.

"Let's go, Miss. The Elder has been waiting for you," the guard said.

Dread filled her stomach as Koen disappeared inside the enormous house. Eric was suddenly beside her, taking her arm from the other man.

"It's time to prove just how strong you two are." He guided her up the drive.

THIRTY-SEVEN

The tall guard led the way while the other followed. Once inside, they were led through the foyer and into the seating area. The guards stopped a few feet away from a long dining table. It was nearly full, and she estimated about half of the elder Clan members were present, almost forty sets of eyes watching her.

She pulled her shoulders back and searched for Koen. He was between two large men near the bar on the other side of the table, watching her unflinchingly. Even from this distance and from among so many other males, she marveled that she was able to pick his earthy smell out of the crowd.

Shoes clicked on the tile floor behind them and she turned to face Res.

"Rebellion breeds rebellion, does it not, Emerick?" Baden's grandmother's voice was bitter. "I should have known you were behind this little stunt of hers." She stalked through the group; her icy glare aimed at Eric.

Eric's tone and scent were calm and soothing. "Your Leis is the wisest woman I have ever met. You've taught her well."

Res startled at the compliment, her brows crashing together. "Thank you for saying so, but current circumstances being what they are, I apparently did not."

Leis caught sight of her parents and couldn't stop the tears. Her mother glared at the back of Res's head, and Leis's breath hitched when she met her Father's gaze. His hand rested lightly on her mother's shoulder.

"*I'm so sorry,*" he mouthed.

Leis bit her lip and blinked furiously to keep the tears from falling. She swung her focus to Eric when he cleared his throat. He crossed his arms and defiantly widened his stance as if braced for a fight.

"We came willingly to discuss the situation in a civilized way," he said.

He easily took command from Res, as the authority in his voice turned everyone's attention to him.

"Mr. Koen Lockton and I have come to notify you that Baden Dietrich has given Leis a written release from the Pledge, and Mr. Lockton has formally asked to claim Leisel in his stead."

Gasps sounded throughout the room, and all eyes turned to Res. Most of them registered surprise at the revelation that Koen was one of them, but Res, Samuel, and a couple others didn't flinch.

"She is here to ask your permission before they complete the bonding," Eric said.

He lowered his voice and spoke directly to Res. His scent was deeply apologetic, and Leis was sure she saw a flash of pain in the woman's eyes.

"We are here because it is her desire not to repeat the wrongs others have done," he said.

Leis thought she might soften, but her face only hardened further.

"The Blood Exchange cannot be completed with a human." Res flicked a hand toward Koen in dismissal. "Leis will take her rightful place as mate to the male we approve."

Res glanced over her shoulder, and with a chill of fear Leis met the unwavering stares of two males standing behind her.

"Since Baden has chosen to forfeit his claim, we have selected two suitable challengers. Both of their families are in need of a mate for their heirs." Res's eyes narrowed on Leis. "The Koch's have honored us by being willing to overlook your shortcomings, and Mr. Fertig personally requested the opportunity to meet you. I expect you to treat both men with more respect than you did my grandson."

Leis's heart pounded first in anger, and then in terror as two men stepped forward. The tallest, and largest, spoke first. The eyes he fixed on her were a piercing shade of green filled with lust so intense her stomach turned.

She recognized him as the man who had been talking to her father before Andrew's ceremony. He was more than six feet of muscle dressed in a tailored yellow shirt and gray vest. Hair nearly as long as hers and even redder was knotted at the back of his neck.

Sweat broke out along her neck as his sharp scent stung her nose. His arrogance was thick in the air as he stepped forward.

"My name is Alexander Koch. I ask the Elder's permission to challenge Mr. Lockton's claim," he said.

His smoothly accented voice made her cringe. Cold fear raked her spine, but she stared back refusing to let it show.

She heard a low growl from Koen's direction, then a grunt of pain. Before she could move, one of the guards caught her upper arms and held her in place as Koen straightened with a hand over his stomach.

She squeezed her eyes shut as Koen hissed, "I'm fine, Leis. Don't fight them."

"The Clan accepts your challenge, Alexander," Res said.

Leis glared at her, but she was smiling at Alexander as if nothing had happened. Before her sentence was finished, the man to her left stepped forward. Leis riveted her attention on him and away from the overwhelming gaze of Alexander.

"I am Stewart Fertig." He bowed slightly, and his wink seemed more friendly than flirtatious. "I ask permission to challenge both Mr. Lockton and Mr. Koch's claims, and I ask permission to meet with her first."

Res's smile grew wickedly. "Permission granted, Mr. Fertig. Your time with her will begin tomorrow, though you understand the rules require you forfeit one day for the privilege." Stewart acknowledged her with a curt nod. Res continued, "Each of the challengers will be allowed three days with Miss Gottschalk. You will be chaperoned, and no physical contact beyond holding hands will be permitted. Because Mr. Fertig has forfeited a day, he will have two days and Alexander up to four. If a decision cannot be reached between the two by the end of Alexander's time with her, the Clan will make the final decision."

Calling Alexander by his first name clearly showed Res's favoritism, and Leis's stomach turned. The man was terrifying. She waited for Eric to speak up, but he said nothing. Unable to stand the silence, Leis twisted free of the guard and pointed.

"*Koen* is my chosen! He is my mate, I have accepted his pledge, and his claim is valid. No challenge can be made!" She flinched at how weak she sounded, and frustration tightened her throat. "You can't do this," she croaked.

Eric closed his eyes and drew a breath. Leis had a sinking feeling when he stepped close and gently freed her other arm from the guard.

"I'm afraid Koen's claim is not validated. His family has yet to give their formal consent," Eric said.

The blood drained to her feet. Raising her eyes to Koen, he looked completely resigned.

He knew this would happen.

Fear rushed through her as she realized that meant Koen would be kept from her until the challenge was decided.

"What about Koen?" Leis whispered.

Her eyes burned, but she refused to let the tears fall. Without needing to look at Res, she knew the answer.

"He will be allowed to remain until his influence has been replaced." She spat the words as though it burned her mouth to admit the truth of who Koen was. "He will be dealt with at the end of the challenge."

Angry and terrified beyond words, Leis whirled on Eric. "Do something!" She searched his eyes for some explanation but found no emotion in them.

He looked past her and sized up the two she would spend the next week with. His brown eyes were focused and unworried.

"There is nothing we can do now but wait." His dark eyes were full of compassion when they fell back to her. "And follow the rules."

"Well, Eric." Res clasped her hands in front of her chest. "It appears you still know how to devastate a woman's heart, but at least you've learned nothing good ever comes from breaking the rules."

THIRTY-EIGHT

KOEN

Koen had prepared himself for outright animosity from Leis's family. Instead, he was ignored.

When the meal began, he was seated at the end farthest from Eric and Leis, still flanked by the two goons who escorted him through the house.

Before being seated for the meal, he was shown to a guest room. A single bed, tiny dresser, no bathroom, and a door connecting his room to the one next door likely meant the room was designed for a child. The insult of it chafed him, but he accepted the offer as graciously as he could. He was trying to be thankful he was being allowed to stay for the challenge. His guards implied more than once that after it was over, he would be escorted into the surrounding desert and left to fend for himself.

In a similar state of dismissal, Leis's parents sat across from him. Stefanie refused to look at him, and when she spoke quietly to Hadyn the devastation in her voice was clear.

Being publicly disgraced had noticeably broken her. Haydn made eye contact with him once, and the sorrow in the man's eyes gave him pause. Her parents were obviously crushed by what was happening.

Koen cleared his throat and addressed them gently, "Your daughter is an amazing woman. You should be very proud of her."

Stefanie's eyes burned into his, looking so much like Leis his breath caught.

"We can hardly be proud of her for choosing to associate with the likes of *you*." She leaned forward, and the echo of her barely controlled rage tightened around him. "Your meddling has cost us our little girl. I would appreciate it if you did not speak to any of us. Ever. You are not welcome here." She gritted the last through her teeth.

Haydn laid his hand over hers, but she shook it off. Ignoring Stefanie's glare, he replied, "Thank you. Your courage is impressive, but your continued interference will only make this harder for all of us." Haydn smiled slightly then returned to his meal.

Steeling himself for a long week, Koen resigned himself to wait. Eric, Ellen, and Baden still had a plan. He just hoped six days was enough.

Not surprisingly, Leis was seated between Alexander and Stewart. The longer she was next to Alexander, the more frightened she became. His presence was commanding, and his harsh scent left no doubt about his lewd thoughts.

Alexander talked freely about the places he visited and the wealthy clients who paid him premium fees to design and oversee the construction of their multi-million-dollar homes.

Despite the churning in her stomach due to his less than polite thoughts, she found herself surprised by his genuine intentions to give his clients the very best for their money. It was his desire for the luxuries and pleasures of his success that made her sick.

When he proudly announced his most recent project, a third home for a well-known actor and comedian being built in the mountains of Costa Rica, the timbre of his voice changed, and his crisp scent slipped over her skin like oil.

"He enjoys his time away from the public." Alexander's rough voice lowered even more. "Private parties are a bit more his style, so I designed the interior of the house to accommodate his need for...secluded spaces." Hidden by the tablecloth, he slid a hand onto her thigh. "His parties are quite the event. If you enjoy that sort of thing."

Disgusted, Leis pushed his hand from her leg, barely registering a spike of pain in his scent at the contact. Though he tensed, the exchange seemed to entice him, and his large body curved toward her. Deciding a direct approach might work, she lifted her gaze and then hesitated when his hungry green eyes bore into hers. Stiffening her back she leveled her chin and spoke coolly.

"Secluded spaces usually mean someone is trying to hide something they are ashamed to let others see. It's my understanding such behavior is offensive to the Clan." His eyes darkened at the implication. Forcing her hand not to shake, Leis reached for her water glass and took a small sip. "Since you've apparently attended his parties, Mr. Koch, *are they* the kind of event you enjoy?"

His lips curled, giving her the impression she had just baited a hungry animal.

"I simply like knowing what other people would prefer to keep hidden." His eyes roamed down her body. He smirked again as a shiver racked her. "Everyone has secrets. Wouldn't you agree?"

Res lifted her wine glass and addressed Stewart. Her smile was brittle as she raised her voice loud enough for the whole table to hear.

"Mr. Fertig, you've been especially quiet this evening. Where are you planning to take Miss. Gottschalk for your first day together tomorrow?"

Until now, she had kept herself from looking down the table at Koen, but when she turned to hear Stewart's response, Leis searched him out. A carefully guarded expression shielded the emotions from his face, but his eyes were twin blue flames. Almost imperceptibly he nodded, encouraging her to play along. Tearing her focus from him she met Stewart's eyes.

In sharp contrast to the piercing green of Alexander's and the raging blue waters of Koen's, Stewart's eyes were a soft, dark hazel.

Searching her face, he spoke softly, "I thought I would ask Leis to show me around Scottsdale."

His calm confidence soothed her, and his sweet musk smelled so similar to Koen's it calmed her nerves. His intentions were vastly different from Alexander's, and the tension in her neck eased slightly. He watched her carefully as he continued.

"I've never been to this part of Arizona and would like to visit through the eyes of a beautiful woman," he said.

Blushing, Leis looked down the table again. Koen's expression was furious before he sat back out of view.

"I would be glad to show you around," she said quietly.

"Meek when she wants to be." Alexander chuckled and raised a glass toward Stewart. "Better watch your backside with that one tomorrow."

Leis remained quiet the rest of the meal and listened to the conversations going on around her.

The four of them - Alexander, Stewart, Koen, and herself - were the youngest at the table. The others were all her parents' ages and older, representing thousands of years.

Their conversations were superficial at best. Casual questions were asked about one another's lives, children and grandchildren, but no one really cared about the answers, and not one person admitted to having a single struggle or difficulty. As hands gestured and bodies moved, her sense of smell allowed her to see through the masks. The couples surrounding her had erected thick walls to hide the truth.

The woman sitting next to Samuel was terrified of her mate. His posture and the dull trace of the scent she was able to detect was bitter and angry. His name was Marcus, but Leis couldn't catch the woman's.

The couple laughed and talked about how well things were going, but when she stood and excused herself to the restroom, Leis caught a glimpse of a row of faded bruises on the back of her neck like the imprints of large fingers. Marcus' glare challenged her to say something.

She dropped her eyes and wanted to scream. She understood her inability to smell kept her from seeing the truth for so long, but why had no one been willing to do anything to change this? Koen's presence proved there were others out there, and she had no doubt his existence wasn't really a surprise.

Bitter anger chewed at her nerves as her eyes marked those who hadn't been shocked. Res, Samuel, Marcus, and the guards. None of them had been caught off guard by Koen's existence.

As each couple said their good-nights, Leis was expected to shake their hand and believe the words they said when they told her they were glad she was home. However, with each hand shake she saw more unhappiness and began to realize most were sorry she had not been able to get away.

Though their comments and tones of voice indicated they agreed with Res, the bitterness and frustration she picked up from the males made her question how they truly felt.

When the final guest was gone, she turned to see Eric and Koen near the table watching her.

Alexander was seated on a caramel-colored leather sofa in the sitting room with one long arm stretched along the back of it. A wine glass spun idly in his long fingers; his eyes focused on the fireplace.

Stewart leaned against the bar on the opposite side of the room, arms crossed and staring at the floor.

Behind her, Res's heels clicked on the tile and Samuel's measured strides followed her into the kitchen.

Koen looked as weary as she felt. His eyes softened and he opened his arms for her.

"Eric told me that after tonight I won't be able to see or talk to you until the six days are over," he said.

He enfolded her in his arms and pulled her tightly to him. As his rich musk washed through her, the sobs she had held back all day burst free. He lay his cheek against the crown of her head and his arms tucked her more securely to his chest.

"Shh. It will all be all right. Trust us, remember?" His whispered words fluttered through her hair, breathing his pledge to her again as she melted against him.

"That's enough.*"* Res's snapped with disgust. "It's time for you to step aside."

He straightened but Leis tightened her hold on him. She pleaded in a ragged whisper, "I can't do this." Sobs choked her throat as she fisted his shirt in her hands. "I won't let them keep me away from you!"

For the corner of her eye, she saw Alexander stand and Stewart straighten. Both moved toward Koen but stopped when he spoke.

"Leis." Koen freed his shirt and held her hands between them. "We'll get through this. Right now, we have to do what we came for." He released her and stepped back. "I love you, always." He met the eyes of the two challengers, then, inclining his head to Res, Koen turned on his heel and climbed the stairs. Leis watched until the door to his room closed behind him.

Trying to gather herself together as best she could, she ran her palms down her face. When she opened her eyes, she locked glares with Res.

"You are making your last mistake. You can't force people to obey your precious *rules* forever. Mark my words, Elder. I. Will. Not. Bow," Leis rasped.

She turned and stalked toward her own suite, shoving Alexander aside as she passed him.

FORTY

The next morning, Leis woke up feeling like she hadn't slept at all. Her dreams were full of Alexander's decrepit stare, Stewart's kind smile, and Koen watching her from behind panes of glass.

Repeatedly, she tried to get past the two males to get to Koen, but they held her away from him. When she did get past them, she was left pounding her fists against the glass while Koen stood inches from her.

Shaking off the dreams, she stumbled out of bed and into the small bathroom attached to her suite. She had visited the compound many times, but she had never stayed overnight as a guest. For the next week, she would share the guest wing with Alexander, Stewart, and Koen.

The section of the house they were staying in had four more suites and two additional adjoining bedrooms for children. She was furious when she found out Koen was being forced to stay in one of the children's rooms. It was no surprise Res was determined to humiliate him in every way possible.

She let her hair down and shook it out. The hot water relaxed her tense muscles, and she wondered why Stewart was so anxious to be the first to meet with her. She didn't think he was the type to go along with Res's schemes, but no one could be fully trusted.

Not even Eric apparently.

His willingness to submit to Res's rules caught her off guard. He said very little once the challenge was issued last night, and she still couldn't believe he hadn't at least *tried* to stop it. She understood Baden needed them to go along with his grandmother's schemes for a time, but Eric's admonishment to follow the rules still hurt.

She leaned against the tile of the shower, resting her head on her forearm.

Six days. I can do this. I have to.

She dressed casually in slim fit jeans and a long sleeve gray and burgundy t-shirt. Though it never really got cold, any temperature below seventy brought out long sleeves and scarves from those native to the Arizona heat. She slipped her feet into a pair of white Toms and reached for her purse.

Laying on top, was the phone Baden had given her. Other than the one text, he had not contacted her and every time she tried to send one to him; it bounced right back. She tried again.

> L - Your grandmother is challenging Koen. I wish you were here.

She was unsurprised when the message returned.

> Number unknown. Message not sent

She dropped it in the bag, wondering why she bothered with the phone at all, but Baden went through a lot of trouble to make sure she had it.

The clock at the bottom of the stairs chimed eight AM. Breakfast would be on the table any minute, and Stewart and Res would be waiting. Stewart would be permitted to spend as much or as little time with her as he wanted over the next forty-eight hours.

Being treated as nothing more than a commodity was humiliating, but she gritted her teeth and pulled the purse over her shoulder.

When she opened the door, her stomach rumbled at the smell of waffles and bacon. The memory of Koen teasing her about waffles made her smile as she stepped onto the balcony and headed for the stairs.

"You look rested this morning," Stewart said. He was also just leaving his room, his expression friendly. As he got closer, his eyes seemed more green than brown. He was dressed in a similarly casual style with khaki pants, an untucked red and gray plaid shirt and bright red sneakers. His short hair was stylishly messy and swept upwards from his face.

"Then I look better than I feel," she replied. He smelled faintly of the outdoors and reminded her of the woods behind her apartment in Ohio. He was calm and inquisitive, and she was relieved his intentions from last night hadn't changed.

When they reached the dining room, Res and Samuel were already seated and ready to eat. The long table from the night before was gone, and there were now only six place settings.

"Good morning, Stewart. Leisel." Res's voice was casual, but she watched intently as Stewart held out Leis's chair. "Did you sleep well? You must be excited for your day together."

"We are," Stewart said, and rounded the table to sit across from Leis. He met her eyes. "Waking up to see such a beautiful face makes for a great start to the day."

Unable to help herself, she blushed and reached for the pot of coffee to disguise her embarrassment.

"I slept well enough," she said. Pouring a cup, she met Res's eyes. "What I'm looking forward to is getting this over with."

Res laughed softly. "Oh, Stewart. You have your work cut out for you with this one."

His smile never slipped. He lifted a hand to the waiting servants.

"I'll have the waffles and an order of bacon." He looked at Leis. "What would you like? The waffles smell incredible, don't they?"

Before Leis could respond, Res made a disappointed sound and set her fork aside.

"Oh, I'm so sorry Stewart. I must have forgotten to tell you about Leisel's...disability." Res's expression was sorrowful. "Our Leisel was born without the ability to smell." She patted the back of Leis's hand, and it was all she could do not to yank it away. "We think that's why my grandson finally gave up on the poor thing." Her soft expression belied the treachery in her cold brown eyes. "I'm sure you'll still find she is quite intelligent and capable, regardless of her shortcomings."

Anger flashed, followed by the pain of all the times her mother told Baden those exact words. Leis started to push away from the table when Stewart's quiet voice stopped her.

"If I've learned anything in my short life, Res, it is that often the ones who seem at the greatest disadvantage can surprise you when you least expect it," he said softly.

When his eyes met hers, Leis read the silent plea asking her to be patient. Settling into her seat, she addressed the servant awaiting her order.

"The waffles do sound good. No bacon," she said.

Stewart thanked the man as he turned toward the kitchen. Leis sipped her coffee and stared out at the brightly lit day. The sun glared off the buildings in the valley below, and she longed to find Koen and get away.

As though sensing the direction of her thoughts, Stewart gestured at the view.

"It would be a shame to waste such a beautiful day indoors. I thought we could do some shopping in Old Town. I was hoping to pick up a few new pieces of art for my family. How does that sound, Leis?"

"That's fine with me," she said.

Doing her best to control her nerves, she finished the breakfast and refilled her coffee.

Samuel spoke for the first time, and Leis was surprised by the strong accent he carried.

"Ray will accompany you wherever you wish to go." He indicated a smallish gentleman dressed in gray slacks and a white polo shirt near the door who inclined his head to them. "Ray will drive, and you will not be permitted out of his sight."

Wiping his mouth and setting the napkin aside, Stewart stood. He stepped around the table and offered his hand.

"Perfect. I'm ready to go when you are," he said.

Leis accepted his hand, then pulled back and reached for her purse.

"Thank you for breakfast." She nodded to the staff then turned to Stewart. He extended his arm toward the door as Ray opened it. "I suppose we will be back for dinner?"

"I don't think so. I was hoping for something a little more relaxed tonight," Stewart said.

He followed her outside, resting his palm lightly at the small of her back. She flinched and walked faster, making his hand fall away.

"Have them back by midnight, Ray," Res instructed.

The man nodded and settled into the driver's seat of the Town Car. It was closer to a limousine, and Stewart surprised her when he leaned forward and spoke to Ray.

"You are here to make sure we don't break any rules, but I don't think you need to hear all of our conversations. Would you please raise the glass?" Stewart asked.

When he sat back, a clear, glass partition slid into place behind the front seats, sealing them off from the front of the car.

Unsure how to respond, Leis glanced at the male next to her. His scent filled the car with carefully guarded emotions.

"I think you and I have some things to discuss." Flecks of gold flashed in his eyes as he asked, "How long have you been able to smell?"

Rocking back, she gaped. "What do you mean?"

He tilted his head in amusement. "How much do you know about your voice?"

"Enough to know you can read my emotions through them. Why?"

He smiled. "For the average male, you're right. We can read emotions and detect truth from lies. However, I have abilities much deeper than that. For example, when you said the waffles sounded good, you really wanted to say *smelled*, but you knew it would give you away." The shock must have been evident on her face because he grinned from ear to ear. He crossed his arms. "Am I close?"

"How can you know that?" she whispered.

"*How* do I?" He shrugged. "I have no idea, I just do." He glanced out the window. "It started when my older brother was pledged by the Clan's directive. Everyone interpreted the girl's hate for my brother as a product of the Elder's decision, but I knew she hated him because he wouldn't stop the Clan from forcing them together. He left, and no one has seen him since." He leveled his gaze at her, a sharp bite of something in the air making her lungs burn. "We have to stop Res. You know that, right?"

Leis nodded and decided to trust him with a little of her story. "The first time I was able to smell was when Baden told me he was not going to go through with the bonding — because we're related." Stewart's eyebrows shot up, and she continued, "His father was my uncle. They were twins."

Anger tightened his features, and she scented his genuine disgust.

"Cousins? No wonder you two kept so much distance between you that night," he said.

Leis's memory jogged. "We were at your gallery opening!" A twinge of regret spiked her heart. "That was the night Baden first told me he loved me." Her thoughts drifted back. "I wonder how long he knew something wasn't right."

Stewart shrugged again. "Hard to tell. When he told you the two of you were related, did he say anything else?"

"He told me Res was hiding what she was doing by using our mothers' last names instead of our fathers'." She absently pulled her hair over her shoulder and began to braid it. "That was also when he told me we're not the only Clan."

"I always suspected there were more after I read the histories. There were too many of us all over the world for them to all have been killed during the Middle Ages." Stewart lowered his chin and picked at his fingernails. "When did you find out Koen was one of us?"

"I didn't know until we were already on the run." She could still smell the damp leaves they knelt in when Koen whispered the Pledge to her the first time. "I thought he was going to take me to Baden until I read the letters Baden left for me. He tried to explain everything, even tried to warn me this would happen. He tried to warn us both."

Stewart narrowed his eyes on her. "Why trust me by telling me all this? How do you know I'm not working with Res?"

She studied his eyes and inhaled deeply. "Because I can smell the honesty in you. I can smell your intentions." As they studied one another, Leis felt the air in the car shift and closed her eyes. "Like now. I can smell your attraction to me." She blushed at her own boldness. "You also know that what you're feeling can't go any further, because I am not yours." She opened her eyes and was surprised to see jealousy in Stewart's eyes.

He smiled and it was gone. Maybe she'd imagined it.

"You love him very much, don't you?" he asked.

The truth of his words scattered her feelings. "It scares me how much I do."

Stewart lowered his gaze and spoke quietly. "Maybe you and I could have been one of the lucky ones." He crossed his legs and glanced out the window beside him. "My sister loves her Matthew, but I haven't seen them in years. They moved out of the country right after their bonding." He looked back, and the longing in his face nearly undid her. "I only hope one day I will be as lucky as Matthew and Koen."

"Don't let Res control you." Leis implored. "Get out. Koen is proof there are others out there as desperate to meet us as we are to meet them."

"I wish it was that easy," he murmured, rubbing his arm.

Leis didn't know how to respond to the shift in him. Something was off, but his scent was still even and calm. It must be her own frustration she was sensing.

FORTY-ONE

The car pulled up to the curb in front of a large wooden cutout of a cowboy holding a lariat. Ray parked the car and rolled the glass partition down. His voice was heavily accented like Samuel's.

"You will not leave my sight. No more than ten feet between us. You may hold hands, but that is all. I will determine what is appropriate and what is not. Ja?"

Stewart held a hand to her palm up. "Ja, Sir." Winking, he pushed the door open and helped her out.

The weather was a perfect mid-seventies, with a light breeze that carried smells from the restaurants and tobacco shops. It was early, and the shops were just opening. There weren't many tourists yet. She shaded her eyes and looked up at Stewart.

"Did you say you were looking for artwork to take home?" she asked.

He nodded, glancing up and down the street. "That and maybe a piece of jewelry or two."

Leis jerked her head toward the outskirts of the shopping center.

"I know the perfect place to get beautiful near replicas of Native American sand art. The colors are amazing."

They spent the day browsing the shops and talking to the artists. By dinner time, Stewart had purchased three large sand paintings, several hand hammered silver bracelets inlaid with Arizona turquoise, and three large, colorfully woven baskets. Though he claimed never to have been in the area, his knowledge of what was authentic and what was a knockoff impressed the artists he spoke to. Several of them were willing to bargain with him, and one of the basket makers gifted him with a matching handwoven blanket.

Though Stewart was polite and easy to talk to, she hated every moment she was forced to be away from Koen. Disappointment rolled from him as the day wore on and she grew more withdrawn. Twice Stewart nudged her when she paused to stare at couples holding hands and laughing.

"Let's eat and head back," he said tightly.

They chose a tex-mex style restaurant near where the car was parked.

They were being led to their table when her purse vibrated against her hip. She carefully drew the phone out and did her best not to react when she saw the words.

B – I got your messages

She cleared her throat to hide the tears threatening to fill her eyes and flinched when Stewart touched her hand under the table. Ray was seated one table away watching them carefully. His eyebrow lifted at the contact, and Leis shifted away from Stewart, shielding the phone from Ray's view.

"*How* did you get a text message?" Stewart removed his hand, glancing at Ray and lowering his voice. "Res has all of us locked out this week."

She forced herself not to look at Ray, focusing instead on appearing to dig something from her purse.

"It's Baden," she whispered.

The phone vibrated again, and she coughed to cover her flinch.

B - Hold on. We're on our way

Stewart pushed the water glass toward her. "How did he do that?"

She picked up the glass and lifted a shoulder. "I don't know." She couldn't keep the smile off her face. "He's a genius." She glanced back down. "It went to someone else, too." Pushing her phone and hands into the bag, she quickly typed a reply.

Almost instantly it bounced back, and she groaned in frustration. Trying to appear unconcerned, Stewart leaned back in his chair.

"Delivery Denied?" When she nodded, he blew out a breath. "Yeah. They have the cell towers locked out for all our phones right now."

Leis startled when it vibrated again, and covered it with another cough, hoping Ray still hadn't noticed. Her breath hitched when she saw the screen.

Leis? It's Koen

She looked up at Stewart. "It's Koen. His phone is working too."

He picked up his menu as Ray moved closer. "Cover it up." He waved to the server. "We're ready to order." He smiled at Ray as the escort slid into a seat next to Leis. "Something spicy will help clear your head, Leis. What would you recommend, Ray?"

The man leaned over to peer into her purse. "The steaks here are the best, but if you want spicy try the four-alarm chili."

Leis turned back with a cough drop in her hand. "Found one!" Unwrapping it, she flinched at Ray's closeness. "Is something wrong?"

"*Nein*." Ray picked up his menu. "After we eat, we head back to the compound."

When Ray focused on the server to order his food, Stewart whispered, "Nice job."

Flushed with fear and excitement, she took a drink of her water. *Baden is coming back.*

Throughout the rest of the meal, Stewart engaged Ray in conversation, and though Leis's mind was racing, she managed to laugh at his stories. The man had lived most of his life in Germany working with Samuel and came to the states when Res moved the Clan to Arizona in the fifties. Though the tension eased, Ray was all business when Stewart tried to put his arm across Leis's shoulders.

"Holding hands only. Rules are not to be broken," he snapped.

Thankful Ray had intervened, the admonishment still needled her. Her jaw clenched so hard she thought she would chip a tooth.

"Stupid rules!" she muttered.

Stewart laughed. "So do I have a chance?"

Her eyes met his. "A chance at what?"

He leaned close. "Getting you to break the rules?"

"Uh, no." For the third time blood rushed to her face. She ducked her head and glanced at her purse.

His shoulders shook as he laughed quietly and bumped playfully against her. "Good to know. I'd hate to have to break the news to Koen tonight."

When they were safely in the car with the glass in place Leis tentatively asked, "Will you see him tonight?"

"Koen?" he asked. She nodded and he crossed his arms. "Somehow we have adjoining rooms." He shook his head. "Not sure how that happened."

Leis held her purse on her lap, wishing she could pull out the phone, but Ray was watching them in the mirror.

"Five more days." She sighed.

"They'll go by fast." Stewart tipped his head. "I saw an advertisement for a horseback ride in the desert. Have you ever ridden?"

"Not since I was a girl. Baden and I used to go at least once a summer." She laughed. "He always fell off. After the third time, he claimed he would rather ride a motorcycle, because it didn't have a brain of its own."

All the lights were on inside the compound when they arrived. She resisted flinching when Stewart guided her up to the entryway with his hand on her back again.

"Thank you for a relaxing day. I hope your family likes the pieces you bought," she said quietly.

As they reached the front steps, movement in one of the upper windows caught her attention, and her breath caught when she saw Koen watching them.

His chest was bare, and a pair of purple shorts hung just below the v of his hips. When their eyes met, his hands tightened on the towel around his wide shoulders. A wicked smile bloomed on his face, and he flexed just enough to make his chest muscles jump. Her eyes widened and he whipped the towel from his shoulders, nodding to her before he turned and strode away from the window. The sight left her breathless.

"Feel better?" Stewart's breath on her cheek jolted her back just in time to keep her from tripping over the steps. Her eyes flicked to his then to the windows above them. He chuckled as Ray stood waiting with the door open.

"You're welcome," he said with a glint of amusement and something darker in his eyes.

Sure her whole body was bright red; Leis hurried toward the stairs and the safety of her bedroom.

"How was your day?" Res called.

Halfway up the stairs, she looked down to see Stewart and Res watching her thoughtfully.

"Enlightening," Stewart said. He crossed his arms and inclined his head to her. "Goodnight, Miss Gottschalk. I look forward to spending tomorrow with you."

Still reeling from her first glimpse of Koen's body, she mumbled a good night and hurried into her room. She turned the lock and rested her back against the door.

Five days. Five more days! She chanted to herself until her purse vibrated again.

> K - Good timing?

Though there was no name or number indicating where the text had come from, she knew it was Koen.

> L - Very. Are you all right? How is this working?

There was a long pause before he responded.

> K - I'm fine. No idea but we should keep this only for emergencies. We can't afford to get caught.

Her heart pounded at the thought.

> L - I know. Five days

He didn't respond and she set the phone aside. Sleep didn't come for hours, and when it did, she was left with dreams of glass walls keeping her from Koen. At least tonight he was shirtless.

Though it infuriated Koen at first, being ignored worked to his advantage. No one questioned him using the gym, and no one gave him a second look when he wandered the compound, even with his ever-present escorts following him.

Koen pulled a black t-shirt over his head and exited the gym. He heard Stewart and Res's voices down the hall and knew Leis would be on her way to her suite. Her reaction to seeing him through the window had been priceless, and he grinned.

Wanting to see her again, he paused near the doorway to his room. The stairway and her room were right around the corner. The taller of the two men assigned to him lifted his chin toward the bedroom door.

"Out of sight, human."

Koen's lip curled at the insult. They all knew he was Vampir, but the slur was all they would use to address him. His fists wanted to connect with the male's face, but he forced himself to relax knowing they were intentionally trying his patience. As much as he wanted to instigate a challenge of his own, causing a scene would get him kicked out, and he couldn't leave Leis here. Taking a deep breath, he opened the door and politely responded to the towering guard.

"I could use a shower. Since my room apparently doesn't have one, what are my options?"

A condescending smirk was his answer as the man waited for Koen to step inside his room, and then pulled the door closed without saying another word.

"Nice." Lowering himself onto the bed, Koen picked up the phone.

> B - I just landed in Ireland. There are many of us coming. Keep texts to emergencies only. It won't take them long to figure out we're in the system. How long until Res forces a decision?

Koen quickly replied.

> K - Two challengers, five more days

Make allies? Koen snorted.

He deleted all the messages and set the phone aside then picked up the bottle of water and towel he brought from the gym.

"Make the best of it, right?" Koen muttered and swore as he poured some of the water over his head and wiped his face. Just as he was about to pour the rest of it, the was a light knock on the door joining his room to Stewart's. Cautiously, he unlocked his side and cracked it open. Stewart was leaning casually in his doorway.

"She loves you, you know," Stewart said.

Koen opened the door wider, assessing him. Stewart's eyes narrowed, and a slight smile broke the tension.

"It looks like you could use a shower," Stewart quipped.

"Are you offering?" Koen asked, and raised an eyebrow when Stewart stepped aside, gesturing for him to enter the larger room.

"Why the olive branch?" Koen asked. He stepped inside, cautiously willing to accept at least a shower.

"I know a good bet when I see one." Stewart said over his shoulder.

He pushed open the bathroom door and snagged a pair of shorts from the back of it. Tossing the shorts on the bed, he unbuttoned his shirt sleeves and sat in one of the wingback chairs near the window.

"The way I see it; you, Tate, and Baden have some sort of plan to stop Res. I only know Baden through friends, but he was always an upright guy. And Leis..." Regret crossed his face when he leaned forward to rest his arms on his knees. "If they both trust you, then so do I." He ticked his chin toward the bathroom. "Take your shower and let's talk."

FORTY-THREE

The next morning, Stewart was waiting in the hallway, dressed for their horseback outing in a snug fitting pair of jeans, a bright blue henley shirt, and scuffed boots.

"Good morning." He stepped toward her. "Sleep well?"

"Well enough." She shrugged. Truth was, tension and nightmares had kept real sleep from her. Inhaling deeply, she pulled together her best smile as his friendly scent greeted her. "You're ready for today I see."

"Born to ride." He swept his arm down his body as they started down the stairs.

They froze halfway when they saw Alexander seated next to Res at the table.

Stewart stiffened and then preceded her the rest of the way. His friendly scent evaporated or was buried under the weight of Alexander's. Either way, Leis wanted to bolt back up the stairs.

"I thought the rules stated Mr. Koch's time didn't start until tomorrow," Stewart said tightly.

Leis jumped when Stewart caught her arm and guided her to a chair before she could escape.

Alexander rose from his seat at the table with the lithe grace of a jungle cat, which was impressive for a man his size. She couldn't help staring but dropped her eyes when his almost feline-like gaze made her squirm.

"I was just leaving." Alexander said. Leis couldn't stop a shiver of revulsion as his oily scent slipped over her. "I apologize for my late departure." Alexander bowed slightly to Res. "I will have all the arrangements settled tonight." He crossed behind her and leaned close to whisper, "Until tomorrow, Leisel."

She closed her eyes and turned her head, resisting the urge to flinch when his shoulder brushed hers. Stewart was unmoved and took her elbow, encouraging her to take a seat. He waited for her to sit, then rounded the table to his chair. His scent was sharp and the undercurrent she had yet to identify was stronger.

He was clearly hiding something, but it was so faint she wasn't sure if he was hiding it from her, Res, or both.

"Leis and I have decided to go horseback riding," Stewart said, derailing her thoughts.

He had recovered completely and appeared unbothered by the tension lingering in the room. He served himself some of the oatmeal from a warmer in the center of the table and offered to fill hers. Leis handed him her bowl and added a scoop of fresh berries when he handed it back.

"Will Ray be accompanying us again today?" Stewart asked.

"He is running errands for Samuel." Res shook her head and frowned. "I'm afraid it will be impossible for you to leave the grounds today." She clucked her tongue. "I'm sorry. You'll have to find other things to do around the house."

"Isn't there another *servant* who could go with us?" Leis said. Her hand shook as she set her spoon down. "I know you have a car we can borrow."

"I'm afraid not." Res's tone made it clear there would be no more discussion. "You'll be staying here today. You had your outing yesterday."

"That's all right." Stewart cleared his throat and tapped the table with his finger, a calculating glint in his eyes. "I'm sure we can find something to occupy ourselves with. There is a chipping green just below the breezeway." He lifted his coffee mug. "Do you golf, Leis?"

I've been once or twice," Leis gritted. Clamped her jaw so hard her teeth ached and forced herself to reply in a civil tone. "I could probably use a lesson or two before trying it again."

Stewart bit his lip, hiding his amusement and nodded. "Golf it is then." He resumed eating. "I hear you can't come to Scottsdale without playing at least one round of golf."

Res made a dismissive sound. "I'll be going into town today. If you need anything, my staff will always be close by."

Stewart chuckled when Leis threw her spoon down as Res excused herself from the table.

"No wonder she calls you a rebel." He refilled her coffee mug. "Following instructions isn't your thing, is it?"

"It's not that." Leis huffed. She gestured over her shoulder as Res left the house. "She and my mother want to make me feel like I'm not smart enough to think for myself."

"They aren't trying to make you *feel* that way," Stewart said. "They expect you to *believe* it." He leaned forward. "I'm glad you're smart enough not to."

He was calm and friendly again. Leis relaxed a little and grudgingly admitted she was beginning to admire Stewart's unflappable poise. She set her mug aside and pushed away from the table.

"Well, I suppose we don't need jeans and boots on the putting greens." Her eyes drifted around the oversized house and out toward the view of the Saddleback mountains. "At least we'll still be outside."

"Why don't we change and meet outside? Nothing we can do but make the best of it, right?" Stewart said. "You should probably hurry before she comes back and changes her mind."

"Right," she said suspiciously. His mood shifted to amused and she narrowed her eyes. He waved her on, and Leis took the stairs two at a time.

She hit something hard and suppressed a scream. That something was Koen. He caught her in his arms. Relief swept through her.

"Shhhh!" he cautioned.

He slid out of sight and took her with him. His scent welcomed her but there was an edge of pain in it.

"I've only got a couple seconds before the guards realize I'm not in my room." His blue eyes lit with laughter and her tension eased. "Hang in there. Stay as close to Stewart as you can."

His pain flared, making her concerned, but before she could ask anything, he kissed her forehead and hurried away. He rounded the corner just as she heard his escorts ask where he had been.

She quickly ducked into her room and closed the door. Her skin tingled where Koen's lips touched her and she inhaled deeply, trying to hold his intoxicating scent in her lungs as long as possible.

Thankful for his resourcefulness and hoping she'd been mistaken about the pain, Leis quickly changed clothes.

A few more days and this will all be over. A shiver raced up her back. She still had to endure the time alone with Alexander. *Focus on today, Leis. You can do this.*

FORTY-FOUR

As it turned out, the impromptu golf lesson was fun. Stewart was a patient instructor, and after sinking her third putt in a row, she turned to him with a triumphant grin.

"So, am I ready to go on tour?" She leaned on the club and struck what she hoped was a debonair pose.

He raised an eyebrow and shook his head. "Maybe." He picked their balls up off the green and touched her cheek with his knuckles. His eyes were a cool amber against his pale skin. "Maybe not. But you *would* make a gorgeous sales model." He stepped away before she swatted his hand down.

Though she knew he wasn't completely serious in his attraction, she also knew he wished he could be. They stood staring at each other for a moment. Uncomfortable, Leis turned away.

"Now that I've beaten you on the green, what's next?" she asked.

"No idea," he replied. He hefted the golf bag over his shoulder and reached out a hand to her. "Let's head up to the house and see what's going on there."

He was casually affectionate, and had she detected anything more from him than a desire for friendship she would have been more concerned. As it stood, she saw no reason to make a big deal out of it and took the offered hand.

On the way up the stairs carved into the hillside, they lagged behind the man who accompanied them outside. Stewart slowed, putting more space between them.

She looked up curiously. "What's wrong?"

"About tomorrow...Alexander is...intense." Stewart rolled his neck and trailed his gaze toward the house. "There's something not right about him, and it's made him a very angry man." He glanced down. "You're smart, and you've already proven you won't back down. It's just...He's broken every rule and gotten away with it by being the sole heir to the fortune that keeps this place going. He's clearly Res's favorite." The way his thumb caressed the back of her hand reminded her of the way Koen tried to calm her. "I guess what I'm saying is, be careful and don't let your guard down. Alexander and Res are planning something."

It wasn't anything she hadn't guessed, but hearing her suspicions confirmed chilled her to the core. They reached the patio, and she crossed her arms as though that would keep her warm.

"Thank you for the warning, but he already creeps me out." She glanced up at the vacant windows of the mansion. "I just wish this was all over with."

Today had made it into the high seventies and a warm breeze carried the smell she recognized as pine up the hill to them.

"And I'm curious, have you seen Eric? It's like he disappeared right after the dinner." She pushed her hands into the back pockets of her shorts, to hide the shaking.

"I haven't. He's around somewhere, I'm sure." Stewart said. He wouldn't look at her, and he was suddenly very nervous.

"Stewart?" Dread settled in her gut when his eyes met hers. "Just tell me he's all right."

He sighed. "For now." He lifted a hand when she stepped toward him. His eyes flicked to the man who stood at the patio doors watching them. "I haven't seen him either. I just know he's still on the grounds."

She gritted her teeth. "How was I ever so blind to all of this?"

He lowered his voice. "We all were. But we know now, and better than that, we have hope of changing it. Right?"

Mutely, she nodded and reached for the pendant at her neck. His gaze followed her hand.

"Okay, then," he said. "We play along until Baden and Eric do whatever it is they still have up their sleeves." He touched her shoulder. "Let's go eat."

Discouragement tore at her as the gravity of her situation continued to settle in. She was completely at Res's mercy, and the Elder would decide the outcome of the challenge. She knew they would never allow Koen's claim to be validated even if they had to kill him to prevent it.

Sensing her disquiet, Stewart did his best to distract her. They ate on the patio. He talked about his love of art, and all the places he traveled to collect the pieces he owned.

He had been all over the world collecting fine art for his parent's galleries in New York and Seattle. They had given him management of the Seattle location two years ago, and he was expecting they would do the same for the one in New York once he was settled. With or without his mate.

At the mention of settling down, his eyes clouded, and he reached for the glass of wine. "I wish we could have met under different circumstances."

Leis realized she could easily care about Stewart. He was kind and encouraging, and once this was all over, she hoped they would remain friends.

"Me too," she sighed. She imagined Koen dressed in a tux and escorting her to one of the Clan's many galas. "I'd much prefer to be hanging out at your gallery. Maybe when this is all over Koen and I can come visit you."

He took a sip of his wine and pressed his lips together. "Maybe."

Sunset exploded onto the mountains behind them, and the glass walls of the house reflected the brilliant colors. Stewart moved to the couch facing the valley. His scent turned mischievous and even playful.

"Come sit," he said, and patted the seat beside him.

She sat at the end opposite him, and the servant that shadowed them all day cleared his throat. Stewart shook his head and waved the man off.

"Relax. We're just going to watch the sunset," Stewart said.

As the sun sank lower, the sky bloomed into a brilliant mix of pink, purple, and orange, the red rock of the mountains amplifying the colors. Tucking her feet under her, she sighed at the beauty of it, then stiffened when behind and above them a guitar began to play softly.

Tears gathered then rolled down her cheeks as Koen's low voice floated down from the deck above them. She squeezed her eyes shut, fighting the need to race through the compound to find him.

Koen's songs plowed through her heart, and as he sang, the ache in his voice grew to match hers. As Koen's smoky voice coiled around her, she reached for the hand Stewart rested along the back of the couch. Sparks of pain ignited along her forearm at the contact.

"Thank you," she managed. He pushed their palms upward and laced their fingers together. Though it hurt to hold his hand, she was grateful he had helped make it happen.

"Anything for a friend," he said.

Koen played until the sky went black. When his last note faded, Stewart pulled her to her feet.

"It's time I got you inside," he said and turned her to face him.

With a glance at the distracted guard, he cupped her face in his palm. Like it always did when Baden touched her, her skin itched faintly under his fingers.

"Thank you for two wonderful days," Stweart said. "Please remember to be careful." His hand fell. "Be strong, and we will see you in four days."

The man at the door finally noticed how close they were standing and called out, "The day is over. Inside."

Taking a step around the couch, Leis growled under her breath, "I'm really getting tired of this place."

Stewart chuckled behind her. "You'll be thankful for it very soon. Stick close to the guards, Leis. Alexander won't make it easy."

The house was quiet when she made her way into her room. Koen's pain was growing. She could feel it in her chest. But why? Had someone hurt him?

She flung herself onto the bed in frustration.

Four more days.

FORTY-FIVE

LEISEL

Early morning sunlight filtered through the curtains of her room as Leis rolled over. For a moment she thought she was still in the hotel with Koen. Disappointment fouled her mood when she remembered where she was and what the day held.

She pushed the covers back and crossed the suite toward the bathroom. Rubbing the sleep from her eyes, she paused at the garment bag hanging ominously on the closet door. It hadn't been there when she fell into bed. Her heart raced when the fog of her vision cleared, and she made out the name on the garment bag. Neiman Marcus.

Pulling her top tighter, she glanced around the room wondering who had put it there. A small card with her name on it was tucked into a pocket on the outside of the bag. She drew it out and tucked her hair behind her ear.

The card was rich cream-colored vellum with bold black ink. Written in all caps, square and precise, obviously a man's hand-writing.

I SAW THIS DRESS IN TOWN YESTERDAY
AND IT REMINDED ME OF YOU.
WOULD YOU WEAR IT FOR ME TODAY?
ALEXANDER

HER HANDS TREMBLED as she unzipped the bag to reveal a soft peach sundress with a coordinating pale blue sweater draped over it. The top crisscrossed and tied behind the neck. The skirt was knee length and as she looked deeper into the bag, she found a pair of matching peach and blue sandals with cork wedge bottoms.

The fabric felt like raw silk, and the sweater was whisper soft. The label on the sweater was a designer she had never heard of and leaning close to read it, saw that the material was 100% angora. She wasn't surprised to see the shoes were Marc Jacobs.

Gritting her teeth, she sealed the bag back up and left the shoes on the floor. This was something her mother would do. If Leis brought home anything that wasn't designer, her mother would remove the offending item from her wardrobe or bedroom and replace it with something she deemed more appropriate.

Angry and a little unnerved, Leis flipped on the bathroom light and froze. On the counter and in the shower, her personal products had been replaced with all new bottles and lotions from L'occitane. The towels she'd used were also gone and lush grey ones were in their places. Another note was propped on the counter.

I HOPE YOU ENJOY THE NEW PRODUCTS.
THEY ARE SOME OF MY PERSONAL FAVORITES.
I LOOK FORWARD TO OUR TIME TOGETHER.
ALEXANDER

• • •

CLOSING HER EYES, she repressed a shudder, wondering when and how someone had gotten in her room. One more shock waited for her when she opened her hair case and found all her hair ties gone. A simple note was lying on top of the empty box.

YOUR HAIR LOOKS SO MUCH BETTER DOWN.
ALEXANDER

"UGH!" She exclaimed and slammed the box shut. "Of all the nerve!"

Angry beyond words, and feeling like a child who was unable to dress herself, Leis reached into her closet and chose a deep emerald green maxi dress with mid length sleeves and a scoop neck. She wrapped a brown infinity scarf around her neck and slipped into the pair of brown flats she purchased at the store where Koen embarrassed her by trying on the heels.

Thankful for the memory, she couldn't stop a giggle and wished he were the one taking her out today. She searched her purse and found a hair tie at the bottom. Defiantly, she swept her hair into a low pony. "Much better."

The clock chimed eight AM, and she needed to get downstairs before someone came looking for her. Sighing and wishing she could delay, she tossed the purse over her shoulder and opened the door. As the air swept into her room she cringed. She steeled herself and stepped into the hallway.

"Good morning, Leisel." Alexander's rough voice spoke quietly.

"Good morning, Mr. Koch." She met his gaze, and his dark expression gave her pause.

He was leaning against the wall opposite her door in sharply creased dress pants, a pale blue oxford, grey waistcoat, and a black leather belt. His sleeves were rolled just past his wrists, and she cringed at the Rolex he wore around his thickly veined wrist. His flaming hair was loose about his shoulders and appeared to still be slightly damp.

His glittering eyes took in her outfit, and he frowned. The neatly trimmed beard didn't hide the tick of the muscle in his jaw. He cocked his head in feigned confusion. "Didn't you like the dress I bought you?"

"It didn't fit." She swallowed as he pushed his towering form away from the wall and gestured for her to precede him down the stairs to breakfast.

"Hmmm. What a shame. I'll have to take you for a proper fitting later."

She stumbled when his strong fingers slid up the back of her head and through the length of her hair taking the elastic band with them. When she turned to face him, he held onto the ends and draped them over her shoulder.

"Much better," he purred.

His nearness set off all kinds of alarms in her chest, and she could smell his adverse reaction to touching her. She was surprised when hurt and disappointment wafted through the air, but Alexander still grinned as she glared at him.

She held out her hand for the return of the hair tie. "I'll take that back, please. I believe the rules state you are not allowed to touch me."

"I'll keep this for now." He lowered his chin and chuckled, the sound greasy in her ears. He tucked it into his pocket and turned to Ray who had appeared behind him. "I didn't actually touch her, did I Ray? I was simply adjusting her hair for her."

Ray nodded. "The same rules apply to you Mr. Koch that applied to Mr. Fertig. You know the rules and I will decide what is appropriate and what is not. Ja?"

Alexander motioned toward the table. "Of course. I promise to be the perfect gentleman where Miss Gottschalk is concerned."

Ray inclined his head, and Leis growled under her breath. Alexander held a chair out for her, lifting and smoothing her hair over the chair back.

"Did you like the new products? Yours were department store brands I believe. Not good for your skin or hair."

Res lowered herself into her chair at the head of the table and patted Samuel's hand as he pushed her closer. "I hope you don't mind that Mr. Koch and Ray paid your suite a visit last night." She signaled to the wait staff while Leis stared at her wide eyed.

"You let him in my room while I was sleeping?" *Playing favorites was one thing, but letting him in my room*? She pointed across the table at the wickedly grinning Alexander. "Surely *that* has to qualify as breaking a rule!"

"No. It doesn't. Mr. Koch was in your suite to deliver gifts, and he was never alone." Res dismissed her protest. "Besides, it appears you didn't even have the good manners to wear what he bought you." She sighed and turned toward the waiter approaching the table. "We'll be having omelets this morning. I'll have my usual."

Alexander stared at Leis and ordered for her. "Miss Gottschalk will have the garden omelet, no peppers, extra cheese and mushrooms. I will have the same without the cheese." His glittering eyes dared her to contradict him.

Her mouth hanging open, she nodded, and real fear settled over her. With a slight nod he released the waiter and poured her coffee.

"I believe you and I may have gotten off on the wrong foot, Leisel." He poured himself a cup and added a bit of creamer. "I'm afraid I get competitive when challenged for something I want. I hope you will allow me to spend the next few days making it up to you."

His piercing eyes still shocked her every time she looked into them. They were the clearest and brightest green she had ever seen. Having them completely focused on her was unsettling.

Setting aside the fact that his scent was no less slippery, but she sensed something underneath. Trying to push aside her fear, she did her best to do what Baden told her and pay attention to his emotions, not just his intentions.

Stewart told her Alexander hadn't had an easy life. Though he scared her, she knew he wouldn't do anything to lose his opportunity to claim her. Deciding a truce was safest, she pulled her shoulders back and smiled.

"I would be grateful for that. We did meet under less-than-ideal circumstances." She sipped her coffee and did her best not to cringe at the victorious smile he gave her. "What did you have in mind for our day, Mr. Koch?"

"I thought you might enjoy a taste of my lifestyle." He settled the plate the man handed him and lifted his fork. "I have an appointment in Seattle with a client, and I thought you could fly out and back with me." He lifted a shoulder. "It's only a couple hour flight and we should be home by nightfall. My jet is waiting for us as soon as we finish our breakfast."

Leis paused with her fork midway to her mouth. "Your jet?"

"Of course." He chewed and tipped his head at Res's delighted smile. "My compliments to the chef. The omelets are perfect." He returned his attention to Leis. "The home is nearly complete, but the owner called the office with a lingering question about the ability of the structure to support his helicopter." He smoothed a hand down his beard. "So, we will be taking my bird from the airport and landing at his residence. There's nothing I like more than making a grand entrance." Res laughed with him, and he added, "Besides, it's two birds, one stone. He will know I am willing to stake my reputation on what I build, and he will see for himself that the structure is sturdy."

Leis was surprised by and taken aback by his genuine honor. She inhaled slowly, trying to read him. Underneath all the bluster of his words and flash of his wealth, he craved the approval of those for whom he worked. He was a puzzle.

"Is something wrong, Leis?" Res watched her.

"Nothing at all," Leis lied. "I haven't slept well."

Alexander appraised her. "The flight should take about two and a half hours. There is a private room on board if you wish to take a brief nap before we arrive." He pushed away from the table when everyone was finished, and she marveled at the way such a large man moved with his incredible grace. "If you are ready to go, Ray?" He came around the table and pulled Leis's chair out for her. "I've reserved an extra seat for both of you on the plane and the chopper so you can stay with Miss Gottschalk the entire time we are away."

Ray looked to Res, then Samuel, before answering. When both nodded their approval, he started toward the door. "I'll pull the car around."

"No need, sir." Alexander took her hand, tucked it into his elbow, and guided her toward the door. "My driver is just outside. You will ride in the back with us." His smile was tight as he looked down at Leis. "I'm sure she would feel more comfortable if you rode with us and let someone else do the driving."

Completely taken off guard, Leis studied his eyes and tried to breathe in without being obvious. "Thank you, Alexander. I appreciate your thoughtfulness." She couldn't get a read on him.

His scent almost reminded her of the lemon from the apartment. Crisp and clean, but stronger, with a sharp edge of a deep pain she couldn't identify. She was going to have to stay on her toes for sure.

Outside, a sleek grey stretch limousine waited for them. Leis pointed. "Yours?" She couldn't help the smile that broke out on her face at the preening expression on Alexander's face. His display was already starting to border on ridiculous.

"As I said, I like to make a grand impression."

Leis turned to step inside and looked sideways up at Alexander. Just as she was about to lower herself into the seat, her smile slipped when she caught sight of Koen in the gym window again.

His hooded eyes bored holes into the back of Alexander's head, and his face was pale and strained. He was taping his hands, and with each turn of the tape his biceps flexed. Her breath caught when he viciously ripped the tape and turned away.

Alexander's scent turned dangerous, but he said nothing until he slid in across from her next to Ray. "Do you box, Miss Gottschalk?"

She met his stare evenly. "No. I was never a fan of any kind of violence."

Alexander leaned back in his seat and stretched an arm along the back of it. The sleeve slid up his heavily veined forearm as his hand dipped casually down. Leis's eyes were riveted in fear to his powerful arms, and she shuddered. His wicked smile told her he noticed.

Making a fist and causing the muscles in his forearm to slide provocatively under his skin, he spoke lightly. "Violence has its place, when necessary, but the primary goal of martial arts is discipline and defense. Knowing how to defend yourself is always a good idea. Especially for beautiful women like yourself." His eyes slid over her, and she stiffened.

Leis held her voice steady and changed the subject. "You said we were flying into Seattle. Where is the home located?"

"It's in a new subdivision just north of Seattle." Idly he pulled the hair tie from his pocket and used it to knot his own hair. "Only seven homes will be built in total, and the lowest price is three million in construction costs." Satisfied with his hair he shot her a knowing smirk. "The home I'm overseeing is considerably more expensive than that. I think you'll like it."

She shook her head at him. "I can't wait to see it."

Just then, his phone rang, and her anger burned again. Stewart told her Res had shut down cell calls. How was he getting them? "I thought all the cell towers were locked out."

Lifting the phone from his pocket he raised a brow. "Res is willing to make exceptions when necessary. Business must go on." He swiped the screen. "Hello, Rebekka." Alexander paused and once more raked his eyes over her. "We're on our way to the plane now." The voice on the other end replied sharply, and he became agitated. "This should have been taken care of already." He listened for a moment more, then relaxed. "Very well. Let Mark know I'll call them. Call me if anything changes."

He glanced at Leis and Ray. "Excuse me, but I'm going to need to make some calls before we arrive."

By the time they arrived at the airfield twenty minutes later, Alexander was growing more tense. After his fourth phone call, he closed his eyes and took a deep breath. Leis did the same and waited for him to explain. His citrus scent had gone sharper than before, and his anger was too close to the surface. He released the breath and leveled his eyes at her. Leis was surprised once again by the honesty in his jewel toned stare.

"It appears there has been some confusion in regard to the layout of the home." His voice was rough and even Ray sat straighter. "I will need to take several hours once we arrive to meet with the contractors and the homeowner to get it straightened out." His eyes moved to Ray. "It appears we will be spending the night in Washington State." Leis's stomach dropped at the reminder of Stewart's warning not to let him get her alone. "Please let Res know I will make arrangements for you and Miss Gottschalk to stay in my penthouse. I will take the helicopter to the client's home and my driver will take you on to my home. You, of course, will remain as her escort. I will do my best to resolve this and meet you for dinner."

Koen's breathing shortened when he realized neither Leis nor Alexander returned to the compound. Stewart had been genuinely worried about her and the time she would be spending with the architect. They talked long into the night about Res and the way she ran the Clan, but Koen hadn't shared anything with Stewart the other male didn't already know. He trusted no one, especially when two days ago he discovered his inhaler missing. With the way Stewart helped him and Leis, he was reasonably sure he wasn't the one who hadn't taken it, but who knew.

After their first talk, he and Stewart met at the gym to work out together. Now that his time with Leis was over, Stewart spent most of his time there. Koen entered and looked around as his guards took their usual places beside the door.

"Koen." Stewart was taping his hands when he entered the room. "I saw you at the heavy bag yesterday. Are you any good in the ring?"

Koen shook his head. "I can hold my own, but I was planning to lift today." His chest was already tight after two days without the inhaler. He didn't want to draw suspicion by avoiding the gym, but a full sparring match would be too much.

Stewart blocked his path. "Did you know Leis stayed overnight with Alexander in Seattle?" His face was bright red.

"I heard." Koen crossed his arms. "But taking swings at me isn't going to change it. And pounding your face won't help me. I just want to push out a few sets and get out of here."

Stewart shoved him. "You think you can pound me?"

Koen forced himself to relax, but his blood pressure skyrocketed. "Stew..."

The impact caught him completely off guard when Stewart sucker punched him in the gut, and he dropped to a knee. The blow knocked all the wind out of him, and he sucked in a ragged breath.

"What is your problem?" he wheezed.

Koen watched Stewart's feet and when he saw them shift, dodged to the side. Still gasping for breath, Koen caught Stewart's right hand as he swung again.

"Knock it off!" Koen twisted his body and wrenched the other man's arm behind his back.

Cursing, Stewart rose on his toes to lessen the strain. Koen held tight and heaved a painful breath to fight back the blackness creeping into his vision.

"We're done. I don't know what your problem is, but you need to chill out." He pushed Stewart away and braced himself as best he could in case he attacked again, but the fight was drained from him.

Stewart was breathing hard and glaring at the ground. Koen's ribs were on fire as fear constricted his chest. There was no way he would be able to hide the effect this would have on his breathing.

Keeping his eyes on Stewart, he lowered himself onto a weight bench and did his best to try to breathe through the searing pain in his side. From the corner of his eye, he saw the guards smirking.

Stewart rolled his shoulders and rested his hands on the smith machine next to him. "Are you all right? I don't know why I hit you. It's Koch I want to get my hands on."

Koen huffed. "I'll be fine." The adrenaline drained from his body, and he ran a hand down his face to hide the grimace. "That's a heck of an uppercut you've got."

"Sorry." Stewart straightened and his expression was unreadable. He watched Koen for a minute. "You sure you're all right?"

Koen stood. "I'm fine." His shoulders pinched and he coughed to cover the shaking. "I think I'll pass on the workout though. Looks like you're not really up for a partner today." He glanced back to see Stewart still staring at him. "I'm going to take a shower. Is your room open?"

"Yes."

"Thanks." Koen stepped into the hallway and stiffened when one of the guards taunted him.

"I thought humans were tough." He was about Koen's height and on a good day, he would have challenged him. Instead, Koen ignored him.

"Guess not. Weak lungs and all," the other replied.

Fear shot through him. He wondered why they hadn't confined him or restricted his access to the mansion, and now he knew. All they had to do was take his inhaler, keep him away from Leis, and watch him suffer.

Last night he felt the first real pangs of the separation from Leis. Nothing more than a pinch in his chest, and nothing he couldn't handle. Eric had warned him this might happen, but told him it would take days for the pain to set in.

Koen pushed the door to his room open and shoved it closed behind him. Without his inhaler, he suspected his weakening body would feel the poisoning in his blood sooner than they anticipated. He collapsed onto the bed and rubbed his bruised ribs. *Three days.* He had to make it three more days.

FORTY-SEVEN

Much like the penthouse she and Koen stayed in with Eric, Alexander's top floor residence in the downtown Seattle high rise was spacious and extremely modern. There were three bedrooms, each with private attached bathrooms. The main area was large and just as open as the compound. Only one wall divided the eating area from the main living space, and a fireplace open to both sides kept even that from being intrusive.

As promised, Alexander's driver met them at the airport and escorted her and Ray to his building. Literally the building was his. Alexander's name was etched into the stone facade beside the covered entrance.

Inside, they were greeted by staff who served them lunch, and Leis was genuinely surprised when a seamstress arrived. Not only did she take Leis's measurements, but the woman had returned this morning with several clothing options currently laying on the futon at the end of her bed. All of them in brilliant jewel tones of blues, burgundies, and golds.

Sighing, she picked up the least dressy of the outfits, a pair of wheat-colored slim fit pants, an oversized cream top and matching tank. Sitting on the edge of the bed, she pulled on a pair of knee-high brown boots. Though she refused to look at the labels, the fit and quality of the material told her they were expensive.

When she explored the space last night, she was unsurprised to find the penthouse decorated and furnished in pure understated luxury. Every chair was upholstered in glove soft leather and suede. The surfaces of the counters and the long-wet bar were natural stone and gleamed with polish, the tables and chairs all rich brown woods. The entire space felt both large and cozy. After it got dark and Alexander still hadn't arrived, she slid open one of the patio doors despite the chilly air just to take in the sounds of the city around her. She didn't like living in a big city, but somehow the distant sounds of cars and trains soothed her until she was able to sleep.

Ray had kept to himself, reading silently beside the fireplace. She went to bed while he was still in the same leather lounge chair where he spent most of the day. He seemed content to leave her to herself.

The room she was sitting in was as functional as it was beautiful. Behind her and tucked around a low wall, the king size bed was fitted with incredibly soft linens in colors of blues, greys, and greens. There was a tall armoire, a wide chest of drawers topped with a mirror and a pair of matching clear glass lamps. The bathroom she showered in was all marble and polished glass. The blue, green, and grey towels echoed the colors of the bed linens, and the same L'occitane personal products waited neatly on the counter and in the shower.

A knock on the door made her jump, and Alexander's baritone spoke from the other side. "Wear what would be most comfortable today. We'll be shopping in Beverly Hills this afternoon."

She rolled her eyes. Apparently spending money was his idea of a good time. "I'll be out in a minute." Leis tried not to sound ungrateful.

After zipping the boots over the pants, she stood and surveyed herself in the mirror attached to the front of the armoire. She smoothed a wrinkle in her blouse and opened the door.

Alexander and Ray were standing near the fireplace. Alexander gave her a genuine smile as she approached.

"Just a touch of cream, correct?" He handed her a mug and swept his eyes over her chosen outfit. "I thought you might prefer the neutrals." His eyes gleamed. "Wait here."

Leis took the offered mug and watched curiously as he crossed the room. His black dress shoes clicked on the stone floor. As he walked away his fluid grace kept her fixated on him. His broad shoulders tapered smoothly to a narrow waist, and the restrained power in his movement was both fascinating and intimidating. He stopped beside the door and reached into what looked like a small suitcase, withdrawing a piece of leopard print fabric.

"I picked up this scarf on my way home yesterday and thought you would like it." He expertly tied the ends to create a loop and held it up as though to place it around her neck, then paused to look at Ray. "May I?"

When Ray nodded, Alexander stepped close, laid the scarf around her neck, picked up the front loop to twist it, and settled it behind her neck. He stayed close to her as he lifted her hair free of the scarf and let it fall down her back. His wide chest filled her vision and though his closeness still made her want to step away from him, his lemony scent was relaxed and easygoing this morning.

"Isn't it amazing how a scarf can make all the difference in an outfit?" Without ever touching more than her hair, he stepped back to admire his addition to her ensemble.

Leis adjusted the silk scarf and shook her head. He continued to confuse her. "You seem to know a lot about women's clothing." She narrowed her eyes at him. "Why is that?"

He took the still full mug from her and gestured to the door. "I'll explain on the way. My pilot is waiting for us."

The three of them once more seated themselves in a limousine for the ride to the airport. They were escorted to a fenced outdoor area and up the stairs into the waiting Learjet. She was too nervous yesterday to observe much more than the four sets of tan leather seats that were paired and facing one another with a small table in between. But behind a narrow wall she noticed the short hallway that must lead to the sleeping area and restrooms.

Alexander allowed her to choose her seat, then settled gracefully across from her. Ray sat in the row behind them. Once they were belted in, the pilot signaled that they would be taking off soon. Alexander thanked him and then refocused his catlike eyes on hers.

"I sincerely apologize for yesterday. I enjoy my work, but it can be demanding of my time." A stewardess approached, offering them breakfast and more coffee. After ordering, he chuckled. "You look so confused, Leisel. What's going on in that beautiful mind of yours?"

His oily voice was back with the compliment, and Leis tried not to wince. "So much money. Spending it so freely on things like a private jet, *a helicopter,* servants, expensive clothes — seems like a waste to me." His head tilted as defensiveness crept into his eyes.

The same defensiveness her mother always had when she would bring up the same subject to her. The last thing she wanted was to annoy him, so she conceded a little.

"It's your money. I suppose you can spend it any way you like. But you never did answer how you know so much about women's fashion." She gestured to the clothing she wore. "You have excellent taste in clothing."

He rested an elbow on the armrest. With an amused smile his eyes followed the flick of her wrist, and he laughed softly at her blush. A different Rolex sparkled around his wrist and the pale green shirt and grey waistcoat toned down the brilliance of his eye color. She inhaled and was grateful to sense he was as relaxed as he appeared.

"Architecture wasn't my first choice as a career field."

The plane bumped along the runway then smoothed out and glided to the left as they lifted off the ground. He raised his mug and took a sip.

"Interior design was my choice. Color and texture translate easily to clothing choices, especially in women's clothing." He lifted a shoulder. "But my father refused to pay for my schooling unless structural engineering was my major. He didn't care what I did otherwise, but he was going to make sure I was prepared to take over the family business." His tone softened and the pain she sensed earlier surfaced. With two deep breaths he reined it in. "One day he didn't come home, mother couldn't live without him, and here I am." He gestured around him. "Heir to a fortune and destined to carry on the Koch legacy of mega home design."

Leis took a bite of her meal. "You've done well for yourself. I'm sure your parents would be proud."

He made a noncommittal sound and raked a hand through his hair. "They would be satisfied I suppose." He folded his hands on his lap. "But I don't want to spend today talking about them." His brilliant gaze lit on hers. "Have you ever shopped in Beverly Hills?"

"Only once with my mother." She shook her head, and her hair fell into her face. She pushed it back impatiently and glared at him. He didn't react. "Too expensive for me. Clothes are clothes. They don't have to cost a fortune."

He leaned forward and his eyes were as sincere as his fresh lemon scent. "Perhaps, like me, she simply believed you deserve only the best." He tucked a strand of hair behind her ear before she realized how close they were.

"Thank you, Mr. Koch. That is very nice of you to say. I just prefer things a bit simpler." She sat back and coughed, hoping to hide the blush creeping up her cheeks. One minute he disgusted her, the next his sincerity intrigued her.

Her reaction infused him with some of his original cockiness. "Well, today couldn't get any simpler for you, Miss Gottschalk." When she met his eyes questioningly, his hand covered hers. "You shop. I pay."

She hastily withdrew and looked out the window at the city below them. Across from her, Alexander's phone rang, and he was once again fielding calls about wall placements and foundations. Leis listened halfheartedly until they landed.

"Rebekka, you will hold all calls for the next two days." He gripped the phone a little tighter and his forearm muscles jumped.

Leis swallowed, marveling at the sheer power he exuded, and then rolled her eyes when she saw the gleam in his that told her he caught her watching. *Again.* It wasn't that she was attracted to him, but his precise control of movement was fascinating.

"Yes, I am aware." He continued. "But there is a family matter I have to attend to. I will be unavailable. Please make whatever decisions are necessary in my absence." He disconnected the call as the stewardess unlatched the door and assisted the groundsman in securing the stairs for their departure.

This time, a dark blue sedan was waiting for them. Ray took the front passenger seat, leaving Alexander and Leis together in the back.

"So, my dear." Alexander relaxed into his seat and lifted a slip of paper from his shirt pocket. He held it between two fingers. "Where would you like to start? The seamstress has already sent your measurements to the boutiques on this list. They will have everything ready for us."

She took the slip from him. Seeing the first two store names she started to protest. His finger shot across the distance between them and pressed against her lips as he snagged the paper back from her. She was too shocked to recoil.

"No arguments. If you won't decide, then I'll direct us."

When she sat silently glaring at him, he raised his voice and gave the name of the first shop to the driver.

"Yes, sir."

To Leis's frustration, the four of them spent the day going from boutique to boutique while Alexander insisted on buying at least one outfit from each.

The owners practically fell over themselves as they offered choice after choice, insisting anything could not only be altered, but custom ordered. By the end of the day, Leis was mentally exhausted from arguing, but Alexander's choices of color and style were flawless. All together he purchased eight complete outfits, three dresses, and to her horror, a pricey ball gown she had no idea when she would ever wear, though she had to admit, the cut and rich sapphire blue satin of the dress suited her perfectly. She'd be able to nearly replace her entire existing wardrobe.

At least my mother will be pleased.

FORTY-EIGHT

Hours later, back at the airport, the steward hung the dozen or so garment bags in a small closet near the rear of the plane before letting them know they would be serving dinner as soon as they were in the air.

Alexander sat staring out the window, apparently deep in thought. Leis seated herself across from him, while Ray seated himself farther toward the rear of the craft. Her attention wandered out the window as the sun set and wondered how Koen was.

She couldn't imagine how angry he must be knowing she was kept away from the compound overnight. She leaned her head against the back of the seat as tears filled the corners of her eyes. Her heart clenched remembering the pained look on his face when she climbed into the limo with Alexander yesterday. Blowing a soft breath through her pursed lips she wished for the hundredth time she hadn't refused him. Had she been willing to break the foolish rules her mother drilled into her, she wouldn't be stuck on this plane dreading the next several days.

Alexander touched her hand lightly, and her eyes startled wide.

His face was soft and concerned. When he relaxed, she could easily acknowledge how handsome he was. Comparing Alexander's almost brutal magnetism to Koen's refined strength, she let her gaze slip over his face, and he turned her hand in his. She watched the muscle under his closely trimmed red beard rise and fall, then the muscles in the wide column of his neck strained. In a moment his scent changed from citrus and fresh to sharp and sour. His powerful presence filled the plane, and she drew away from him.

Her skin buzzed where he touched her, and she knew immediately he felt the same reaction to her. He sat back in obvious disappointment, and she boldly challenged his attempts to entice her.

"Is this what you really want?" His eyes narrowed in question. "This." She lifted her hand from where it rested near his and gestured between them. "We're not intended for one another." A sudden realization hit her. "It *hurts* you to try. Why do you keep doing it?"

Defiance lit his eyes. "The pain will go away. It simply takes both parties being willing to work through it."

"No. It doesn't." She leaned forward and took a huge risk. "What I felt when Koen and I met could never be described as pain." She held her ground when his eyes flashed in warning. "Even when I didn't understand, I at least knew there was something between Koen and me that was very different than what I felt for Baden. Believe me when I tell you, Baden and I *wanted* it to work, but now we know it never could have." She huffed with an ironic smile. "He knew before I did that Koen is the one I'm intended for."

Her words were only making him angrier, so she tried a different approach. "What if your true mate is out there waiting to meet you?" She leaned toward him in emphasis. "You are the only one created for her, and if you choose to go through with Res's plan, you're taking away her chance to meet *you*."

A flicker of hurt crossed his face before it hardened again as he too leaned across the table. "Mr. Dietrich was not willing to do what it takes to make it work. I, however, believe in the traditions of the

Vampir. If, in the next two days you and I are still having difficulty, we will let Res and the rest of the Clan decide what should be done." He sounded like he was repeating someone else's words. His grimace told her the words sounded hollow even to him.

"Res is wrong." Alexander lifted his chin. Ray shifted into the seat behind her, but she ignored him. "Koen is proof she is."

"Just because you stumbled on one rogue family doesn't mean there are any other Vampir Clans out there." Alexander's voice was tight, but she could tell he was having trouble reconciling the logic of her statements with what he thought he knew.

"Think for yourself, Alexander! You're a logical person. If there is *one* family, wouldn't it stand to reason there would be more? Wouldn't you want the chance to meet them? What if..."

Ray stood. "That's enough." His accent was thick with anger. "What the Elder decides is final. There are no others." He took the seat next to Alexander and crossed his arms.

She lowered her head. "Repeating a lie doesn't make it true."

Ray glared at her, and she fell silent. Alexander's expression closed. He leaned a shoulder against the window frame and stared at her thoughtfully while idly stroking his beard. When they exited the plane and entered the limousine, he was deep in thought and didn't speak to her.

Good. She thought. *He's an intelligent man. Surely, he has to see the truth of what I'm telling him.*

They arrived at the compound just as the sun dipped below the horizon. Alexander unfolded himself from the car and reached in to help her out. Tucking her hand into the bend of his elbow, he walked her through the entryway and up the stairs. She could feel his tension grow with each step. He released her arm but caught her hand to place a gentle kiss on her knuckles. Despite the tingle of distaste on her skin, she was sure something had shifted in him.

"Thank you for a wonderful day." He murmured before he straightened and turned down the hall. She stood with a hand on the doorknob. Alexander glanced over his shoulder, his rich voice carrying softly. "You've given me a lot to think about, Leisel." His eyes, still bright even from a distance, fell then returned to her face before he turned the corner. "Sleep well."

FORTY-NINE

LEISEL

L eis was surprised when Res was absent from breakfast the next morning. She approached the table where Alexander was casually reading a newspaper. Seating herself across from him, she reached for a slice of toast and marveled at how relaxed the house felt. Even the servants she never heard talking spoke in hushed tones.

Alexander chuckled. "Something wrong?" He lifted his coffee mug and regarded her over the rim.

"No." Leis's brows creased. "In fact, things in the house seem better than usual." Alexander's eyes were darker, almost the color of jade when they met hers. She lifted her chin slightly toward the kitchen where two of the men who were always waiting on Res spoke in low voices, their heads close together. "Everyone seems relaxed."

Flicking his eyes toward them then back to hers, his face lifted into a small smile. "Res isn't here. She's...distracted. She'll be back for the event tonight."

"What's tonight?" Leis poured her coffee. When he passed the cream, there was a hint of weariness in Alexander's broad shoulders, and his sharp citrus scent was almost dull. "Are you all right? Did you sleep last night?"

His smile broadened. "No. I didn't sleep much last night." Alexander ducked his chin and glanced at Ray who crossed the wide space to approach the two men who hastily stepped apart. Alexander leaned slightly forward, the paper in his hand crinkling against the table. "Would it surprise you to know I spoke with Emerick Tate last night?" He took a long draw from his coffee, darkening eyes boring into hers.

Leis's heart pounded in her ears. "You did? Why?" Her voice was barely a whisper. She glanced at Ray. "What did he tell you?"

Alexander set his mug aside, folded the paper, and kept his eyes on hers. He raised his voice. "Ray, Miss Gottschalk and I would like to go for a short hike this morning. Would you mind escorting us?"

Ray huffed. "With Res and Samuel out of the house until this afternoon and security scrambling, I can't leave. I'll send one of the guards with you."

Breaking her stare, Alexander turned a full smile toward Ray. "Thank you. She and I will change and meet him on the patio in a few minutes."

The man nodded and turned. Alexander stood and motioned for Leis to follow. They climbed the stairs and at her door he paused. His crisp scent and muffled emotions confused her.

Alexander lifted a hand from his side as though he meant to touch her, then let it fall back. "Wear comfortable shoes. I'll meet you outside."

Puzzled, she stared after him as he disappeared around the corner. *What in the world?!* Confused and curious, Leis slid into her room to change.

FIFTY

KOEN

Koen glanced resignedly out the small window as he pulled on his shoes. He rested most of the night and his breathing mostly recovered from Stewart's punch. As he suspected, the pinch in his chest had become a sharp cramp overnight. He knew it would suck, but he would be all right as long as he took it easy. He rested his elbows on his knees wishing not for the first time that morning, he could at least speak to Leis.

His hand went to the empty space at his throat then dropped. Every day he was away from her his body would poison itself. His father described the feeling after being away for two weeks for a school trip.

As a college history and ancient language professor, his dad took a group of students on a two-week tour of Germany and Austria. When he returned, his father said it felt like his veins were being pulled from his body. During that same time his mother was very quiet and withdrawn. They explained it was part of their genetic makeup, a physical dependency so strong the male would stay close to his family to protect and provide for them.

Concern for Leis tightened his chest but he forced himself to relax. Stressing himself out over things he could do nothing about would only exacerbate his breathing issues. He knew she wasn't feeling the same pain. His blood already changed in anticipation of their union, but since they hadn't bonded she should remain unaffected. Still, all the doubts and worries he had been able to push aside pressed on him the more he thought about her. He forced himself to take deep even breaths, trying to focus on the breathing exercises he relied on while on stage.

Koen lifted his head and looked at the door adjoining the rooms. Stewart hadn't returned to his room until late last night, not quite slamming his bedroom door, but almost. They left the doors between rooms closed but unlocked so Koen could use the shower whenever he needed, but until he knew what Stewart's mood was like this morning, he decided to leave the other man to himself. He wasn't sure he had the strength to fend off another attack.

Needing to do something to take his mind off Leis and Stewart's strange behavior, he decided to take his chances with a walk. When he opened the door, he was surprised to see Alexander striding down the balcony toward him. The usually overdressed male was not in his normal black slacks and expensively tailored oxford, but modern fitting kakis and a surprisingly casual long-sleeved t-shirt.

Alexander hesitated then cleared his throat. "Mr. Lockton."

"Don't touch her today." Alexander's sharp eyes narrowed at the challenge and Koen squared his shoulders. Picking a fight with a man who could obviously break him in half probably wasn't the wisest thing to do, but at the moment he didn't care.

Alexander stopped a few steps away and sighed. "Being angry with me won't do you much good."

Clenching his jaw, Koen had to admit he was right. He'd said as much to Stewart the day before. He jerked his chin toward the stairs and the quiet house beyond. "Where is everyone?"

Alexander glanced toward Stewart's door. "Out, I suppose." Koen tensed at his flippant answer then stilled when the other man spoke low. "I don't know exactly what's going to happen tonight, but your

Leisel is a brilliant woman and a very determined female." Alexander's steady eyes met Koen's. "She deserves better than what she'll get here." Striding forward, he landed a large hand on Koen's shoulder. "Good luck."

Koen stood frozen as Alexander disappeared around the corner toward Leis's room.

Your Leisel?

Their voices and footsteps faded as they descended the stairs together. He was still standing in place when he heard the front door open and close. He turned to continue on his way out, when he realized something...*where were the guards?*

He turned back, curious, and even looked over the railing into the space below but saw only the few housekeepers and kitchen workers.

There was still no sound from Stewart's room, and he rapped his knuckles against the door. To his surprise the door inched open, unlatched.

"Stewart?" He called and pushed the door the rest of the way open. The room, like the other suites in this section of the house, held a king size bed directly in front of the door. Beside it was a long dresser with a mirror, a lamp and a few leather-bound books stacked obviously for decoration. He glanced around the space and realized the bed had not been slept in.

"Stewart?" He called a little louder, turning in a circle just inside the room.

Koen stepped into the hallway and pulled the door shut. Scratching his head, he descended to the main level and walked toward the back patio. As he crossed the dining area several of the servants' low voices floated toward him and he strained to listen.

A woman laughed. "She won't be back for another hour at least, probably two. And Ray, he's down in the basement with the rest of the guards trying to figure out who got him out."

Another woman responded, sounding concerned. "She'll kill Ray if he was to blame! And all before the ceremony tonight."

Koen backed away as their footsteps headed toward him. "Let's get this done and leave before she gets back. I don't want to be here any longer than we have to." The two workers came through the door carrying what looked like stacks of tablecloths. As Koen crossed the entry way and opened the front door he glanced back. The two watched him curiously.

He stepped outside unguarded, and contemplated leaving, but the compound was in the middle of nowhere. They were surrounded on every side by mountains and desert. On the drive in, he'd noted the nearest house was miles away. There was no place for him to go, and in his current state he wouldn't get far anyway.

He walked around the side of the garage and peeked in. The lone car inside looked like the limousine Leis and Alexander had taken. Stealing it crossed his mind, but he had no idea how to hot wire a car.

Koen's hands tightened remembering the sight of Leis being helped out of the car and escorted into the house by Alexander last night.

He took a set of steps to a lower level and crossed a large patio where linen covered tables lined one side, and a round platform sat in the center. The sun beat down on his head and his breath shortened as sweat trickled down his back. He reached the edge of the patio and let his eyes trail over the hills around him. About a hundred yards away across a deep cleft in the red-orange earth, he spotted three figures walking slowly along a trail. His breath hitched in his throat, hoping he wasn't seeing what he thought he was.

Easily recognizable as Alexander, Leis, and one of the guards, the three figures stopped, and Koen watched in horror as Alexander placed his hands on Leis's shoulders and pulled her close. Leis rose on her toes. His heart stopped as their faces closed on one another and then her arms were around Alexander's neck.

Koen felt sick and reason fled. Anger and jealousy clenching tightly across his chest. Turning away, he launched himself at a run toward the front of the compound and the trail he knew they were on. With every step his fury grew, and the pain spurred him until he was running at an all-out sprint. He rounded the side of the house and searched for the entrance to the trail.

The red stone hillside blurred as the pain in his ribs nearly dropped him to his knees. Pressing forward, he began to sway on his feet. His body began to convulse with the effort of forcing the air in and out of his lungs.

One part of his mind screamed at him not to jump to conclusions, reminding him Leis was his. She would never betray him. The other half sneered. What if Eric was wrong and it *was* possible she had more than one potential bond mate? Could her effect on him be reversed if she chose someone else, or would his blood sour in his veins?

His mind took another turn as his vision began to fade. This was her home. Alexander could give her everything he couldn't, all the luxury she was used to, and here she was surrounded by the people had she probably known all her life. The more his thoughts ran rampant the more his vision became a clouded red haze. His shoulders pinched with the effort to breathe.

He dropped to his knees, his fists crashing into the concrete of the driveway. He barely registered the pain of the skin tearing from his knuckles and resisted the urge to collapse flat onto the cool surface. Koen's violent gasps for air drowned out the sound of running footsteps and someone calling his name. Shiny, dark brown shoes topped by crisply folded and rolled jeans stepped into his line of sight.

"Koen!" The voice above him sounded vaguely familiar. "Koen, what happened? Are you all right?"

Still crouched on the ground while his shoulders hunched painfully against the contraction of his struggling lungs, Koen became aware of more and more feet and legs surrounding him. Male and female voices filtered through the fog, and he heard that same voice again, closer this time.

"Help me get him up." Strong hands gripped him from either side and lifted him to his feet. He closed his eyes and willed his chest to relax, begging his lungs to draw just one deep breath, while at the same time wishing the darkness would swallow him and end the pain.

The men holding him upright slung his arms across their shoulders and nearly dragged him forward. Gritting his teeth, he opened his eyes to see concerned brown eyes focused on his face. It took him a long moment to realize who he was looking at.

"Baden?"

FIFTY-ONE

Leis and Alexander walked quietly around the side of the compound until they reached a path that led them up and away from the main structure. They followed it until they were looking down onto the roof of the building.

The hill dropped off sharply to their left, leaving a wide cleft in the rock between them and the mansion. The guard who was assigned to follow them kept pace a good distance behind and out of earshot if they kept their voices low.

The heather blue long sleeved t-shirt Alexander wore lay close to his thickly muscled torso and with the well fit khakis he looked even larger than he normally did. His fiery hair was gathered at his neck and the ends twisted against his shoulders in the light breeze. From the moment they stepped onto the worn path, he tucked his hands into his front pockets and avoided any contact with her. The wind carried his scent away, giving her no read on his emotions or thoughts.

Alexander finally spoke; his eyes focused on the horizon. "When I turned twenty, two years before my father died, my parents and I went to Res and made a deal." He ran a hand down his beard. "We agreed to allow the Clan to choose my bond mate in exchange for allowing me to live outside the Clan's rules until I was ready to settle down."

Leis stumbled and he reached out to catch her arm then pulled his hand back immediately. "Thank you." She breathed. "Why would you want that? And why would Res agree to it?"

Alexander slid his hands into his pockets. "My parents were demanding, but they loved me very much. I'm the youngest, a surprise baby actually." He blew out a breath. "To say I was spoiled would be putting it mildly." He shrugged. "But they also expected a lot from me academically and professionally."

"I did not live up to those expectations, and they thought giving me time and space to sort myself was the best choice." He turned his brilliant eyes toward her and the sunlight glittered across them. His face paled then turned as red as his hair. "I am not proud of those years, and knowing what I know now..." He trailed off, running a hand over his scalp. "Knowing what I know now, I realize I was looking for what I thought I could never have. I want what you and Koen have."

Stopping, she grasped his wrist and was startled when he flinched away from her. "Alexander..."

He cleared his throat and angled away. "Please, let me finish." He exhaled and seemed to gather his thoughts. "For most of us, touching the one we are not intended for is uncomfortable. Just enough to let us know we should keep our distance. It can simply be a lack of attraction, or it can cause an itchy feeling. For me, it is much more severe. I've never been able to touch a Vampir female without it causing me excruciating pain. " His gaze returned to hers. "When I got to college and found I could touch the human girls I met there..." His eyes glazed and he tipped his head to the sky. "I had no hope of ever attempting a bonding. So, I reasoned it would be a waste of time to guard my reputation with the Clan if I could never..." He looked down at her and shades of past anger simmered in his expression. "I grew to hate the females my parents brought home to meet me. Every handshake reminded me of what I couldn't have. I knew I would never be able to have a physical relationship with any of them. When I was twenty-one, I sent away the last one they chose for me without ever meeting her. I didn't care anymore. I was getting what I wanted in the only place I thought I would ever get it."

He shuddered and closed his eyes. "And it didn't matter to those at home. No one cared about a few human girls so long as I was still the Koch heir." His lip curled in disgust. "My parents thought it would be easier for me to eventually settle down if I were allowed this...behavior while I was young." He grunted. "But even though they pledged me to someone, I had no intention of stopping. How could I let them tie me to her? If I had, I would never have been able to touch her." His hands fisted inside his pockets. "Then one day, she ran away. I don't even know where to look for her. If I could, I would bring her back to her family and release her like Baden did you. But I've been so selfish...and every day the pain continues to get worse."

Tears felt cool against the heat of her skin, and when his eyes met hers she covered her mouth with the palm of a hand.

He smiled slightly at her and his stance softened. "And now I've met you." His hand drifted toward her again and then fell back at his side.

She found her voice. "I had no idea it was so strong, but I know you feel pain when you touch me. I can..." She paused and his eyes were so open, so honest, she decided to tell him the truth. "I smell the pain of it from you."

With a huff and a shake of his head he laughed lightly. "Why am I not surprised? You let Res keep believing you couldn't. Wise. She would have approached this challenge much differently if she'd known that." He gestured forward and led the way toward a wide, flat space ahead. "No. I can't touch you, but what you helped me realize is that it's by design." He waved a hand. "Obviously I have a stronger response than most of our kind." He grinned roguishly. "Apparently I need the pain, I just haven't been listening to what it was telling me." He sobered. "I may need the pain, but I can't let anyone else suffer. I have to find her."

They reached the clearing and stopped. "Why tell me this now?"

"I'm telling you because after talking to Emerick I realized my mate is out there somewhere. What if she hurts like this every time she touches anyone but me?" His voice roughened. "When Eric talked about you and Koen, how you met, the intensity of your relationship...Leisel, I realized I want that. I *need* that."

The wind caught and drifted his familiar citrus scent to her, and she stared at him. This couldn't be the same man she'd met only a few days ago. He was so changed, and though she was glad, it made no sense until the wind shifted.

Hope.

His hope washed over her, filling her senses as he continued. "I want you to know that I withdrew my challenge last night, and so will Stewart. We won't stand for what Res and the rest of *our* Clan have been doing. She's kept us in the dark for too long, and honestly, I'm ashamed none of us figured it out sooner. She convinced us all we were victims who needed to stay hidden, and at the same time fed into our arrogance and superiority. We've been brainwashed into believing we're better than everyone else." He shook his head. "The bravery you, Koen, and Emerick demonstrated coming here has forced us to see the truth."

The sobs started low in her stomach and before they could reach her throat, Alexander's hands were on her shoulders. She tilted her head to look up, and in his eyes and crisp scent she could read the division in him. He wanted to comfort her, but their contact was causing him severe pain. Covering her mouth with her hand again she meant to pull away, but his hands tightened.

"Some things are worth the pain." He pulled her closer. "I finally have hope it won't always be this way. Hope you gave me."

She rose to her toes and threw her arms around his neck.

"Thank you, Alexander." She held on until he trembled with pain, and she stepped away. His hands fell in fists so tight the knuckles turned white.

Seeing such a strong man in so much pain from a simple touch broke her heart. "I hope you meet her soon." She swiped the last of her tears away. "I believe she'll be a very lucky woman."

He glanced behind them toward the guard who was watching something across the ravine. "I may get my chance tonight."

Her head whipped up to stare at him. "Tonight? What do you mean?"

His cocky attitude slipped back over him, and she shook her head knowing it was as much a part of him as his brilliant eye color. "Well, it seems your Baden has come home. And he didn't come alone."

By the time Leis and Alexander returned to the compound, tables full of food and appetizers lined the wall just outside the patio doors. Clusters of people were already gathered beside the pool and had settled on the sofas and loungers that spread across the large stone terrace overlooking the valley below. There were far more people here than she had ever seen, and the staff looked overwhelmed. The usual guards were nowhere in sight.

Alexander escorted her into the house where more people milled around. The mansion was full, and Leis gaped. She caught sight of Koen's escorts standing near the door glowering as more people flowed inside.

Alexander ignored the commotion and followed her up the stairs. They paused outside her room.

"Stewart will accompany you to the celebration since Res is expecting him to claim you." He smirked. "Judging by the number of people we've seen, he, Emerick, and Ellen should be on the grounds now." He paused at several agitated voices around the corner, then continued when they moved the other direction. "Once everyone is in place, Baden, Koen, and I will join you. Baden and I will make sure no one interrupts you and Koen."

She gave a small cry and hastily reached inside the collar of her shirt. Untying the strap from the back of her neck, Leis removed

Koen's necklace. With tears stinging her eyes, she laid it in his large hand, careful not to touch him. "Please give this to Koen. He'll know what it means."

He slipped it into his pocket. "I will make sure he gets it as soon as I leave you." His smile was rueful. "One day I hope to make someone as happy as he obviously makes you." Alexander backed away and bowed at the waist. "*Auf Wiedersehen*, Miss Gottschalk."

FIFTY-TWO

KOEN

K oen was vaguely aware of voices surrounding him. It sounded like absolute chaos. No one stopped them but he thought he heard Baden comment that they didn't have much time to get out of sight.

"What *happened?*" Eric and Ellen exclaimed together as Koen was maneuvered into Stewart's room.

Stewart swore and helped them settle his heaving body onto the mattress. Koen immediately rolled onto his side in an effort to ease his breathing. He forced his eyes open and saw Baden nod his thanks to someone as they left the room. The noise diminished and he picked out Ellen's soft voice as she knelt next to him.

He was sweating and though his breathing deepened at Ellen's quietly spoken words, he still struggled. "Where is your inhaler?"

"They took it." He whispered. He forced himself to focus on the people around him and saw Baden standing with his hands clasped behind his head.

"We found him collapsed on the driveway." Baden said. "Good thing I expected this." Dropping his hands, he tossed an inhaler to

Ellen, then looked sideways at Stewart. "Do you know what happened?"

"No." He shook his head. "I've been off the grounds all day. Maybe Alexander..."

Koen snarled. His voice was harsh both from his lack of breath and anger. "Alexander kissed her!" Pushing himself to sit on the edge of the bed, Koen took a puff of the precious inhaler, then braced his hands on his knees, fighting for enough breath to speak. His words rasped. "I will kill him."

Baden stared. "Are you sure you saw him kiss her?"

"That's not possible." All eyes turned to where Eric lowered himself into the chair next to the bed. Clearly weary, his hand rested on Ellen's back while she crouched in front of Koen. Eric opened his mouth, but Alexander's low voice snapped their attention toward the door.

His large frame filled the room and his voice was flat. "I think I can clear things up."

Alexander started to cross the room toward Koen, but Baden stepped between them, stopping him before he reached the bed. The tall man straightened, his face expressionless.

"Let's hear it." Baden leveled his stare and waited.

Alexander spoke directly to Koen. "I formally withdrew my challenge last night after the conversation Stewart and I had with Emerick. And for the record, Emerick is right, I *cannot* kiss your Leisel, or any other Vampir female. I would guess you saw us on the trail?" When Koen nodded Alexander's face tightened. "Jumping to conclusions about people is dangerous, my friend. What did you think I meant when I called her yours this morning?" Ignoring Baden, he took another step forward and pulled something from his pocket, extending it to Koen. "Leisel asked me to give this to you. She said you would know what it meant."

Baden stepped aside as Koen took the necklace from Alexander. Koen's shoulders immediately relaxed, and he drew a deep ragged breath.

"As long as my heart beats," he whispered and met Ellen's brightly smiling eyes. "He's telling the truth?"

"He is." She patted his knee and rose to stand behind Eric. "But Stewart is hiding something."

FIFTY-THREE

Leis took a quick shower and swiftly braided her hair down her back. Her hands shook with anticipation as she dressed in a salmon pencil skirt and carefully tucked in a creamy lace blouse. Grinning with excitement, she buckled on the matching wide strapped suede sandals Koen insisted she buy.

She smoothed the skirt over her thighs and glanced in the mirror, pleased by what the shoes did for her short legs and couldn't wait to see Koen's face when he saw them.

She hurried across the room and opened the door when someone knocked. Outside her door, Stewart was staring away down the hall.

"Ready to go?" he asked distractedly, then turned toward her and froze.

The hands that were nervously raking through his hair fell slowly. Stewart swallowed hard as his eyes slid down her body and back to her face. His blond hair was bright against the dark navy suit coat and the white v-neck shirt made his hazel eyes dark.

"You look beautiful," he breathed, and she blushed.

"Thank you." His earthy scent greeted her with his usual friendliness, but she paused at a ripple of emotion in him she couldn't identify. Writing it off as nerves, she cleared her throat and stepped into the hallway, laughing at his stunned expression.

"You all right?" She poked him in the shoulder.

Stewart shook his head. "Yeah. I'm good." His eyes grazed over her again before he turned and offered her his arm. "I think everyone is waiting for us."

Nervousness rushed from him, and she took the arm he offered, thinking about how much it must have hurt Alexander all the times she had done the same with him.

Stewart grew tenser the closer they got to the stairs, and whatever he was trying to hide pushed at her.

"Stewart, what's going on?" He covered her hand with his and drew her down the stairs without answering.

With every step, her stomach clenched in dread, and by the time they reached the bottom his warm friendly scent had dissolved into a throat stinging anger. His grip tightened viciously on her hand when she tried to pull away and she yelped in pain.

"Stewart! Let go, you're hurting me!" She hissed.

He loosened his grip just enough to ease the pain but didn't let go. He leaned over to speak into her ear.

"I'm sorry, Leis." Her head twisted to look him in the eye and his gaze fell to her lips, his breath hot on her face. "After hearing what Eric had to say, I truly thought I could give you up." Stewart's jaw tensed as his discomfort rode through both of them. He guided them toward the patio doors. "But I've changed my mind. You, Leis, are too stunning to let get away."

Her heart banged painfully against her chest as the murmurs and muffled laughter from the crowd outside grew louder. The buzzing of her skin increased where they touched, and she knew he felt it too.

"This will never work, Stewart. Koen is the only one for me. You'll hurt both of us if you force this. Please let me go!" She leaned away from him, then caught sight of Res approaching the sliding glass doors with a triumphant smile.

Looking every bit the hostess of the party in a crisply tailored grey pant suit and silver pumps, a large onyx stone lay against her chest in the deep v of the jacket and her long silvery hair was swept into a clip at the nape of her neck.

She laid a hand on the door and turned to address the crowd behind her. Everyone backed up to form an arc of bodies around the perimeter of the patio. Leis's stomach churned as the people gathered outside then turned their attention to her and Stewart.

Leis recognized many of her parents' friends and several of the elder Clan members before returning terrified eyes to Res. Satisfied, the woman slid the glass silently aside.

With a wide gesture and her steely brown eyes locked on Leis's, Res welcomed the two of them onto the patio. "Mr. Fertig and Miss Gottschalk have news."

Unable to do anything else, Leis let Stewart lead her past the grinning Res and into the early evening air. The back of her throat was burning and staying this close to Stewart was becoming increasingly uncomfortable.

The discomfort should have been enough to warn him away, and Leis struggled to understand the sudden change in him. She could smell his pain increasing, but he refused to let her go.

Her eyes flew through the rows of familiar faces. Smiles slipped when they saw the fear in her eyes. Some looked on in sympathy, but most were growing concerned. Gulping a breath, she tried one more time to disengage her arm from Stewart's. Res came up behind them and with a hand on each of their shoulders, locked them in place. The crowd was quiet as all eyes settled on the three of them.

"There has been an attempt to interrupt our festivities tonight, but I assure you, nothing can stop me from presenting our newest pledged couple." Res leaned forward and whispered in Leis's ear. "You will bow, my dear. No one defies me."

Before anyone could react, a familiar voice caused all their heads to turn in confusion. The voice sounded exactly like Res's.

"Res. It's time to end this." Ellen stepped out from behind one of the large, stuccoed pillars with Eric on one side and Baden on the other. Baden's eyes burned with outrage and hope leapt in Leis's heart.

Res's hand tightened on her shoulder, and she laughed in Leis's ear as she straightened.

"My dear sister and her traitorous mate, Emerick. Together again." She pushed Leis and Stewart until they were all directly in front of the other trio. Res sneered, "When he came back here dragging Leis and that human they picked up along the way, I figured he abandoned you just like he did me."

Murmurs swirled from the crowd, and Baden stepped forward. His voice was clear and strong as his dangerous glare moved from Stewart to the woman behind them. "Grandmother, what you tried to do to Leis and I — "

Res cut him off, her nails digging painfully into Leis's shoulder. "What? Give you a future together? A family?"

"By forcing me into a bonding with my uncle's daughter after killing your own granddaughter to cover it up?" Baden responded angrily. The crowd gasped. "Leis's father is my uncle. My *murdered* father's twin brother, which I believe, makes Leis and I practically siblings." He kept his gaze on Res but angled his head toward the shocked onlookers. "Guess you hadn't told them that, had you?"

"Your parent's death was a horrible accident that led to a mistake which has now been corrected." She released her grip on Stewart and stepped around Leis. "I am truly sorry for what happened, but as you can see, the Clan has released *you*, and suitably matched Leis."

Questions were shouted from every corner of the crowd, and Leis suddenly realized she didn't recognize any of the men and women surrounding them.

"How could you not know they were related?"

"What does the female want?"

"Murder? Who's responsible for that?"

Res whirled toward those questioning her. "You are too young to understand such decisions!" She pointed toward Eric and Ellen, who moved closer. "Their betrayal is proof! Without the Clan Elder enforcing the rules..."

"Whose rules, Res?" Eric raised his voice just enough to interrupt and pull everyone's attention back to him. "The ones your parents worked so hard to write to *protect* us, or the ones you twisted to rule with?"

"Don't talk to me about what my parents wanted! You brought division to us all when you decided you could do whatever you wanted, with whomever you wanted." She stepped toward Ellen, shaking off Samuel as he tried to hold her back. "You never cared about our parents!"

Toe-to-toe the sisters glared at one another, looking so alike aside from their clothing, it was as if each were glaring at their own reflection in a mirror. Leis couldn't believe she missed the resemblance.

"What Eric and I did to you was wrong. We were young and made a choice that hurt you terribly." Ellen pulled her shoulders back, hurt and tears in her eyes. Eric rested his hand on Ellen's shoulder, and she covered it with hers. Her voice lowered. "We are very sorry for what we did, but that is no reason to punish everyone else."

"Crescentia...Res..." Eric spoke imploringly, begging her to see reason. "You know what you are doing here has to stop. Our people are dying." He gestured to the waiting crowd. "Re-uniting the Vampir Clans is our only hope. Stop this nonsense."

Res's hand covered the red imprint on her cheek. Thoroughly enraged, she squared her shoulders, her words shrill. "Look at the chaos you've brought to my house! This proves I did the right thing by leaving the rest of you behind. I will not allow *our* children to run rampant without proper guidance. If you wish to live like animals and let your instincts rule your intellect, then that is your choice, but you will have no say so in what happens here!" She pointed to the ground. "This is *my* Clan! Who are any of you to think you can *stop me?*"

FIFTY-FOUR

KOEN

Eric shook his head, a sad huff escaping him as Res realized her mistake too late. Her eyes flew wide as the crowd froze then erupted in shouts from young and old alike.

"Your Clan?"

"The Clan doesn't belong to you!"

"Who do you think you are?"

As the crowd pushed closer, Stewart pulled Leis backwards and around one of the wide pillars. She thought he was moving her out of the way, and it wasn't until he turned to push her against a hard concrete surface that she focused on him.

"Stewart, it's over. Let me go." She planted her palms against his shoulders and pushed, but he was stronger. The hazel eyes that had once been so friendly were hard and possessive with violence shining clearly just under the surface of his control. She shoved at him. "What is wrong with you?"

Stewart's voice was deep and harsh. "Years ago, I wanted to meet you, but Res wouldn't allow it because you were pledged to her precious grandson, *Baden*." Leis shuddered as anger and lust quickened his breathing and soured the air around them. "When he ran away, instead of choosing *me*, the one she knew wanted you, she called her pet. Koch."

He spat the name and pressed closer, slipping a knee between her thighs. He shoved her hands off his chest as his hips slammed into hers, pinning her lower back painfully against the rough stucco.

"I hate what Res has been doing as much as anyone, but it still should have been you and me all along." He caught her hands and held them down, leaning in to kiss her neck. She tried to twist away, but his lips grazed up her skin until they met her chin. "I've wanted you for years, Leis."

"Stop it!" She bucked against him, but his muscled body pressed her harder against the pillar. As she struggled, the rough texture of the stucco tore into her back, and she cried out in pain.

Releasing one hand, Stewart gripped her chin and forced her to face him. She tried to whip her head away, but his fingers tightened like a vice on her jaw. She grabbed his wrist and tried to pull it away, but he held her still as his lips lowered toward hers.

"You are mine, Leis. I claim you."

Stewart's moist breath and bitter scent made her gag as panic seized her chest. Bile rose in her throat as his upper lip touched hers, then she tumbled sideways as the weight of him suddenly disappeared with the sickening sound of a fist meeting flesh.

Strong arms wrapped around her as she stumbled but her momentum carried them to the ground. Leis pushed away from the one holding her until she registered who it was.

Gripping the slick black fabric of his shirt, her eyes began to focus. Beneath her hands were wide shoulders that rose and fell rapidly, and her eyes trailed up the buttons of a dark grey vest until her gaze landed on a familiar pendant resting in the smooth hollow of a tanned throat.

Warm hands smoothed back the hair torn from her braid during the struggle, and Koen's raspy voice repeated her name. "Leis! Leis, are you all right?"

Koen's eyes searched hers, concern turning them an even deeper blue. His thumbs swept across her cheeks as a whimper escaped her lips. He pulled her tight against his chest whispering in her hair. "Please tell me you're all right."

Sobs tore from her, and she shook her head. He ran his hands down her back, and she winced in pain when his palms crossed the scrapes and bruises from her shoulder blades down to her lower back. When he looked over her shoulder and saw the torn and bloody fabric his body went still with anger. Koen gently slid his hands to her sides.

"Can you stand?" Unable to speak through the sobs, she nodded.

Koen tenderly lifted her away from him so they could stand, a growl of anger rising from his chest. They leveraged off the stone floor of the patio, and he pulled her close to his side. Her knee ached from the fall and her back was on fire. Another soft cry escaped when she tried to straighten and the skin of her back pulled. Shaking too badly to walk, she tugged him back when he tried to lead her away. Koen dragged a chair over so she could sit.

He dropped to his haunches in front of her and swept the tangled hair away from her tear-stained face.

The tight black shirt stretched around his biceps and the deep v of the shirt exposed the skin of his upper chest lightly coated with sweat. The heart pendant rose and fell with his breaths, and in fascination, she watched the rapid beat of his heart in the veins of his throat. He urged her to look up and his concerned eyes probed hers as his rich scent soothed her.

"Talk to me."

"Koen," she whispered, "I love you."

His face collapsed as the worry ran out of him, and his head fell to her lap. He pressed his face into the fabric of her skirt. Her hands slipped into the soft curls of his dark hair as his shoulders quaked with what she thought were quiet sobs. They sat that way for a few moments, and when he finally lifted his eyes to hers they glittered with tears. He touched the pendant at his neck.

"Did you mean it when you gave this back?" His voice was coarse and low.

"Of course I mean it. Why would you think I wouldn't?"

He exhaled slowly. "I saw you and Alexander on the trail this morning." His eyes drilled into hers, their blue suddenly stormy. "Did you kiss him?"

"No! Never." She knew he would hear the truth in her voice and already she could see him relaxing. "He was telling me he had withdrawn his challenge." Her voice cracked, remembering Alexander's painful confession. "I love and want *you*. You have to know that."

He closed his eyes, the skin under his dark lashes almost blue. For the first time, she realized he was struggling to breathe. Before she could ask if he was all right, his eyes opened, and she gasped. The gold around his pupil sparked like amber shards of glass.

"I love you, Leis. Tonight, you will be mine." There was no room for argument. "No one will ever keep us apart again."

CHAPTER

FIFTY-FIVE

LEISEL

S houts broke into the quiet moment and pulled their attention back to the group surrounding the patio. Koen took Leis's hand and helped her painfully to her feet. He supported her as they rounded the pillar to see Baden being forcibly restrained by Alexander. A circle of people five or six deep surrounded them. She and Koen stepped into a clear space slightly to the left of the commotion.

Baden's shout cut through the rising clamor. "Let go!" His soft-spoken voice was rough and angry. "I'm done."

He shook them off and straightened his shirt, lifting the back of a hand to his bleeding lip. One shirt sleeve was neatly rolled up while the other hung loosely over his wrist, his dark brown hair was sticking up wildly.

On the ground in front of him, Stewart bent on one knee shrugging his jacket in place. Blood dripped from his nose and onto his white shirt. Alexander stood between the two of them, his arm partially raised toward Baden while he watched Stewart climb to his feet.

Ellen offered Stewart a towel and murmured something to him.

His eyes slid from her and Eric to glare at Baden, before catching sight of Leis leaning against Koen. Stewart's shoulders sank and his eyes fell to the ground. Ellen reached out to touch his arm, but he shook her off and turned to push through the crowd, into the house, and out of sight.

Alexander dropped his hand as Baden spotted Leis and cursed. He crossed quickly to her, her father and Andrew right behind him. Baden reached for her, worry creasing his handsome face. "Leis! Are you all right?"

She glanced up at Koen. With a nod he removed his arm, and she embraced Baden.

"I'm okay." She pressed her face into Baden's shoulder, and he tensed when she couldn't stop the whimper as his arms went around her back.

Her father and Baden turned her to get a look at her battered shoulders, swearing at the same time. Koen recaptured her hands as her family gathered around. Relief, anger, and doubt swirled in his eyes.

Carol touched Koen's arm. "Let us take her inside."

He gripped her tighter and shook his head. "I'm not letting her go."

A deep chuckle followed his statement, and Leis looked up in shock to see both her brothers standing beside her father. Seeing Andrew and Baden together was natural, but their older brother, Josh, had left the Vampir years ago.

"Josh! How are you here?" Still clutching tightly to one of Koen's hands, she reached out for him.

He took her hand and leaned in for a careful hug. Brushing a hand down the back of her head he smiled. "It's a long story, Red. There's time to explain later."

She shook tears from her eyes. "Where is Mom? Is she here?" It would take time to forgive her mother, but Leis wanted to try.

Her father reached back and drew her mother forward. When their eyes met, her mother's jaw tightened. Disappointment crashed in on Leis when she saw the defiance still in her face. Leis bit her lip against the angry tears as her mother spoke bitterly.

"You have a lot of explaining to do, Leis." Leis stared at her mother in astonishment. "All of you are spoiled little brats! We gave you everything. You've cost us everything!" Her father pulled her away before she could say anything else.

Carol was the first to speak. "She'll come around, Leis."

A gentle hand rested on her shoulder, and she looked up into the eyes of Josh's wife, Gina. "She's still angry with Josh and I for letting her believe I'm a human." Her eyes were bright with amusement as Leis's jaw fell open.

Josh kissed her cheek. "Let your sisters get you cleaned up." He pointed to Koen who was anxiously watching the family. "He'll be waiting for you when you come back down, and we can explain everything." He grinned. "Well, maybe we'll explain after..."

Her sisters-in-law's pushed everyone aside and guided Leis inside.

She glanced back as the glass door slid closed behind the three of them. She watched Josh extend his hand to Koen. He clasped Josh's hand, looked up at her, smiled slowly and winked. Despite the ache in her back, a rush of heat coursed through her.

His flirtatious grin earned him a slap on the back from Baden and all the men laughed at something he said.

Carol shook her head. "Come on, Leis. I'm sure you don't want to keep him waiting."

She blushed and followed her sisters-in-law up the stairs, a sudden thought causing her to stumble. *If* his *family isn't here, how will we get their approval for the Pledge?*

FIFTY-SIX

KOEN

J osh was still shaking Koen's hand when Baden slapped him on the back. "Snap out of it, Lockton." He laughed. "She'll be back."

"Thank you," he said humbly. The effects of being without his inhaler were fading and though the adrenaline of the last few minutes gave him a burst of strength, Koen needed to sit. He knew he would recover, and if what he suspected was true, after tonight he wouldn't need the inhaler ever again.

Baden clasped him on the shoulder. "Let's talk."

Koen searched the crowd, but Res and Samuel were nowhere to be seen. The five of them sat on two wide outdoor couches flanked by matching chairs. "Where is Res?" Koen asked.

Alexander smoothed his tie and crossed an ankle over his knee. Pulling his pant leg straight, he nodded toward the front of the house.

"Some of the elders have escorted her off the premises." He glanced at Baden. "With the information Baden has, Emerick and Ellen will help us reorganize. It's a complicated mess right now, but I suspect after tonight we'll have enough support to untangle it all."

Baden leaned forward as he re-rolled his shirt sleeves, the blood smeared towel in one hand. "I'll be helping them develop software that will enable all the Vampir to keep in touch." He folded the towel over his thigh and leaned on his elbows on his knees to look around at the crowd. "We'll also be planning regular gatherings like this in different locations to give everyone an opportunity to meet." He looked at Alexander. "Hopefully allowing those, like Alexander, who have not found their intended the chance to."

Alexander inclined his head and swept his eyes across the crowd. "I look forward to it."

Koen shifted nervously next to Baden, unsure what to say. Josh and Andrew were seated across from him and looked at each other. The younger brother cleared his throat.

"We know Eric accepted your claim for Leis, but the laws state it must be the next of kin who accepts. We know what he was trying to do, and we give the two of you credit for waiting. That couldn't have been easy." Andrew's eyes were unreadable. "However, you should know our parents won't acknowledge it." Frustration boiled inside Koen, but calmed when Andrew continued. "But they didn't refuse it either."

Josh nodded and Koen's stare swung to him. "Eric and Ellen have kept me up to date on what's happened over the last few months." Koen noticed his eyes were the same shade of green as Leis's though his hair was light brown, almost blond. His gaze never wavered. "Leis is my baby sister, and as long as she's happy, I'm happy. From what I've seen and heard, you make her happy, Koen."

Andrew nodded in agreement. "We're still trying to wrap our minds around how Res managed to keep us from finding out about you and the others." He gestured around the patio. "But there is no denying this, and there's no denying you and Leis are meant for one another."

Josh relaxed. "As her oldest living brother, I am willing to accept your claim, once we have confirmation from your family."

Koen fell against the cushions, trying not to let disappointment crush him. He looked at Baden. "Are we able to make calls now? I haven't exactly been able to talk to them since we left Ohio."

"No phones yet. Kinda makes a person wish we still had land-lines, doesn't it?" Baden grinned. "But Ellen and I made a little pit stop on the way here." He reached beside him for the messenger bag Koen hadn't noticed and withdrew a laptop. "I would have had service restored tonight, but this morning Res managed to figure out how we were communicating and crashed every piece of software in the place." He opened the lid and pulled out two envelopes. "It's going to take me a couple days to rebuild the network, and we'll all need new phones and computers. The virus she used corrupted any hardware linked to it." He shook his head, holding the papers out to Koen. "She's *almost* as thorough as I am."

Koen took the envelopes Baden offered him. "What's this?"

Baden set his useless computer aside. "Open them and find out."

Koen recognized his father's handwriting on one of the envelopes and his mother's on the other. Biting back the burning in his throat and trying to focus through the stinging in his eyes, he carefully tore open the heavier of the two. It was from his mother.

When he pulled the folded pages out, several pictures floated to the ground. He heard the other men rise as he bent over to pick up the photographs. Alexander caught one as the wind flipped it just out of reach.

Handing it to Koen, he said, "We'll give you some privacy." Then he followed the other four as they stepped away.

Hot tears fell down his cheeks as Koen read her short note.

My Dearest Koen,

I know you haven't been able to contact us, and I miss you. Mr. Dietrich and Mrs. Tate let us know you and Leis are safe and will soon be bonded.

Your father and I are so very proud of you,

and we can't wait for you and your mate to come home and meet your sister.

Her name is Johanna Elaine Lockton. We call her Anna.

With all our love,
Mom

THE PICTURES DREW a ragged exhale from him, and he held them carefully in his shaking fingers. The first was his only sister wrapped in soft white blankets, her tiny hands clasped in fists under her chin. Dark hair covered her head, and her full cheeks were almost as pink as her pouted lips. The other was of all three of them. His father cradling his mother's shoulders as he placed a gentle kiss on Anna's head.

Choking up, he looked to the sky and did his best to wrestle his emotions under control. Running a hand down his face, he carefully folded his mother's note and slipped it and the pictures back into the envelope, reaching for the other.

Tearing it open, he smiled at his father's sharply slanted handwriting. As he quickly read the brief letter, typical of his father, it was direct and to the point.

Koen,

I'm proud of you. We would be there if we could, but with Anna's birth and my illness, the distance is too much for your mother and me.

I always believed you would one day find her. Without reservation, I give you my consent.

Make her yours, Son. We can't wait to
meet her.
    Joseph Mikal Lockton

RELIEF FLOODED THROUGH HIM, and Koen sat for a moment letting it all sink in.

For the past week and a half, he felt like he was on a runaway roller coaster. Gripping the letter from his father in both hands, he rested his elbows on his knees and pushed his fisted knuckles against his eyes, completely overwhelmed with emotion. Lost in his thoughts, he jumped when a hand lightly touched his back.

Ellen's comforting smile greeted him when he looked up. "Are you ready?" Though she was outwardly as calm as ever, her brown eyes danced with excitement.

With the heel of one hand, he scrubbed the moisture from his cheeks and shook his head. "I still can't believe you knew all along. I can't believe I never knew what you were."

Ellen's laugh was light. "I think you did, you just couldn't recognize what was right in front of you until you met her." Ellen ticked her head toward the patio doors where Leis's sisters-in-law stood expectantly.

Koen felt his heart stop and then beat wildly when his eyes slid past them and landed on the beautiful woman behind them. He slowly rose to his feet as his eyes caressed every inch of her.

Leis's luxurious hair was loose and the sky-blue blouse she wore made the soft waves look like a net of fire around her shoulders. The early evening sunlight glinted across the windows, highlighting her silhouette and his gaze slid lower to her tiny waist and the curve of her hips. White pants were tucked into tall grey platform boots that hugged her slim legs, and with every step she took he felt the heat he suppressed for so long building low in his stomach.

When his eyes rose to hers, her cheeks flushed as red as her hair. He pulled his waistcoat straight and ran a hand through his hair, never taking his eyes off Leis as she walked toward them.

"You're right, Ellen." A smile he couldn't stop spread across his face and he exhaled. "Meeting her changed everything."

Leis shook with nerves as she crossed the wide, tan marble floor of the dining area and approached the patio where Koen and the rest waited. Her sisters-in-law had carefully washed and treated her back. She had one long scrape across her shoulder blade that needed a bandage, but the rest were shallow scratches that had hardly broken the skin. Excitement and anxiety made her skin flush, and Leis twisted her hands together.

Carol walked beside her. "Are you ready for this, Leis?"

"Yes." She laughed. "And no."

Carol reached for the patio door with a grin. "I have no doubt he's just as nervous, but you'll both figure it out pretty quickly."

Leis looked up and saw him.

Koen.

Her breath caught at the sight. He was talking to Ellen and emotions she couldn't begin to decipher were smeared across his beautiful features. The door opened and Ellen's head moved in her direction. With his strong arms still folded over his knees, Koen's eyes drifted toward her.

Their gazes collided and the sound of the voices around her were drowned out by the rush of blood in her ears. As they continued to stare at each other, he stood, and the breath whooshed out of her lungs as her stomach clenched. He was staring at her with a look so intense she blushed in embarrassment. His black hair ruffled softly in the breeze and his high cheekbones flushed with red. Koen's bright eyes were luminous as they swept down her body, and she let herself do the same to him.

His hand gripped the bottom of his vest and pulled it straight, rippling the cords of muscle in his forearm. A familiar rush flowed through her stomach as his toned bicep flexed when he ran a hand through his hair. The black shirt had a slight sheen to it and accented the defined muscles of his chest and shoulders while the snug vest lay smoothly across his flat abs. He dropped his hands to his sides and tucked the fingers of one hand into the pocket of his pants as he watched her walk toward him.

Lowering her chin, she looked up at him through her lashes, and his blue eyes continued to burn into with a heat she could feel in her bones.

Ellen touched him on the shoulder as she passed, and then Leis was just a few feet from him. For a moment they stood, neither willing to break the silence, until Koen stretched out a hand. Quaking a little, she slid her hand into his and they both exhaled at the contact.

"You look so beautiful, Leis." His brow furrowed and he shook his head. "I don't even know what to say."

She squeezed his hand, relishing the way his palm felt so good against hers. "I love you, Koen."

He exhaled in a puff and pulled her to him, enfolding her in his arms. One strong arm crossed her shoulder; his hand splayed around her ribs. He buried the other in her hair and cupped the nape of her neck. She sank against his chest in relief and wrapped her arms around his waist, her hands bunching in the fabric of his vest.

"I love you, too, Leis." His lips pressed against her hair as a throat cleared behind her.

"Are you ready to make this thing official?" Koen rubbed his cheek against the top of her head and released her enough to allow her to turn and face Eric. He was smiling widely at them both.

"I've never been more ready for anything in my life." Leis let Koen pull her against him, his chest firm against her shoulders, his arm around her waist. She shivered when his deep voice resonated through her body. Her knees nearly gave out when Koen's lips grazed her ear. "And you?"

She leaned her head back to look up at Koen. "I'm ready." Her brow creased, almost afraid to ask, "But what about your parents?"

"All taken care of." He pulled a letter from the pocket of his vest and handed it to Eric with a flourish. "A letter from my father giving his approval." His playful eyes met hers. "No getting out of it now, Miss Gottschalk." Koen tightened both arms around her. "You. Are. Mine."

She crossed her arms over his and laughed with relief while Eric turned to lead the way to the center of the patio.

"Let's get the formalities out of the way." He winked. "Then you're on your own, kids."

FIFTY-EIGHT

KOEN

Unwilling to let her go for even a second, Koen tucked her arm into his and wove their fingers together. They followed Eric to the patio doors where Ellen, Josh and Gina waited for them. The rest of the crowd milled around the edges of the patio, watching and talking quietly.

Eric cleared his throat, and all eyes turned to them. Leis stepped closer, clamping her hand on his arm like a vice.

He chuckled and whispered in her ear. "Nervous?"

She shivered, then looked up at him as Eric began to speak. "You're not?"

He raised an eyebrow and gave her hand a quick squeeze before tuning into what Eric was saying.

"Today starts a new chapter in the history of our people." Everyone quieted and even the shuffling of feet stilled. "We've been divided by hurt and fear for nearly two centuries now, and it is up to you to move past the mistakes of your elders and unite our people once again." Ellen laid a hand on his back, and he lifted an arm to wrap it around her shoulders. "It's fitting that tonight not only do we celebrate having representatives from as many of the world's Vampir as possible, but we will celebrate the bonding that helped bring about the reunion of our people."

Eric laid a hand on Koen's shoulder. "Koen Joseph Lockton, with the letter I hold in my hand, it is my privilege to validate the Blood Pledge between you and your bond mate, Leisel Rene Gottschalk." He nodded to Josh who stepped forward. Mummers drifted toward them from those watching.

"And, as Leis's oldest brother, I accept the validation and release her to his care." Josh tilted his head at Koen with a challenging smile. "Do you have the traditional gift for your mate?"

Koen's heart skipped as he realized he'd forgotten this part. He had no way to get her anything, much less a crib. He turned to look down at Leis, his face reddening. "I don't."

She was shaking her head, clearly about to tell him it wasn't necessary, when Baden called out, "Actually, Lockton, you do."

To their right the crowd parted. Baden and Andrew came forward carrying a crib partially covered with a large quilt. The quilt was made of alternating squares of pink and blue stitched together with a wide white ribbon. A silver envelope was pinned to the top.

Leis trembled against Koen's arm as she began to cry. She extracted herself from him and took a step toward Baden and the intricate piece they were carrying.

Koen himself had only seen this crib once, carefully stored and preserved in the basement of his parents' house. His father had shown it to him the same day he gave Koen the heart pendant. On each end was a carved medallion with an L in the center, but the highly detailed carvings surrounding them were very different.

Glancing at Andrew and Baden in awe, Koen tucked Leis under his arm and ran a hand down the rail closest to them. The wood under his palm looked like the flames of a dragon's breath shooting from one end of the crib to the other. The end they originated from was decorated with a tall castle behind the medallion, a large heavily scaled dragon appearing to fly between them. Its tail curled over itself to rest along the ground near intricately carved taloned feet. The dragon's head and neck were outstretched toward the top rail, a stream of fire belching from a wide toothy mouth.

As they walked around, the other end was just as detailed as the same castle, this time covered with fluttering banners and vines full of delicate flowers and sweeping leaves. The vines wrapped around the medallion and curled around the L in gentle swirls. He watched as Leis reached out to run her fingers along the rail that looked like a row of flowers of all shapes and sizes, stitched together.

Attached to the blanket that had always been folded along the end of his parent's bed, Koen's mother had written both their names on the envelope in her flowing script. With a wide-eyed glance, Leis reached out, unpinned the envelope, and handed it to him.

He swallowed against the burning in his throat. Leis slipped an arm around his waist as he pulled open the flap and withdrew the note. He held it out so they could both read it.

> Your father and I want you and your Leisel to have these. This crib was hand carved by your grandfather and given to your grandmother on the day of their mating and she made the blanket the day you were born. They always believed you would one day find your mate. They would be as proud of you as we are.
>
> May your daughters be as beautiful as Leisel and your sons live long lives as protectors and providers for the generations to come.

Koen looked up to meet Baden's eyes. He handed the note to Leis before reaching out a hand to the other male. "Thank you, Dietrich. We wouldn't be here if it weren't for you." Koen shook his hand firmly. "I can't thank you enough for all you've done for us and for the way you took care of Leis all those years. She's lucky to have you as a friend. If there's ever anything you need, let me know."

FIFTY-NINE

LEISEL

Seeing the two men who meant most to her standing together in friendship sent more tears to Leis's already burning eyes. Leis stepped away from Koen to embrace the boy she had spent her whole life with. Baden would always be her best friend.

"Thank you, B. I'll always love you." She kissed his cheek, then reached again for Koen. "Your intended will be a very lucky woman."

Baden blushed and cleared his throat as a huge smile spread across his face. "I'm the lucky one." He lifted a shoulder. "Her name is Dani. I hope you get to meet her sooner than later."

Leis's hand covered her mouth, and she held back a very girlish squeal as Baden reddened further.

"We can talk about me later. Today is your day." His amused brown eyes moved from her to Koen and darkened slightly. "Take care of her, Lockton."

Koen dragged her back to him again. "Always." His deep voice rumbled against her ribs. The rich and faintly sweet smell she had come to love intensified around her. "I'm ready if you are."

Searching his eyes she whispered, "I'm ready to be yours, Koen."

His chin lowered with a slow and determined inhale, and he

turned, leading her toward the patio doors where Eric and Ellen stood. Leis could smell the nervousness rolling off Koen as he stopped in front of them.

His voice was low and soft. "Is there anything else we need to do?"

Eric jerked his head toward the inside of the house. "Go on. You've waited long enough."

Leis glanced out at the smiling crowd and caught Alexander's eye. He was again dressed to the nines, his broad shoulders and ginger hair standing above most of those around him. He inclined his head then turned to mingle with the others.

Koen's hand moved to the small of her back making her stomach flip as he guided her through the doors and across the marble floors toward the stairs.

She heard the glass doors slide shut, silencing the sound of the party that would continue without them. In a few short strides, they were on the landing.

Nervousness heightened her already hyper aware senses and she could not only smell the intensity of his expectancy, but it tingled against her skin, doing strange things to her heartbeat. By the time they reached the door to her room, she was shaking with anticipation and tension.

Koen leaned a shoulder into the frame and waited for her to enter first. As she stepped past, her hand trailed across the satiny fabric laying close to his stomach and he sucked in a breath. He captured her hand as he took one last look down the empty hallway then pulled the door closed behind them.

Her nervousness tipped further into a fear she couldn't explain, and thankfully Koen picked up on her need for a moment to catch her breath. With a brush of his hand down her hair, he crossed the room to pull the sheer curtains closed.

After pulling the light fabric over the windows, and keeping his back to her, he tucked his hands into his front pockets and turned his head sideways, revealing his sharp profile. While she wrestled with her nervousness, she watched his shoulders rise and fall with each breath.

Leis leaned back against the door as his hands left his pockets to unbutton the vest and slip it off his shoulders. Folding it neatly, he laid it across the chair next to him and slowly pulled his shirt untucked. Her knees went weak as his tugs revealed a sliver of skin before the fabric lowered over the slim line of his brown leather belt. She'd dreaded this moment most of her life, but watching Koen remove even one piece of clothing changed everything.

He didn't turn as he unbuttoned his shirt. She looked in the direction he faced and locked eyes with him in the mirror above her dresser. Raw want raged across his face and the intensity of his need burned in his eyes.

Her head fell against the door with a thunk as all the air seemed to be sucked out of the room. When he turned to face her and slowly unbuckled his belt to slide it loose from his hips, she pressed a hand against her chest in an effort to keep her heart inside.

Rolling it around his hand and setting in on the dresser as he passed it, his blue eyes glowed as he stalked toward her. Every muscle in his body tensed as Koen slid his shirt off. He tossed the shirt aside with a flick of his wrist as his steps slowed and his dancing eyes dared her to get her fill of him. Her fingers curled, itching to feel his skin under her hands.

In the swirl of air his movements created, she inhaled and tasted the sweetness of his desire. Breathlessly, she let her eyes travel down the chiseled lines of his torso. His shoulders were pinched together slightly, the fibers of the muscle taunt and clearly defined under the sun kissed skin. His breathing was ragged and with each breath his chest contracted, causing the lines of his abs to ripple as though each exhale caused him pain. Her eyes landed on the v of his hips where they disappeared into the top of his jeans and any rational thoughts she had vanished.

He reached her and deliberately placed his palms on either side of her head, leaning forward onto his elbows. His biceps framed her ears and caged her firmly against the wooden door.

Rich and warm, the distinct smell of him washed over her like the heavy air after a summer rain.

He leaned in closer, and she shivered as the ache in her upper jaw intensified. His pupils nearly disappeared as his eyes darkened to black with desire. Pain spiked in her cheekbones and her lips parted in anticipation.

Her fangs flashed down as a short cry of pain escaped her throat. She could taste the blood on her tongue, heavy and coppery from the roof of her mouth. She ached with the need to taste his.

She lifted trembling hands and placed them flat on his chest, sliding her palms up to rest on his shoulders as he moved even closer. Their bodies met slowly and the weight of him pressed her gently back against the door.

One hand still around her ribs, he braced a knee between hers and trailed the fingers of the other hand down her jaw. His tender fingers lifted her chin as he ran his thumb across her lower lip, pulling it down to expose her fangs. His breath hitched at the sight of them.

Koen lowered his head and angled his mouth toward hers. "Leis," His moist breath filled her mouth and lungs as he drew closer. "I offer my blood to you. Will you accept my offering?"

She barely whispered, "Yes," before his upper lip touched hers, and his soft tongue lightly followed the path his thumb had taken. His tongue stroked her mouth, tracing back and forth before sliding easily between her parted lips and slicing against her right fang.

Her blood alone tasted heavy and coppery, but the mixture of their blood together was like freshly browned butter.

For just a moment he lifted his mouth from hers as he swallowed, and with a thrum of energy, she felt strength flood his body. The shoulders under her hands lifted up and back as his chest expanded, air filling his lungs.

In her next breath, the smell of relief and wonder washed over him before he mashed his lips back to hers. They savored and explored one another, tongues reaching and tasting while his hands moved lower to wrap around her waist, his thumbs caressing the bottom of her ribcage. Breathless and shaking, Koen leaned his forehead against hers as his eyes fell closed.

She let her hands glide down his shoulders to rest on his upper arms. When his eyes opened they were a rich sapphire, sparkling with joy.

"I love you." He breathed.

She lifted her chin to press another quick kiss to his lips. "I love you, Koen."

She squealed in surprise and delight as the hands at her waist effortlessly lifted her. Her legs instinctively went around his waist, and her arms wrapped tightly onto his neck. He turned toward the bed while pressing light kisses along her collarbone.

Her fingers slid into the softly curled hair at the nape of his neck and across the leather necklace. His lips stayed against her skin as he lowered them both onto the mattress before allowing his mouth to slide lower, stopping just above the swell of her chest.

His low, raspy voice felt cool against the now moist skin above her heart.

"Together, as long as our hearts beat," he whispered.

EPILOGUE
ALEXANDER

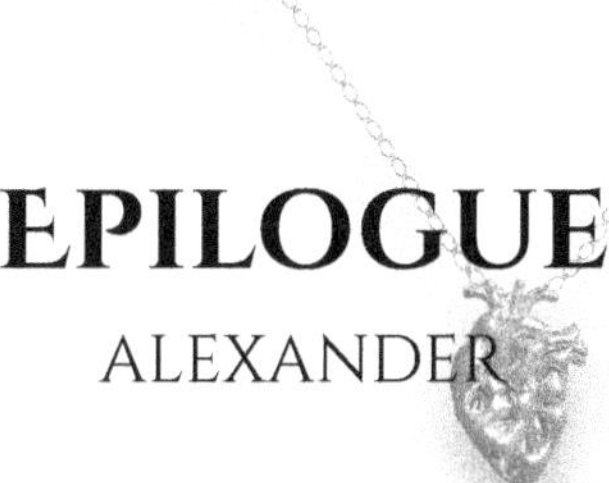

With a tired smile, Alexander watched Koen and Leisel disappear into the compound. Steeling himself against the agony, he shook the offered hands of those gathered as often as the pain would allow him.

He watched as Vampir mingled, several times seeing the light of recognition in their eyes when a potential match was made. Hope and a sense of renewal permeated the cooling air as the night wore on.

Unable to stand the constant touching, Alexander made his way to the edge of the crowd near a table where one of Res's remaining servants was replenishing the drink table. Alexander picked up a bottle of water and turned to see Baden and Emerick approaching.

"Alexander." Emerick smiled. "Thank you for all your help." The elder man still looked worn out.

Lifting his water bottle in salute, Alexander inclined his head. "You are of course welcome, Mr. Tate." He gestured around them at the crowd. "Seems the plan worked."

Baden's grin was wide. "Yes. It did, and it looks like we're onto something with gatherings like this." His eyes swept across the crowd and landed on two couples seated together, their heads close as they laughed. "It will take time for Res's inner circle to accept it, but we're well on our way it seems."

Emerick took a long drink from the bottle in his hand and met Alexander's eye. "We would sincerely like to have you involved in the leadership of this new union." Alexander stiffened, suspecting the next question. "We would like to ask if you would be willing to serve on the first Council."

Alexander cleared his throat and let his eyes travel over the horizon. He sighed. "My company demands a great deal of my time." Lowering the bottle of water to his side, he pushed the suit coat aside and slipped a hand into his pocket. He met Baden's eyes. "Who else has been asked?"

Baden chuckled. "I've been asked, mostly because I can get the network up, I think."

Emerick shook his head at both of them. "You've both been asked because you've proven yourselves to be open-minded." Emerick pointed at Baden. "You, young man, put together clues no one else was able to pick up on for years, and you were able to persuade Leis's hard-headed brother to listen to you."

Baden shrugged. "Josh already knew. It was his wife Gina that got through to him."

Alexander's brows lowered. "So, Gina was the so-called spy?"

Emerick grinned. "Yes. She was willing to learn how to disguise her voice and pose as a human to get us close to Leis and Baden." He shook his head. "We knew some of what Res was doing, but when we found out she was going to force the two of them together, we couldn't wait any longer." He caught sight of Ellen across the patio and smiled. "My Ellen arranged everything at the college in Ohio, getting them both far enough away from their families to prevent interference until everything was in place."

Alexander was impressed. "That's a lot of planning."

"Almost ruined when Res forced Hadyn and Stefanie to bring Leis home." Baden shook his head. "Now *that* took some quick work to get out of."

Emerick patted him on the shoulder. "But here we are." He looked up to Alexander. "So, what do you think? Will you serve on the counsel?"

Smoothing his tie, Alexander nodded. "I would be honored. My offices are in Seattle, but in light of recent events I was thinking of making some major changes to the company anyway."

"Glad to hear it. We'll be in touch to let you know when we have the first meeting arranged." Emerick's tired eyes lit up as Ellen reached them. "But for now, this old male needs some rest."

"I believe the term is ancient." Ellen's sweet voice made them all smile. "If you boys don't mind, I haven't been alone with this one in a long time." Her arm snaked around Eric's waist, and she looked up at him with adoration. "Are you ready, my love? Let's let the kids enjoy the party."

"I'll follow you, El." Together they waved and made their way through the open house and out.

Baden jerked his head toward the crowd. "You go ahead. I have a flight to Ireland to catch tomorrow afternoon." He offered his hand. "She's out there, Koch. Hopefully closer than you think." With a wink Baden turned and left the same way the Tate's had.

Alexander took a long swallow of water and joined a group of males who were discussing the latest cars. Over their conversation about horsepower and torque, chrome wheels versus aluminum, he heard a swirling laugh rise from a larger group behind them.

The sound caressed his sensitive skin, and he spun toward it. His eyes raked the crowded space trying to locate her, but her voice got lost in the mix of the other voices.

Excusing himself from the group, he threaded through the crowd, doing his best to control the painful flinches every time a female brushed against him.

In the midst of the most crowded section of the patio, a gentle hand swept across his back and instead of pain, a wash of relief rushed through his entire body. His whole world tilted.

"Excuse me." A softly cultured voice with only the faintest of echoes sent chills up his spine. Her sharp intake of breath confirmed she felt it too.

He wanted to reach out and catch hold of her, but shock delayed his reaction time. Sensing her retreat, he whipped his head around. The woman was backing quickly away, but not before their eyes met and locked.

Hair as black as gunpowder framed her delicate face, and the ends that curled around her shoulders were a darkly saturated purple, bright against the creamy woven top that hid her shape. Wide hazel eyes rimmed with dark liner registered the same shock that must be shining in his. But he was confused when her shock melded into fear.

"You weren't supposed to be here." She was inching away, and before he could react, she was pulled away by another female.

"Come on, Jessi! I promised Kevin we'd be home by midnight."

Jessi's pale lips parted in surprise, and she appeared ready to say something else, but at her friend's insistent pull, she turned and vanished between the bodies surrounding them.

"Wait!" Alexander was taller and broader than most of the others in the crowd, but it did him no good when he tried to follow her.

She was tiny, and her petite form was quickly swallowed by the other bodies. By the time he excused and pushed his way through to the edges of the crowd, all he saw was the glimmer of her purple highlights behind the wheel of a tiny red car already rolling down the driveway. She glanced over her shoulder with a look of muted terror, and then the car turned right, and she was gone.

"Jessi." Alexander breathed her name. "I will find you."

THE END

ABOUT THE AUTHOR

Michelle Bolanger is a Christian author of contemporary and speculative fiction. She also writes non-fiction articles that share the hope of Christ through daily life lessons as a wife, author, and child of God. In addition to her writing, she is also a talented vocalist and enjoys painting. She lives in small town Ohio with her husband. Together, they enjoy going on long cruises, motorcycle rides along side roads and back roads, and cheering for their favorite professional hockey teams.

After 30+ years of mid-level management in banking and finance, Michelle left the corporate life to pursue her creative passions. She has co-lead Biblical courses on personal finance and budgeting, and served as the women's ministry co-ordinator for her local church where she crafted Bible studies and taught women how to apply Biblical principles to their daily lives. As a vocalist, she has served as a member of her church's worship team, leading the congregation into a deeper connection with God through song.

She began her publishing journey in 2015 with her urban fantasy debut novel, *"The Kiss"* the first book in a young adult series now titled *"The Divided Hearts Series."* She also published the first two stand alone contemporary novels in a collection of gritty, hot button stories that follow characters who come to faith in Christ after walking through some topics most Christian novelists won't write about. She tackles topics like LGBTQ, human trafficking, abortion, and adultery.

Michelle and her husband host a small group Bible study in their home once a week, and she has plans to expand her teaching and encouraging opportunities in the future by organizing an in person writer's group for writers of all levels in her local area. Her greatest desire is to demonstrate the hope of faith in Christ by sharing the lessons God is teaching her as she continues to publish new stories, grow her business, and encourage other writers and women in their giftings and callings.

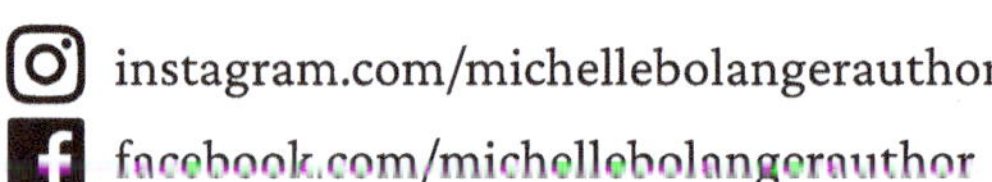

instagram.com/michellebolangerauthor

facebook.com/michellebolangerauthor

CONNECT WITH MICHELLE

Find me online:
Website: michellebolanger.com
Socials: @michellebolangerauthor
Email: Michelle@risenfiction.com